MW01093611

Dean L. Hovey

Print ISBNs
LSI Print 978-0-2286-1215-5
B&N Print 978-0-2286-1216-2
Amazon Print 978-0-2286-1214-8

BWL Publishing Inc.

Books we love to write ...
Authors around the world.

http://bwlpublishing.ca

1

To Brian and Lisa

Like in any publishing venture, the author puts the words on paper (in the computer) after research and consulting with an army of people who provide information, critique, direction, feedback, plot suggestions, editing, proofreading, emotional support, and more.

At the top of the list is my wife, Julie, who reads an early version and provides invaluable insight on the way I've tangled the plot, mischaracterized the key players, and generally works to improve the book and keep me humble.

Frannie, an archaeologist by education, suggested the premise of Spanish coins discovered on Padre Island, which led to the plot. Fran also suggested the devious resolution of a sub-plot that emerged in the previous book.

Anne edits, proofreads, and offers suggestions after flying through rewrite after rewrite despite having a husband, a small child, and two jobs.

I can't express my profound gratitude to the librarians, bookstores, and readers who continue to offer encouragement, on-line reviews, interesting questions, and plot suggestions. Thank you.

Many thanks to Jude Pittman and Susan Davis of BWL.

Prologue

On April 29, 1554 three Spanish Galleons, the Espiritu Santo, Santa Maria de Yciar, and San Esteban sank off Padre Island, near the effluent of the Rio Grande. They were loaded with more than 45 tons of gold and silver coins. The lone survivor led a salvage crew back to the wrecks where the masts of the San Esteban were visible, sunk in only 12-18 feet of water. The Spanish divers recovered only 18 tons of silver coins.

The Santa Maria de Yciar was destroyed during dredging of the Port Mansfield Channel in the 1950s. Only her anchor was recovered.

A 1967 salvage effort recovered 13 tons of coins and artifacts from the San Esteban. After a lengthy legal battle, the recovered coins and artifacts were awarded to the State of Texas. They were subsequently turned over to the National Park Service and are displayed in the Corpus Christi Museum of Science and History.

Roughly 14 tons of coins are still offshore, on the beach and dunes of Padre Island, or in the Mansfield Cut/Padre Island Archaeological District. The National Park Service is charged with protection of the Spanish shipwrecks, coins and artifacts in the waters and on the shore of

Padre Island National Seashore. It is illegal to use a metal detector in the archaeological district. Coins, ship fragments, and artifacts found by visitors must be pointed out to NPS rangers so they can undergo proper archaeological recovery. Most visitors comply with the law…

Chapter One

After solving the Padre Island hazardous waste dumping mystery, my Park Service Investigator's job migrated into the role of training officer for Rachel Randall, the new law enforcement ranger at Padre Island National Seashore. Rachel was green but smart. Lacking any serious crime, there wasn't a lot of training involved in patrolling the mostly empty Gulf of Mexico beach. As we grew as partners, Rachel and I lapsed into small talk and rumors, the lifeblood of cops worldwide.

Rachel glanced at me to make sure I paid attention to whatever she was about to say as the pickup tires sung on the damp beach sand. "Why are you still here, Doug?"

"Where else would I be? It's our twice-daily drive to Port Mansfield Channel and I always ride with you."

"Why are you still in Texas? You're a Park Service Investigator, and there's nothing here to investigate." She paused. "Or, is there something else going on with your personal life that's got you here? I heard a rumor that your roommate is going to be our new interpretative ranger."

"You mean my roommate, as in Jill?"

"Yes, Jill. Is she really quitting her job as the Flagstaff superintendent and staying here?"

"I can neither confirm nor deny that rumor."

"Really? That's the best you can do?"

"Sorry. Jill makes her own decisions, and I'm not always privy to the information."

Rachel took her foot off the gas, and the pickup rolled to a stop. I looked around but saw nothing of interest.

"Why are we stopping?"

"I want answers. Either we're partners, or we're not."

"My personal life is not fodder for the Park Service rumor mill. This has nothing to do with us being partners."

"Matt told me Jill's starting the first of next month. That's a fact, not a rumor. That fact makes me think you're making Texas home."

"What else did Matt tell you?"

"Matt's wife has a realtor friend. I heard she was showing you and Jill a house before the shootout on the canal."

I nodded without commenting.

"C'mon, Fletcher. This is like pulling teeth. What else is going on?"

"My mother's flying in tonight."

"Oh, oh. Jill's meeting your mom. That's significant."

"Mom wanted to see the Gulf of Mexico."

"That just happens to be coincidental with a diamond showing up on Jill's finger?"

I glared at Rachel. "You knew that, but you wanted to needle me until I told you."

"Pretty much," she said, smiling. She stepped on the gas, and we started rolling down the beach. "Did you get down on one knee during a candlelight dinner?"

"Do you really think that's my style?"

"You're a traditional guy who's into marriage and family. I can see you doing something romantic." She paused. "Wait! Jill asked you, didn't she? She's a take-charge person and you're still healing from your divorce."

I pointed through the windshield. "Why is that group of coyotes gathered on the dune ahead of us?"

Rachel shifted the pickup into neutral and it rolled to a stop. "I've never seen several of them together before. They're solitary and usually more skittish than this."

We stepped out of the pickup. The three coyotes looked up, then trotted away.

I flashed back to my first investigation in Arizona. "I've seen them act like that around a dead body in the desert."

Rachel closed her door quietly. "Do you see a conspiracy behind every door?"

"I tend to be a little cynical, but it's served me well. Besides, it looked like two of the coyotes were tugging on something."

"They probably found a porpoise carcass washed up on the dune."

I looked around for vehicle tracks or footprints but saw none of either. We were halfway to the Port Mansfield Channel, and not many park visitors ventured this far down the island.

Rachel froze about ten feet from the spot where the coyotes had been gathered. Flies buzzed in a swarm over the dune. She sniffed the air and grimaced. "That doesn't smell like dead fish."

I walked ahead until a mottled greenish leg and arm were visibly protruding from the sand. I looked back at Rachel, who was frozen behind me. "It looks like I've got something to investigate."

Rachel shook her head. "It's you. You're cursed. There weren't any dead bodies here until you showed up."

I pulled out my cellphone and keyed in the park superintendent's number. "Matt, we've got a dead body."

"Ha. Ha. Very funny."

"I'm not joking. We're not equipped to manage the crime scene. Who should we call?"

"You're not bringing the body in like you did with the guy in the surf?"

"This person is buried in a dune. It should be handled as a crime scene."

"I've never . . . I suppose it'd be the Corpus Christi police."

* * *

It took nearly four hours for the Corpus Christi crime scene investigators to arrive at the Padre Island Park Service headquarters. They were accompanied by an unmarked police cruiser bristling with antennae. The lanky detective who climbed out of the cruiser wore cowboy boots, jeans, a western cut shirt, and a bolo tie. He arranged a white Stetson on his head and walked to the pickup where Rachel and I were briefing the crime scene investigators.

I offered my hand. "Hi, Scott. I assume you remember Rachel."

Detective Scott Dixon shook my hand, then Rachel's. "Nice to see you again, Rachel. I heard your partner is a Jonah."

"What's a Jonah?" Rachel asked, shaking Scott's hand.

"It's a person who brings bad luck with him. In the old seafaring days, people perpetually on unlucky ships became known as Jonahs. None of the captains would hire them as crew."

I attempted to interrupt the narrative, but Scott wasn't to be deterred. "Is this your jurisdiction?" I asked, hoping to change the topic.

Scott smiled. "Kinda hard to say. Officially, it's yours. But I generally come out when the crime scene crew is called out. Why are you asking? Do you want me to back off so you can call in the FBI?" Scott and I shared a distrust of the FBI, and he enjoyed yanking my chain.

"I didn't realize it was 'pile on Doug day.'"

Scott smiled. "Well, you know, you're supposed to call in the FBI when there's a major crime on Park Service property. I was just pointing that out, in case you'd forgotten."

11

"We're not sure there's a crime here. We may be looking at someone who fell overboard and drowned, was wandering the dunes and was bitten by a rattlesnake, or is the victim of a murder that occurred somewhere else. I guess your CSI crew can sort that out."

Scott nodded. "Can I park here and ride down with you guys in the pickup?"

Rachel pulled the back door open. "Jump in!"

Dixon put his Stetson on the back seat and leaned on the backside of the front seat as we drove down the beach. "What's new since the FBI news conference?"

Rachel glanced into the mirror. "Doug's engaged."

Dixon clapped me on the shoulder. "Congratulations! I assume the lucky woman is the skinny one who was with you at the news conference."

Rachel looked at me like she expected me to respond. When I didn't, she went on. "That would be Jill, the former Flagstaff Park Service superintendent. She's really nice."

"She's nice? What's she see in Doug?"

I glared over my shoulder at Dixon, who grinned, broadly.

* * *

The sound of helicopter rotors diverted my attention from the CSI team, who were slowly removing the sand from the body with trowels like an archaeological dig. I'd become attuned to the sound of helicopters during a stint as an MP in Iraq where deep thumping preceded the actual sighting of the helicopters, sometimes by minutes. Helos meant a break from the desert monotony either with the arrival of VIPs, mail, food, new people, injured soldiers, or sometimes body bags.

Rachel shielded her eyes and looked skyward down the coast. "Here comes the Coast Guard."

The radio in the pickup squawked, "Park Service, this is the Coast Guard. Do you copy?"

Rachel ran to the pickup and picked up the mic. "This is the Park Service. Meet you on twenty-two." She switched from the hailing channel to one of the police and rescue bands by the time I arrived at the pickup.

"It looks like you guys are having a party. Do you require any assistance?"

"Thanks, Bruce, but we're doing fine."

"You guys find another floater?"

Rachel paused as if trying to frame her response for the airwaves to whoever else might be listening in. "Not this time. We're working a similar situation in the dunes."

"We're clear then," the helicopter pilot replied.

I gestured for Rachel to hand me the mic. "Bruce, this is Doug Fletcher. Have you guys seen any unusual boat activity in this area in the past few days?"

"Somebody beached a boat a couple days ago after you guys passed that area. A couple people were walking around, looking like typical beachcombers. Nothing really unusual. Does your *situation* look like something that had a boating aspect to it?"

"We've got a dead visitor in a shorty wetsuit as if maybe there'd been snorkeling or diving in the area."

"I haven't seen much scuba activity, and the surf there is rough for snorkeling. I'll ask the other crews when we get back to the hangar."

"Thanks, Bruce."

* * *

The sun was setting, and the rising tide was lapping at the pickup tires when the crime scene team wrapped up. They secured the victim in a body bag and were stripping off their gloves and Tyvek coveralls. I was surprised when a tall woman took off a baseball cap, shook out her strawberry blonde hair, and walked over to us.

Scott Dixon, who'd been leaning on the pickup fender chatting with us, stood up and smiled. "Hi, Connie. What've we got?"

Connie shook Dixon's hand, then brushed him aside. "Please excuse Scotty. He sometimes forgets that not everyone he meets knows everyone else he's ever met. I'm Connie West."

Rachel and I introduced ourselves and shook her hand. Connie was freckled and six feet tall, my mother would've described her as *big-boned.*

She wore blue utility pants and calf-high black rubber boots. Her blue sweat-stained CCPD CSI t-shirt strained across her ample bosom. She smiled exuding professionalism, and her ramrod posture hinted at a previous stint in the military.

"There wasn't much for us to work with. The surf, wind, coyotes, and birds pretty much cleaned up the scene. What I can tell you is that your victim is a young woman with sun-bleached blonde hair. I'll let the medical examiner make a determination of the time and cause of death, but I can tell you she's been dead for a couple days, and she's got bruising on her neck that's suspicious if not the cause of death."

I watched the other techs slip the body bag into an SUV. "Was there petechial hemorrhaging consistent with strangulation?"

"We couldn't tell." Connie was about to expand on her comments and momentarily hesitated when she looked at Rachel's reaction to the body transfer, then said, "Decomposition, maggots, and scavengers made that hard to discern."

"Did you find any scuba or snorkeling gear?" I asked.

"No swim fins, mask, snorkel, scuba tanks, weight belt, or BC vest. She's wearing a shorty wetsuit, and that's the only thing that hints she might've come out of the Gulf."

"Sexual assault?" Dixon asked.

West shook her head. "I'm sure the ME will check, but I'm ninety-nine percent sure that wasn't what this was about. She's zipped into a wetsuit and it's hard to put one on yourself when you're alive much less trying to get a dead body into one."

West's comment piqued my interest. "So, what do you think this was about?"

West smiled like she'd been awaiting the question. She reached into her pocket and pulled out an evidence bag. "This." Connie bounced the bag in her hand.

Dixon took the bag and held it up toward the setting sun. "Is that a gold coin?" He handed me the bag.

"I think the Spaniards called them Ducats or Doubloons," West said.

I passed the bag to Rachel. "Are there Spanish shipwrecks here?"

Connie nodded. "According to my sixth grade Texas history, three Spanish ships sank off Padre Island in the 1500s. The Spaniards recovered some of the treasure freediving on the wrecks in the following years, but about half wasn't recovered. There've been a couple salvage expeditions, and one of the treasure ships was destroyed when the Port Mansfield Channel was dredged in the 1950s. There's still literally tons of gold and silver out there."

I looked down the beach. "The Port Mansfield Channel is just a few miles from here."

Dixon jammed his hands in his jean pockets. "It kinda makes a guy want to buy a metal detector."

Rachel shook her head. "This is an archaeological preservation area, which is why someone might salvage on the sly."

Connie West accepted the coin back from Rachel. "Hurricane Harvey moved a lot of sand around. I bet some of that treasure is shallower than it was before the storm."

"Where'd you find the coin?" I asked.

"Inside her wetsuit," West said. "If there were other treasure-hunters who thought she was hiding coins from them…"

I shook my head. "I don't need this right now. My mother is flying in to meet my fiancé. I don't have time to start a murder investigation."

Rachel smiled. "Your mother is coming to meet your fiancé. Maybe they'll hit it off and won't need you around to entertain them."

"Jill will kill me if I leave her alone with Mom."

Dixon nodded. "I like that kind of crime. Spousal murders are easier to solve, especially where there's clearly defined motive, like dumping your mother on your fiancé and leaving."

I was about to blurt out an obscene response, then stopped and looked at the two women. Connie was smiling.

"It's okay, Fletcher. I'm a Marine. I doubt you were about to say anything I haven't heard or said before."

I bit my tongue. "Have a nice day, Scott."

Chapter Two

It was dark when our caravan pulled into the nearly empty headquarters parking lot. Rachel locked the pickup and looked at the headquarters building where Matt's office light was still on.

"Are we going to tell Matt what's going on?"

I looked at my watch. "Could you cover it with him. I need to pick up Jill and drive to the airport to get Mom."

"I've got it. I hope everything goes well with Jill and your mom."

I took out my pickup keys and nodded. "I'm sure it's going to be fine."

I had a terrible feeling of foreboding as I drove to the townhouse. I'd sprung Mom's visit on Jill, and the news hadn't been met with excitement. I'd offered to make the airport pick up alone, but Jill said that could be construed as a statement, and she wanted to put her best foot forward. I parked the pickup and mentally prepared myself to face my anxious fiancé in our townhouse.

Jill opened the door before I got to the steps. She wore a flowered sundress with a V-neck that hinted at more cleavage than I'd ever seen exposed. Her brown hair had blonde highlights and was carefully combed into a short swept-back hairdo. She wore a hint of pink lipstick, and she didn't seem angry.

I was unsure what to say or how to act, so I went the safe route. "You look beautiful."

"Thanks." Jill spun around so I could see all of the dress and sandals. "It cost us a hundred dollars."

"It cost us?"

She grabbed my hand and pulled me into the townhouse. The house smelled like a florist shop. Cut flower arrangements had been set on the table next to the front door and on the dining room table. There wasn't a speck of dust anywhere, and the kitchen counters looked like an ad from *House Beautiful.*

"Did you spend the whole day cleaning?"

"Not the whole day. The makeover and shopping with Mandy took a couple hours."

I pulled her into my arms and kissed her. I glanced at her chest. "Cleavage?"

"Mandy took me to Victoria's Secret and talked me into buying something other than a sports bra. She told me it was time to quit trying to look like one of the boys and 'give my girls a little lift.'"

"Remind me to thank Mandy. Let's skip the airport and go upstairs."

"Change out of your uniform. I think we'd better get your mother before she thinks we forgot her."

Jill watched as I changed. "How was your day?"

"We found a body partially buried in a sand dune."

Jill looked shocked. "Someone who drowned?"

I pulled on a golf shirt and adjusted it over my holster. "The medical examiner will make the final determination, but the CCPD crime scene team thought it looked like the woman had been strangled." I ran a comb through my hair in front of the bathroom mirror. "Ready to go?"

Jill sat on the end of the bed staring at me. "You don't seem rattled."

I sat down and put my arm around her. "I'm not trying to be calloused, but I've dealt with a lot of murders, and I compartmentalize my job from my home life. It's how I cope with the ugliness I had to deal with on a daily basis as a cop in St. Paul."

She looked into my eyes. "You know that you can talk with me about anything. You don't have to keep your emotions…the horrible things you see…bottled up inside."

I took her hand and kissed it. "I appreciate that thought, but there are things locked away in my head that no one should ever see. I'm dealing with them. If I ever get to the point where I can't, we'll talk."

"Promise?"

I kissed her, then pulled her up from the bed. "I promise, but right now, we have to meet a plane."

* * *

We drove a mile in silence, and I wondered if Jill was thinking about the body Rachel and I had discovered.

She finally turned to me and said, "I'm nervous about meeting your mother."

I reached over and squeezed her hand. "There's nothing to be afraid of, my mother won't bark or bite."

"No, but you said she worshiped your pretty ex-wife, the college professor. I'm hardly a gorgeous young thing, nor am I a college professor."

"You're cute even without the lipstick or new hairdo. And she'll love you for who you are, an educated, smart, self-confident woman who has a career."

"I bought new underwear, too."

"To impress my mother?"

"No, to enhance my figure."

"You've piqued my curiosity."

"Down, boy. We're picking up your mother."

We waited near the baggage claim until most of the passengers had arrived and claimed their bags. I was starting to get concerned that Mom had missed the plane, then I saw her walking toward us while chatting with a flight attendant. She'd aged in the four years since I'd last seen her, but she was still vibrant and walked with confidence. I grabbed Jill's hand and led her across the baggage claim area.

"Hi Mom," I said, giving her a hug. "This is Jill."

Jill stepped forward with her hand extended for a handshake. "Hi, Mrs. Fletcher."

Mom grabbed Jill's hand and pulled her into an embrace. When Mom released the hug, she reached down and lifted Jill's left hand, examining the engagement ring. "Has Doug turned into a cheapskate? I expected to see a rock on your finger."

Jill shook her head. "Doug wanted to buy something bigger, but this is what I wanted."

Mom smiled. "Doug said you were comfortable in your own skin. I think that's the nicest thing he's ever said about the women he's dated."

Jill's eyes darted between us, and she cocked her head. "Thanks, Mrs. Fletcher."

"Please call me Ronnie."

"Welcome to Texas, Ronnie. Do you have a suitcase?"

"The blue one on the carousel."

I leaned over and picked up the bag as it went past. When I turned around, Mom was frowning.

"What's wrong, Mom?"

"You're wearing a gun under your shirt."

"I'm a federal law enforcement officer. I'm supposed to carry my weapon all the time."

"I'd hoped you'd outgrown the cop thing."

I almost rolled my eyes, then glanced at Jill, who was grinning. "I'm a Park Service investigator. It's not like I'm handing out speeding tickets."

"I've seen you on the news, and I know I should be proud of you." Mother sighed. "Isn't it someone else's turn to save the world from bad people."

"Ronnie, Doug's good at what he does."

Mother sighed and grabbed Jill's hand, apparently willing to move on. "Doug told me that you're the superintendent of the Flagstaff Park Service office. You've done very well for yourself. Have you been married before?"

Jill shook her head as they started walking from the baggage claim. "I've never met anyone like Doug before."

"Did he sweep you off your feet?"

A step behind, I was only catching snippets of their conversation.

"He was sneakier than that. He became my best friend first."

Mother stopped and pulled Jill's hand, so they were eye-to-eye. "It took me a long time to realize it was more important to be married to my best friend than it was to have a torrid romance. You've got something many couples never have and don't realize they're missing." Mom pulled Jill into another hug and whispered in her ear. Jill's eyes darted to me, then I saw tears form before she buried her face in Mother's hair and really embraced Mom.

I waited for an explanation, but they stepped apart and continued to the parking lot. I unlocked the back of the Isuzu and stowed Mom's suitcase.

23

Jill tried to get Mom to sit in the front seat, but she chose the back seat and buckled in. I looked at Jill, hoping for an explanation about her tears, but all I got was a headshake. I didn't know if she was happy, sad, or mad.

Jill gave a running description of the areas we were passing, worthy of a tourist guide. Mother nodded and asked a few questions until we crossed the Kennedy Bridge.

"Is that the ocean below us?"

"We're crossing Corpus Christi Bay," Jill explained. "The other end of the bridge is Mustang Island, where we live. The Gulf of Mexico is beyond the island."

I turned onto the main highway down Mustang Island, and we passed brightly lit hotels and condos overlooking the Gulf interspersed with empty lots and buildings that hadn't been repaired after Hurricane Harvey.

I could see Mom checking out the barbed wire along the bayside of the road. "Why is the left side so dark?"

"That's farmland that overlooks the bay, Mom. All the development is built on the Gulf of Mexico side of the island."

"Seems like a waste."

I pulled into the townhouse parking lot. Jill had Mom on the front steps before I got the suitcase out of the Isuzu. The lights were on, and Jill was giving the downstairs tour.

"What a lovely place. I like the flowers and your decorating. Doug's St. Paul apartment looked and smelled like a locker room. You're a good influence on him."

Jill was smiling. She mouthed *locker room,* and I shrugged.

I thought my sports-themed apartment decorating was appropriate for my lifestyle. Who doesn't want a Kirby Puckett jersey hanging on their wall? I carried the suitcase to our spare bedroom and set it on the bed. Jill and Mom were right behind me. Jill had a maritime-themed spread on the bed, and she'd put up some shadow boxes with seashells and sand dollars.

Jill opened the closet door. "I emptied a closet for you so you can hang up a few things."

"I feel like I'm putting you out," Mother looked genuinely embarrassed to be imposing on us.

"Ronnie, your visit is a pleasure, not an imposition. I'm looking forward to getting to know you and hearing about Doug's childhood."

Mom smiled. "I'm excited to be here, but if I become a burden, I'll move into a hotel. It seems like there are lots of them here."

Jill reached out and took Mom's hand. "It's a privilege to have you here. Let's go down and have a glass of wine to celebrate your first visit to Texas."

Jill took down wine glasses while I searched through kitchen drawers for the corkscrew. Mom wandered the living room, looking at the decorations, but also making a drill sergeant's white-glove inspection of the cleaning. As near as I could tell, Jill's cleaning passed inspection.

I opened and poured the wine, then passed glasses to Jill and Mom.

"Doug said something about your parents driving down from South Dakota."

"They called from Nebraska this afternoon. They should be here in three or four days. I don't think they realize it takes almost a whole day just to travel the length of Texas." Jill raised her glass. "To your first visit to Texas."

Mother shook her head, which made me clench. She'd lost the filter between her brain and mouth after Dad died, and some of her comments had been inappropriate and sometimes hurtful.

"No. I'd like to toast my new daughter-in-law. To Jill—may you and Doug be as happy as his father and I were."

I didn't realize I'd been holding my breath, but I tried to inhale and take a sip of wine at the same time, which brought on a coughing fit.

* * *

We'd finished the dinner salad Jill had prepared and all the wine when Mom announced that she was tired. We showed her the guest bathroom, found a plastic glass for her nighttime drink, and bid her good night. Jill and I went downstairs.

"I think that went pretty well," I said as an opening parry.

"Ronnie is delightful. I think we'll be fine together."

"What did she whisper to you at the airport?"

Jill looked over her shoulder to make sure Mom wasn't coming down the stairs. "She welcomed me to the family."

"That was very nice."

"While you were getting a glass for the bathroom, she told me she hoped we were going to supply her with a couple grandchildren."

I rolled my head back and stared at the ceiling. "What did you say?"

"I told her I couldn't have any children, and she seemed to accept that." Jill paused. "My mother told me the same thing when she responded to my picture of the engagement ring."

I blew out a breath. "I hope they can accept that train has departed the station."

Jill reached out and took my hand. "Would you consider adopting a child?"

"You'd like to have a baby?"

Jill shook her head. "There are lots of adoption options." She paused. "We've never discussed children."

"Based on your lack of concern about birth control, I'd assumed children weren't an option for you . . . us."

Jill shrugged. "Biologically, it's not an option now, and it wasn't when I was younger and working sixty or eighty hours a week. Now, maybe we'd have time to be parents."

"We'd be retired when a child was in high school. I don't think I want to do that to a kid or myself."

Jill patted my hand. "It was just a passing thought."

27

Chapter Three

Jill and Mom were drinking coffee over crumb-covered plates when I came down in my uniform. Jill laughed at something Mom said as I pulled a mug out of the cupboard. I stuck a slice of bread into the toaster and grabbed the crunchy peanut butter, setting it next to Jill's jar of creamy. I chuckled about that being one compromise neither of us was willing to make, so the solution was each of us having our own jar of peanut butter.

I set my toast, coffee, and the peanut butter on the table and sat down. "I'm going to check-in at the park, and if there's nothing pressing, I'll try to sneak away for the rest of the day." I waited for Mom's sarcastic remark about *the cop going off to risk his life*, but it never came.

Jill shook her head. "You take care of whatever you need to do at the park. Ronnie and I are meeting Mandy Mattson for a tour of Corpus Christi. We'll pick up something for supper."

I looked at Mother, who seemed pleased. Jill had predicted a dire outcome if I abandoned her with my mother, but they both appeared at ease. My boss's wife, Mandy, was a Southern belle who oozed charm and lubricated interpersonal friction. I could see the combination of Jill's Park Service professionalism and Mandy's Southern charm as the perfect mix to ease the impact of Mom's sometimes blunt and often inappropriate comments.

"That sounds lovely," I said, spreading peanut butter on my toast.

The words were hardly out of my mouth when the doorbell rang, and Mandy swept into the house without waiting for an invitation. Mandy rushed to Mom's side and took her hand. "Mizz Fletcher, I'm Mandy Mattson, and it's an honor to meet y'all." Mom looked stunned, then immediately charmed. Mandy's genuine smile, Southern charm, and Texas twang disarmed her. "Doug and Jill are just the sweetest people on earth, and I know the apple doesn't fall far from the tree."

Mother beamed. Jill smiled and gave me a look like she'd just pulled off the most significant coup in the history of the world. Mandy was indeed the perfect person to throw into the mix.

"Matt and I talked last night, and you folks absolutely *have to* come over for supper tonight. We'll pick up some shrimp, slaw mix, limes, and a bottle of tequila, and we'll have ourselves a welcome to Texas party."

Jill put her hand on Mom's arm. "Oh, Ronnie, you're in for a treat. Mandy's shrimp, Texas slaw, and margaritas are to die for."

I looked a Jill and mouthed *margaritas*?

Jill gave me a slight nod and smiled.

Mandy looked at me like she was surprised I was still at the table. "Now, Doug, you get out of here so we womenfolk can make some plans."

I grabbed my plate and mug. I was tempted to say *yes, ma'am*, but decided to just bid them goodbye and go to the park.

* * *

Matt was at his desk when I arrived. I sat in his guest chair. "What does Mandy have planned for my mother?"

Matt signaled for me to close the door. "Jill called yesterday morning and told Mandy she needed Valium because your mother was arriving and had no clue what to do with her. As only Mandy can, she talked Jill off the ledge, then took her shopping. That seems to be the remedy to all female problems. They spent the day together, got their hair done, and bought Jill some girly clothes. Mandy said Jill was laughing when they got back to your townhouse, and they decided to take your mother sightseeing today."

"Mandy invited us over for shrimp and margaritas."

Matt stared-off into the top corner of his office. "I swear if she gets your mother drunk on margaritas . . ."

Matt's thought was interrupted by a knock on the door. Rachel stuck her head in. "I hope I'm not interrupting anything. The Coast Guard hailed us to report a boat beached near Port Mansfield Channel and what looks like beachcombers with metal detectors walking the shore."

I jumped up from Matt's chair. "Let's go!"

Rachel got in the driver's seat and snapped her seatbelt as she started the engine. "Do you think I need the lights and siren?"

I snapped my own seatbelt as the pickup rolled. "Seriously? On the beach? Are you going to warn the jellyfish or the seagulls?"

"I don't know. There might be campers or people walking on the beach."

I shook my head. "Do what you want."

Rachel flipped on the lights but didn't turn on the siren. She sped down the beach faster than she'd ever driven. Port Mansfield Channel was almost fifty miles away, and at best, we'd be to the area of the beachcombers in an hour.

I picked up the mic and checked the marine radio channel. "Coast Guard, this is the Park Service. Do you copy?"

"This is Coast Guard station, Corpus Christi. Meet me on twenty-two."

"We've got beachcombers off a boat near the Port Mansfield Channel. We're an hour out. Do you have anyone nearby?"

"We've got a fishing boat dead in the water off Rockport, and we've got the helo and a boat assisting them. Sorry, no one near Port Mansfield Channel."

"Roger that, Coast Guard. If you break anyone free, we'd appreciate eyes on their boat."

"Are you expecting trouble?" Rachel asked.

"Not really, but we won't be able to follow a boat if they push off before we get there." I paused. "On the other hand, we have the Jane Doe who was recovered from the dunes. If these are the same people, they've already committed murder, and they're not innocent tourists who happened to be on the beach."

Rachel slowed just a bit. "Do you want to call Corpus Christi PD or the sheriff's office for backup?"

"No. Let's drive down and see what's going on. Chances are that they're just beachcombers. If they're not, they'll probably make a run for it rather than confronting two rangers."

"They won't know we're armed."

I thought back to an earlier discussion when she'd revealed that her roommate/boyfriend didn't like having a loaded gun in their house. She'd been carrying her gun without a shell chambered. We'd argued, but in the end, she'd understood it was for our safety. She had to be ready to fire her weapon immediately if the worst scenario played out.

"You do have a round in the chamber."

I got a glare and a sarcastic, "Yes."

"Just checking. How's your boyfriend's research going? Is he still trying to test the effectiveness of rehab programs on reducing crack-addicted babies?"

"He's still at it, but his pool of crack-addicted pregnant women is shrinking."

"Is the rehab effective, or do they have fewer children?"

"He's struggling with that question. I guess some of his subjects have disappeared, and he's not getting many new women to study. Lots of them haven't had any prenatal care. The first time they see a doctor is when they're in labor. Toby's cruising the hospitals, but the health privacy laws are keeping him from accessing the records of incoming women unless they self-identify and volunteer for his study." Rachel paused. "What's it like having a fiancé?"

The sudden change of topic caught me off guard. "It's okay. I mean, it doesn't feel a lot different except now we're committed to making things work. We've both been independent for years, and it's strange asking Jill's opinion about something I would've just done before."

"Does it feel different? I mean, it's more than just living together. How is it . . . more special?"

"Are you questioning your open relationship with Toby?"

"I don't know. We're together, and we seem compatible."

I turned. "Jill and I are both committed to making our relationship work. I feel like I'm getting more out of it than I'm putting in. As odd as this sounds, she told me she has the same feeling. It's kind of like having two burning logs. If they're together, you get more heat out of them than you'd get from either of them alone."

"Toby's got a lot on his plate with school and his study. He's frustrated and hasn't got any energy left at the end of the day. It leaves him kind of edgy and angry."

"We all have days like that. We accept them and prop up each other. If it's every day, then it becomes a problem."

Rachel slowed as we crossed an area where rainwater sometimes washed out the beach, then she sped up again. We hadn't seen another person on the beach for miles, so she turned off the flashing lights. She also didn't comment anymore about her relationship with Toby.

"Are we going to watch the autopsy of Jane Doe?" Rachel asked.

"It seemed like the crime scene people had it pretty well sewn up as strangulation." I hesitated, then added, "The last autopsy didn't go really well for you. I didn't expect you to volunteer for another."

"Listen, Doug, you were the one who told me that you learn more from being at the post mortem than you get from reading the report. If you hadn't asked the ME to test the water in the lawyer's lungs, we never would've known he drowned in a bathtub and not the Gulf, where we found his body."

"I spoke with the ME this morning as I drove in. She's doing the post-mortem the day after tomorrow."

Rachel glanced at me. "Were you going to tell me?"

"We got sidetracked before we had a chance to talk. Then I forgot about it."

"I'm going with you."

"Are you going to bring your own bucket?"

"Not funny, Fletcher. I plan on keeping it together this time."

"Eat breakfast."

"What?"

"You're less likely to toss your cookies at an autopsy if you've eaten."

"You're just making that up, aren't you?" She paused, then added, "It's part of the rookie initiation thing. 'Let's convince the rookie she needs to eat before the autopsy, so she has lots of cookies to toss.'"

"Going in on an empty stomach seems to make me more prone to nausea. A couple cups of strong coffee on an empty stomach make me even more queasy. But having some carbs, toast or cereal, seems to keep my belly quieter."

"Scout's honor?"

I put up three fingers, like a scout promise. "Scout's honor."

Chapter Four

The people on the beach looked like black dots from a mile away and were hard to count because they seemed to be cutting back and forth. One of them looked in our direction. There was immediate activity as all the people suddenly ran toward the boat. We were still a hundred yards away when the last person pushed the boat off the beach and jumped aboard.

I pulled out a pair of binoculars, but they were too far away, and the bouncing truck made it impossible to read the boat identification numbers or recognize faces. As soon as they put the motor down, they shot across the surf line and turned south.

"Ease off the gas and stop before you get to the footprints."

Rachel let the pickup roll slowly to the area where we'd seen the activity. She stopped short of the footprints in the hard-packed sand and shut off the engine. The boat looked like hardly more than a speck with white wake pushing away from its sides when we stepped out.

Rachel walked to the bumper. "What are we going to learn from the footprints?"

"I'm not sure, but if we drive over them, we're not going to learn anything." I studied the prints for a minute then stepped next to Rachel. "Do you see how some of them were taking long strides, and the balls of their feet were digging deeper into the sand?"

"Yeah, I suppose that's when they were running to the boat."

"Right. And those prints all funnel together where the boat was beached. But ignore those and look at the other prints."

Rachel stepped behind the pickup and climbed into the bed. "It's easier to see from up here. It looks like they were walking in parallel lines."

Rachel had hopped onto the bumper and jumped the tailgate. I got into the pickup bed, but not as quickly or as gracefully.

"In police jargon, they were doing a grid search. Each person walks alongside another, so their fields of search overlap slightly. When we examine a crime scene, we often get a line of cops and walk, or crawl, in a line to search for evidence. I assume the beachcombers were using the same principle as they searched with their metal detectors. It's more efficient than having people walking around randomly and searching in the same area someone else has already checked."

Rachel considered that for a minute. "That means this was no random group of people who happened to stop here to look for sand dollars. They came with gear and a plan."

"What else do you notice?" I asked.

"They dug some random holes."

I surveyed the sand in front of us. "I don't think there's anything random or accidental about the hole arrangement. I think they dug where their metal detectors found metal."

"But there's like two dozen holes. Do you think they found that many coins?"

"I doubt it. As you pointed out the first week I was here, some campers don't police their garbage very well, and a lot of debris washes ashore from the passing boats. I'm sure some of those holes yielded bottle caps, nuts, bolts, and pop can tabs."

Rachel considered my comments. "The hurricane moved a lot of sand around, and I'm sure some of the Spanish coins were pushed ashore or unearthed. We never used to see many treasure-hunters here, but there are a lot of visitors willing to travel farther down the shore since the hurricane. I'll bet they're not just looking for a quiet section of beach for skinny dipping."

"I imagine the treasure-hunting fraternity is pretty close-knit. I don't think any individual is going to identify his 'honey hole' of artifacts, but just a couple comments in a bar and a general location will probably set off a whole herd of people, trying to make an extra buck."

"Oh, Doug. You're so twentieth-century. Someone mentions a discovery in their blog or on Twitter, and ten thousand people read it, then within hours, it goes viral. If people are finding coins on the beach, we've got a problem. There will be people coming by boat, car, and helicopter if someone reports significant finds on the internet."

"We're not staffed to deal with that kind of beachcomber influx." I climbed down from the truck bed. Rachel hopped over the fender like a gymnast doing a dismount. I felt lucky not to do a face plant. "I think we'll have to ask Matt to step up the beach patrols. I wonder if we can get more support from the Coast Guard?"

"Bruce told me to ask any time I needed help. He said they might not always say yes, but the worst that could happen was they'd say no. He promised they wouldn't shoot or eat me."

I reflected on the comments my archaeologist ex-wife made about people searching the Civil War battlefields. "Gettysburg National Military Park had so many people combing the battlefields looking for bullets, belt buckles, and other memorabilia they 'salted' the battlefield with thousands of metal disks to frustrate the treasure-hunters. Their metal detectors would start beeping like a fire alarm, but when they dug down, all they found was a metal disk."

"Was it successful?"

"I guess it cut down a lot on the casual hunters who had basic metal detectors. I've heard that the technology has advanced, so the high-end metal detectors can differentiate the type of metal, the depth, and the size of the item. It slows down the serious folks. But it doesn't stop them, especially when they're willing to work in the dark when the staffing is thin."

Rachel snorted. "We put up a sign at the park entrance at the end of the day, and no rangers are here after dark. A busload of beachcombers could come in after closing, and we'd never know it unless we saw their footprints when we drove the beach the next morning."

I gazed a distance down the beach. "It's even worse than that. No one comes down here after our last beach patrol. I suppose the Coast Guard might spot an unusual boat, but it's not their job to chase away treasure-hunters."

Rachel looked at the beach ahead of the pickup. "Are we trying to protect a crime scene, or can we walk around?"

"I don't know what evidence we could collect or maintain here. We might as well walk around."

Rachel found a bottle cap at the first hole. I found the metal "bung" ring off a five-gallon pail cast aside next to a hole farther down the sand. Together we collected four additional pieces of metal debris, some unidentifiable and others like something from a boat or drilling platform.

Rachel held out a collection of metal debris to me. "About half the holes had some scrap next to them. Do you think they found coins in all the others?"

I surveyed the area. "If they did, you can bet they'll be back. I'm not sure what a gold 'doubloon' or a silver 'piece-of-eight' is worth on the collector's market, but I'll bet a lot of people will consider it worth the risk."

"What risk, Doug? It's not like you and I pose any threat to them. They can see us approaching from miles away like the boat we just chased off. If they come in by boat, all they have to do is push off, and as soon as the boat's twenty feet from shore, they've effectively escaped. And even if we catch them, what are we going to do? We'll confiscate the coins and send them away."

"Maybe there's a higher-tech solution." I nodded toward the pickup, and we drove back to the visitor center.

* * *

Mom, Mandy, and Jill were already into the margaritas by the time Matt and I arrived at the Mattson's home. We heard laughter from the driveway.

Matt shook his head. "Tequila makes her clothes fall off."

"I have a hard time envisioning Mandy with that much liquor in her."

"Not literally, but there have been a couple times where she's kicked off her shoes and danced on the table." He held the door for me. "We're home!"

"We're on the patio!" Mandy replied from somewhere on the other side of the house.

We stepped through the patio door and found the three women sitting around a glass-topped

41

table, each with a chilled salt-rimmed glass in her hand. On the table were bowls of chips, guacamole, and salsa. Mother's cheeks were rosy, and she was grinning. I'd rarely seen her displaying either of those reactions since Dad died, nor had I seen her in shorts, sandals, or a brightly colored blouse.

Jill patted a chair next to her, putting me across the table from Mother. "Come, sit down. I'm sure Matt can find a beer for you." Jill's outfit was equally summery, although slightly more subdued.

Mandy gave me a wink like she and Jill had pulled off a coup. "Y'all eat a chip and sip a beer while Jill and I set the table," she said with her endearing Texas twang.

Matt showed up with two beers, each with a lime wedge in the bottleneck. He reached across the table and handed one to me. "How was your day, Mrs. Fletcher?"

Mother put her hand on his arm. "Please call me Ronnie."

"Okay, Ronnie, did you have a good time with the girls?"

Mother took a sip of Margarita and nodded. "I'm so pleased Jill invited me down. I haven't let my hair down in years."

I nearly choked on my beer. The invitation had come from me, and Jill was more than irritated that I'd invited Mother down with even a chance that I'd leave them alone. Suddenly, the invitation had come from Jill. I wasn't even mentioned as a co-inviter.

Mom pointed at the neck of Matt's beer bottle. "Matt, tell me why you put limes in the beer bottles. Is that a Texas tradition?"

"It's actually a Mexican tradition. The common theory is that it's a way to get vitamin C into the beer drinkers. The alternate theory is that the Mexican beer is so bad you need a squeeze of lime juice to cover the skunky flavor."

Mother tipped her head back and laughed out loud. She slapped Matt's shoulder like he'd just told the world's funniest joke. "You're just as delightful as Mandy. I understand why Jill dragged Doug here to live."

Matt's eyebrows rose. "I didn't realize it was Jill's idea."

"Mandy explained it over lunch and had us in stitches. Doug, being socially inept, didn't catch any of Jill's girlish hints, and she finally dragged him out for dinner, planted a kiss on him, and suggested they go back to his house for a nightcap. I guess Doug only caught on after Jill was sitting on his lap and nibbling on his ear."

Matt laughed so hard he spilled his beer. "I hadn't heard that version of their first date."

I leaned my head back and took a deep breath. Although, there was a hint of truth to the story, the thread was very thin.

Mandy walked onto the patio and looked at the three of us. "Douglas, I do believe you're blushing."

Matt grinned. "Ronnie just told me the story about Jill dragging Doug into her net and kidnapping him to Texas."

Mandy cocked her head. "And that embarrassed you, Doug?"

I put up my hands in surrender. "I hadn't expected to be the topic of the day."

"Aw," Mandy said. "It's such a sweet story, and Ronnie hadn't heard it."

Matt seized the opportunity to change the conversation before I had a chance to set the story straight. "I think I smell shrimp. Do you need me to do anything?"

Mandy put her arm around Matt's waist and kissed his cheek. "All you have to do is bring your beers inside and eat."

Matt, the perfect gentleman, helped Mother out of her chair and carried her Margarita inside.

I followed, closing the patio door. Mother took a chair at the corner next to Jill and by Matt. I sat next to Mandy, who quickly went into hostess mode and explained the meal, the proper way to peel shrimp, and got people passing platters of food. The meal was sumptuous, and eating interrupted the conversation, which was fine with me.

Mandy and Jill cleared the table while Matt refilled Margarita glasses and brought two more beers. Mandy returned with a pecan pie that smelled like it had just come from the oven. I passed the first slice to Jill, who smiled at me and ran her bare foot up my calf. That nearly caused me to drop the second piece on my lap. I tried to glare at her, but her angelic smile, complete with dimples, melted my anger. Mother mistook the exchange as me fumbling the pie and Jill rescuing me. Right then, I realized that Mom and Jill had bonded, and I'd become extraneous to their relationship.

I'd limited myself to two beers over four hours and knew I was the only one capable of driving back to the townhouse. Jill and Mother left the house after lots of hugs and kissed cheeks. I shook Matt's hand and Mandy surprised me with a hug and a kiss on the cheek. Before she released the hug, she whispered, "Mission accomplished. Ronnie knows that Jill's the saint who rescued you from unhappy bachelorhood."

"You're the saint," I said, kissing her cheek.

She batted her eyelashes. "Little ole me?"

The drive to the townhouse was quiet, each of us with our own thoughts. I unlocked the door and led everyone inside. Mother hugged Jill and suggested she needed a minute with me. I was surprised Jill didn't appear worried as she disappeared up the stairs.

I looked at Mother, who seemed concerned. "You have a problem, Doug."

"What would that be?" I asked.

"Jill might be too nice for you. If you don't pull your act together, you might lose her."

I was flabbergasted. "What?"

"Jill is as sweet as Mandy's pecan pie, and you're damaged goods."

I was at a loss for words, and it apparently showed.

"Jill spent her life waiting for someone special, and she seems to think that's you. She wasn't around when you were the drunk, who couldn't relate to his own wife and ruined a marriage. Are you ready to act like a grown-up and treat her with the respect she deserves?"

"Mother, you're drunk. Let's have this discussion tomorrow."

"No. We're having this talk now. Jill has her poop together. She's excelled in a man's world and somehow thinks that you're the piece that's been missing from her life. What I'm telling you is that I like her. I like her a lot. You're obviously taken with her too, or she wouldn't be wearing a diamond, but I don't want you to mess this up."

I finally understood what she was saying, and I hugged her, something that hadn't happened a dozen times in my lifetime. "Mom, I love her. I plan to marry her and spend the rest of my life with her. She's going to be your daughter-in-law, and I'm pleased that you love her too."

Mom pressed her face into my shoulder. "You're starting to catch on, but you're missing a piece." She pushed me back and held my arms. "I don't want to be standing next to her when someone hands her a triangle-folded flag."

"My funeral?"

"She's waited a lifetime for someone. Don't leave her a widow." Mom pushed away from me and walked up the steps, leaving me stunned.

Jill was already in bed when I closed the bedroom door. I brushed my teeth, put on a pair of clean boxers, and slipped under the sheet next to her. I put my arm around her waist and spooned with her.

"What did Ronnie have to say?"

"She likes and respects you."

"That's nice. I like Ronnie too. She's an interesting woman."

"She's happy that you're going to be her daughter-in-law. But she doesn't want me to leave you a widow."

"What?"

"She said you're too nice, and you've waited too long for the right guy to come along. She doesn't want me to leave you a widow."

Jill rolled over and looked into my eyes. "I can't say I'd argue with that view. On the other hand, it's not my place to change you. I love you for who you are and not the person I hope to mold you into."

"Thank you."

Jill yawned. "Can I go to sleep now?"

I kissed her deeply.

"Not tonight, Doug. Mandy's picking us up in seven hours to go golfing."

"You're taking my mother golfing? Has she ever been golfing?"

"If you'd been paying attention, you'd know that she took lessons and joined a women's league after your father died. Her handicap is nine."

"That's good?"

"She's going to give me a lesson."

* * *

47

Rachel was doing internet searches on Texas treasure-hunters on her ancient computer, using a connection pirated off the neighbor's Wi-Fi. Toby, her roommate, walked in a few minutes after ten PM and glanced over her shoulder as he walked to the kitchen. He wore a stained t-shirt advertising a concert tour that had taken place eleven years before and jeans that were brown with grime. His hair was greasy and wrapped in an old bandana that had been twisted into a headband.

He stopped at the refrigerator and asked, "What's up with the treasure hunt?"

"We're trying to stop people who are digging up the national seashore looking for Spanish doubloons."

"There's actual Spanish treasure here?"

Rachel described their encounter with the boatload of treasure-hunters and the history of the three lost Spanish galleons.

"So, people are finding Spanish coins on the shore, and you're trying to stop them?"

"The area around North Padre Island is the Mansfield Cut Archaeological District, and it's illegal to recover of artifacts. The Park Service is charged with protecting the area from looters."

Toby walked out of the kitchen, eating soy yogurt. "You're talking like you're trying to save the last orange-spotted tree frog. Are there just a couple dozen coins left?"

"Between the three ships, there are tons of unrecovered silver and gold coins."

Toby finished his yogurt and set it on an end table consisting of three cement blocks. "Man, that's nuts. You should be encouraging people to dig them up. The county could use like half the money for social programs. They're doing nobody any good laying on the bottom of the Gulf or buried in a sand dune."

Rachel closed the computer. "They're archaeological artifacts, Toby. You can't let people just dig them up and carry them away."

Toby gave her a look of disdain.

Rachel set her laptop on the floor, deciding to change the topic. "You're kind of late tonight. What's up?"

"You know how it goes. I'm trying to keep track of my mothers who've been through treatment to see if they're staying clean. They're not morning people in the best of times."

"How many have you got left in the study?"

"I'm down to four right now, but I'm trying to convince a couple more that they should be in rehab."

"They're pregnant, on drugs, and you've been trying for seven years to get them into treatment programs. When does it end?"

Toby glared at her. "Listen. I'm doing something that's going to make a real difference in the world. If I can get traction in the community, I'll be able to get these women off drugs before they get pregnant and prevent a bunch of crack babies. That's real social progress. What are you doing? You're chasing down treasure-hunters and ticketing people for

49

littering in a campground. Whose job is more important in the greater scheme of things?"

"We've had this discussion. Both our jobs are important, but in different ways."

Toby rolled his eyes.

"You've been doing this Ph.D. project for seven years. How many women have you convinced to go into treatment, and how many of them stayed clean until their kids were born?"

"It's taken a while to get accepted into the community and develop the programs. Besides, I don't have to worry about some speeder pulling a gun and killing me."

"Right. You're so much safer hanging around with crack whores? Don't you think there's some pimp out there who's ready to kill you for stealing his girls and putting them into treatment?"

Toby walked into the bedroom and slammed the door. The same ending they'd had to a dozen other discussions, each ending with Rachel sleeping on the couch.

Chapter Five

I was drinking coffee and searching the internet for information about North Padre Island treasure-hunters when Rachel walked into my office, looking tired. She dropped into the chair on the other side of my desk.

"Tough night?"

"Toby and I had our recurring battle over whose job is more important. He said we should let people dig up the coins, then use the money for social programs."

I logged out of the computer. "How is his research project going?"

"He doesn't want to talk about it except in general terms."

I knew the statistics on the effectiveness of court-ordered rehab programs. It was dismal, and as I recalled, the one-year success rate was in single digits. "Is he having any success?"

"Based on his evasive answers, I'd say, no. He's working with a couple new people, trying to get them into rehab, but he's up half the night roaming crappy neighborhoods to find addicts who are willing to enter rehab."

"That's dangerous as hell! A white guy roaming drug infested-neighborhoods might as well have a target painted on his back."

"I know. We had a side argument about whose job was more dangerous."

"He's still hung up on you carrying a gun?"

"I said he was at greater risk from a pimp, who sees one of his girls talking to Toby about joining the rehab program."

"What's Toby's educational endpoint?"

"At some point, he has to accumulate and summarize his findings in a doctoral dissertation."

"How many crack-babies has he saved?"

"He won't say. I think that's why his research has gone on for seven years. He can't find an endpoint that shows anything but failure."

"Maybe that's the dissertation. 'After exhaustive attempts, I was unable to make progress in getting inner-city addicted women off drugs until their babies are born.'"

Rachel slid down in her chair. "I'm pretty sure that won't be acceptable to his advisor."

"So, he just keeps beating away at this until he gets shot or his advisor boots him for being ineffective?"

Rachel shrugged. "I don't know if I can face either of those outcomes."

Matt knocked on the doorframe and stopped when he saw Rachel's downtrodden look. "Have you two strategized a way of approaching the treasure-hunters that won't chase them away before you get close?"

Rachel straightened up. "It's going to get worse. I found a website last night where someone with the handle CCRichMan was bragging about the 'honey hole' he'd discovered. He was elusive about the location, as are all treasure-hunters, but he posted a photo showing a handful of Spanish silver coins that looked like they might've been abraded in the surf. The guy claimed they were worth three hundred dollars each."

Matt looked awestruck. "The coins on the beach are worth that much?"

Rachel shook her head. "It depends a lot on the condition and the date if it's visible. The smaller, one-reale silver coins are probably only worth eighty bucks. The larger ones are proportionately more valuable. There were some gold coins on the 1554 shipwrecks and if word gets out that people are recovering those, we'll have to string razor wire on the shore."

Matt shook his head. "Shit."

I pulled my computer over and logged on. "I'm afraid the horses are out of the barn." I turned the laptop so Matt and Rachel could see the screen. "Here's a website where treasure-hunters were soliciting partners for a Padre Island recovery effort." I scrolled down to a post and let them read it.

This is the perfect place to hit because there are literally tons of unrecovered silver, and the Park Service doesn't have the resources to watch the beach. All you have to do is avoid their morning and afternoon patrols, and you've got the whole rest of the day to search.

Matt tilted his head back and stared at the ceiling. "I wonder if there's an opening for a Park Service Superintendent somewhere quiet, like the Ozarks or Mount Rushmore." He paused, then asked, "Do you two have any suggestions?"

I smiled. "Like Rachel said, we could string razor wire on the beach."

Matt shook his head. "That'd be a first—fencing a national park to restrict access."

"Maybe Doug and I could patrol alone and make twice as many trips on an irregular schedule."

"I don't think splitting you up is a good idea. My primary concern is still safety, yours, and that of the visitors. Having either of you alone in the pickups would make me very uncomfortable."

Rachel straightened up and became more animated. "Before Doug came, I used to patrol with one of the interpretive rangers. Put another ranger in the pickup with each of us. With overlapping trips, we'd be closer if something came up and we needed backup. Besides that, I've learned a lot from Doug, and I'm a much better cop than I used to be."

Matt looked at me, awaiting my judgment.

"Rachel's good, but there are still a lot of bad situations she hasn't experienced. There is a lot of money involved here, and there are people who'll kill over thirty dollars in a liquor store hold up. If we arrest someone, they're facing federal prosecution, which is a big deal. I can see some shady characters going to *any* length to avoid arrest and keep a bag of silver coins."

Rachel's face flushed, her gaze dropped toward the floor.

"I'm sorry, Rachel, but you're still green, and I agree with Matt, I don't want to risk your life."

"So, Doug, what's the solution?" Matt asked. He'd told me early on in my Padre Island tenure that my greatest value to him was walking in with a problem and the solution. I was really reaching this time because there wasn't an obvious approach.

I put my hands up like I was as lost as he was. "A helicopter would help."

"That's not going to happen. The Park Service would have to divert a copter from somewhere else and the operational and pilot expense would come out of my budget."

"Can you get a couple more seasonal law enforcement rangers down here?"

"I can call, but I wouldn't bet on that solution either."

"How about the local sheriff's departments?" Rachel asked. "They might be able to access a helicopter, and they have boats."

"That might be a great solution." I glanced at my watch. "Can you ask the local cops if they'll give us some support and maybe put some guys in a boat by the Mansfield Cut, Matt?"

"I can make some calls. If things are slow, they might be willing to help."

Rachel got up. "Let's make the afternoon beach cruise."

Matt looked at me. "Anything else you can think of?"

"I've got nothing, but I'll think about it."

Rachel got behind the steering wheel. "You don't think I can handle this alone?"

"I'm not sure I can handle a boatload of treasure-hunters alone. Controlling a crowd with two cops is a whole different thing than trying to do it alone."

Rachel got quiet.

I hoped she believed me because I told her the truth. If we ran into a dozen hostile treasure-hunters, I would be happy to have even a rookie ranger backing me up.

Chapter Six

I parked the Park Service pickup in the driveway next to my Isuzu. Based on our evening discussion, I expected to find Jill and Mom at home recovering from their day of golf with Mandy. Instead, I heard a woman crying as I opened the townhouse door. My mind swam in the possible scenarios that would have Jill or Mom crying.

I didn't recognize the blonde woman at the dining room table. She wore jeans and a t-shirt with a logo I couldn't read. Her hair had been carefully done up at one time, but now it was in disarray, and I could see that her makeup had run. Mother, still in her golf outfit, held one of the woman's hands, leaning close.

Jill, in a golf shirt and bright green shorts, glanced up at me with sad eyes and raised brows. She slid a chair away from the table for me, then reached across the table and touched the woman's other hand. "Clarice, this is my fiancé, Doug."

The blonde looked up at me and tried to smile politely. Mascara streaked down her cheeks, her lipstick smeared. Her face looked familiar, but I didn't remember the context of our meeting. I saw the two boys racing around in our yard, playing some version of tag, and I put the pieces together. She was our neighbor.

Jill stood and put her hand on my shoulder. "Would you like a beer or something?" She shifted her gaze to our neighbor. "Clarice, would you like something?"

Clarice pulled a tissue from a box sitting next to Mother and wiped her tears. "Do you have anything a touch stronger?"

"I've got some pre-mixed margaritas. It's either that or beer."

Mother looked up. "I'd take a margarita. Would that be okay, Clarice?"

The woman looked out our patio door at the boys, then shook her head. "I'd better not. I have to take care of the boys."

Jill knelt down next to Clarice. "Have a margarita. Doug and I can make sure the boys are fed supper and put to bed."

Jill read the panic in my eyes and sent me a discreet frown that said, *suck it up*.

Clarice set her tissue down. "I suppose one wouldn't hurt."

Jill poured margaritas. Clarice had her eyes closed and occasionally sniffled.

I got up and took a beer out of the refrigerator, then leaned close to Jill as she put the margaritas in the fridge. "What's going on?"

Jill grabbed my elbow and pulled me into the entryway. "Clarice's husband, Charlie, is a flight cadet at the Naval Air Station. An officer and a chaplain showed up this afternoon and told her that Charlie had a mechanical problem and ejected over the Gulf. The Navy and Coast Guard are looking for him.

"Shit."

"They said they have a good idea where his plane went down . . ."

I put the beer back in the refrigerator and went out the patio door. "Hi guys, my name is Doug." I sat in a patio chair to minimize my height, putting me close to eye-level with the boys. They stopped chasing each other and walked over to me, looking more curious than scared. "What are your names?"

The older boy looked through the patio door at his mother, then looked back at me. The younger boy's eyes never left my pistol.

"Are you a cop?" The older boy asked.

"I'm a Park Ranger, and you can call me Doug. Jill and I live here, next door to you."

The younger boy continued to stare at my holster, then he looked up. "Is that a real gun?"

"Yes, it's real."

"Do you shoot people?" he asked.

"I've never shot anyone." Only a slight lie, I'd been caught in a night firefight in Iraq and fired my weapon but had no idea if I'd hit anyone. As a ranger, I'd been in a shootout with a guy smuggling hazardous waste. I'd shot his direction, and he'd died but not from bullet wounds.

"What are your names?" I asked again.

"I'm Danny," said the smaller boy, who looked about four. "My brother is Allen."

59

"We'll have to ask your mom, but if she says it's okay, would you like to ride in my pickup and go out for a malt and a cheeseburger?"

Danny's eyes got wide. "Can we use the siren?"

"I'm afraid not."

Allen finally spoke, "I can't have milk or cheese."

I stood up and put out my hand. "I guess you'll have to get a hamburger and Coke. Is that all right?"

Danny pushed Allen aside and took my hand. "I'll have a cheeseburger."

I reached down with my other hand and took Allen's hand. "Let's ask your mom if it's okay." Allen reluctantly took my hand.

We walked into the dining room where Clarice, Jill, and Mom were sipping green drinks from tumblers. Clarice had stopped sobbing, but her eyes were red-rimmed and puffy.

"If it's okay with Clarice, the boys and I are going out for burgers."

"Can we, Mommy? Doug said he'd drive us in the pickup with lights and siren."

Clarice looked at me with concern.

"We're not using the lights and siren. We're just going to take a quiet ride to the diner."

"Allen's lactose intolerant."

"He's already warned me that he can't have cheese or a malt."

"Can we, Mommy?" Danny begged.

Relief spread over Clarice's face, and tears welled in her eyes. "Sure. You can go with Ranger Fletcher."

"He told us to call him Doug," Danny explained with determination.

"Okay. You and Doug can go to the diner. But you have to behave and do what Doug tells you to do."

"Yay!" Danny yelled. Allen looked apprehensive but nodded.

"Can I bring back anything for you, ladies? Burgers? Salads? Gumbo?"

Clarice shook her head.

Jill walked me to the door and pecked my cheek. "Bring back a quart of gumbo and maybe another jug of margaritas. It might be a long night."

"Did the Navy give her any hope he'd be found soon?"

Jill's eyes turned steely. "His locator beacon didn't activate."

"So, they don't know exactly where he is, but they're hoping to find him visually."

Jill grabbed my bicep and squeezed it, then rested her head on my shoulder. "They found his empty auto-inflating life raft," she whispered.

"The pilots wear inflating vests, too."

Jill nodded. "They do. And they carry dye packs they can release when they see a search-aircraft but none of the search planes have seen dye in the water."

The boys were getting restless standing next to the pickup, so I pulled out my keys. "This is hell for Clarice."

Jill shook her head. "This is purgatory. Let's hope we don't get to the hell stage."

I thought about Mother's comments about not want to be standing next to Jill while someone handed her a triangularly folded flag at a funeral as I drove to the diner. That would be hell.

* * *

The lights were off in Clarice's townhouse when we got back from the diner, so I assumed that she was either still at our dining room table, at the hospital, or the morgue. I steeled myself when I opened our door. The boys raced past me as I carried in the bags of gumbo and margaritas.

Clarice, still at our dining room table, looked like she was melting. Mother looked like a caretaker. Jill was holding Clarice's hand, apparently trying to appear upbeat but at a loss for words.

"Anyone want gumbo?" I asked as the boys fought for Clarice's lap.

Jill took the bag with the tub of gumbo and ladled it into three bowls, then put the first one into the microwave to warm it.

"Anything?" I whispered.

Jill shook her head, then carried the bowl to Clarice with a spoon. The boys were chattering non-stop, and Clarice slid the bowl and spoon over to Mother.

Jill set the second bowl in front of Clarice. "You've got to eat something."

Clarice slid the boys off her lap. "I should put the boys to bed."

"Nonsense," Jill said, using a tone I'd only heard once before when she'd addressed an FBI agent who attempted to take credit for my work. "Doug and I will put the boys to bed. You and Ronnie eat some gumbo."

I held out my hands to the boys. "C'mon guys." The boys looked at Clarice, who hesitated for a second before nodding her approval of the plan.

Jill scooted the boys out the door. "Teeth get brushed, then into pajamas."

"Dad reads to us," Danny protested. Although older, Allen let Danny do the talking.

"You find the book you want, and Doug will read to you."

The boys ran up the stairs, tumbling over each other.

I finished the book, made sure the boys were asleep, and turned off the light when the doorbell rang. When I came downstairs, Jill was talking to a Navy commander in dress whites with aviator's wings and a dozen service bars on her chest. I caught the end of the conversation. Jill said, "Next door."

I trotted to catch up with them but waited on our steps so I could watch Clarice's front door. The commander sat at the table while Jill and

63

Mom tried to stand back at a discreet distance. I overheard the word *hospital* and sighed in relief.

The commander and Clarice stood. "I've got to get the boys."

Mother stepped forward. "Jill and I've got that under control. You go and take care of your husband."

Clarice hesitated for a second, then nodded. She followed the commander to our door. "Commander, I've got a Park Service vehicle with lights and a siren."

The Navy officer smiled for the first time. "There's no rush. He's a little waterlogged, but he's going to be fine."

I followed Mom to Clarice and Charlie's house and stood awkwardly in the living room. Mother went upstairs to check on the boys. Jill waited until she was out of sight, then engulfed me in a hug.

"That was godawful," she said into my shoulder.

"Worse than dealing with bickering rangers?"

"Oh, this was at the top of the Park Service awfulness scale. Right next to waiting to hear if lost hikers were alive or not."

"At least, this sounds like there's a happy ending."

Jill sighed. "Clarice is going to try and talk her husband into dropping out of the flight cadet program. She's hoping he'll take a nice quiet job on a ship or at a desk."

"They'll be okay when the dust settles."

"I hope so because it sounds like he's dreamt of being a pilot his whole life. If they can't get their heads together on this, I think there will be a parting of the ways."

"I'm sure the Navy has great counselors who've dealt with this dozens of times."

Jill leaned back and looked into my eyes. "This scared me."

"You want me to give up my badge." I made it a comment, not a question.

"I don't want to change you. It just makes me realize how much I want to treasure every moment we have together."

I noticed the microwave clock. "It's almost midnight. I have to be up in five hours."

Jill gave me a kiss. "Good night."

"You're not coming to bed? I think Mom's got this."

"Are you kidding? There's no way I can sleep right now with the adrenaline that's been pumping through my system all evening. I might curl up on the couch later."

Chapter Seven

Although Jill and I had only been a couple for a short time, it was odd not feeling the warmth of her body next to me when I woke up. I reached for the alarm and saw the bleary red numerals staring at me. I'd only been asleep for a little over four hours. The hot shower pounded on my shoulders but failed to make me feel awake. I smeared shave cream on my face and shaved as the shower stall filled with steam. I stepped out of the shower to a kiss, and a towel still warm from the dryer.

"Clarice got home a couple minutes ago. Ronnie is helping her get breakfast for the boys. I was in the way."

I toweled off. "How's Charlie?"

"He probably has a concussion. He's bruised, but nothing is broken. They're keeping him for a concussion protocol."

"Do they know what happened?"

Jill shook her head. "Clarice said he had a flameout."

"Rachel and I are going to the hospital morgue. Maybe I can see Charlie when we're through with the autopsy."

I hung up my towel and looked closely at Jill. "Did you get any sleep?"

"Their couch isn't comfortable. Every time I turned over, I found another toy hidden under the cushions." She watched me dress from the edge of the bed. "You don't look like you got much more sleep than I did."

"The Army trained me to operate on almost no sleep."

Jill snorted. "Your Army basic training was a long time ago, cowboy. You're not the kid you used to be."

I pulled on my duty belt and checked the Sig, then kissed Jill gently. "Get some rest."

"I think Clarice is going to need some help today. Maybe Ronnie and I can tag-team support, and each of us can get a catnap."

Allen stood on the corner wearing baggy shorts and an orange backpack that looked big enough for a high schooler. I was pulling out of my parking spot when the bus stopped to pick up Allen. He stepped off the curb across the street from the bus when I heard the bus horn. A car raced along in the open lane next to the bus where Allen was crossing the street. I lit up the flashers, hit the siren, and pulled between Allen and the car.

The teen who drove the car was oblivious to the flashing lights on the bus and the pickup until he looked up from his phone when he heard the siren. He panicked, locked the brakes, and swerved onto the curb where he hit a mailbox. I waved the bus driver on, then radioed for backup.

The impact set off the airbag, and the young teen staggered from the car with cuts on his face and a bloody nose. He glared at me. "What the hell?"

I grabbed the kid by the collar and spun him around, so he was leaning on the hood of his car with my hand in the middle of his back. "I hope whatever you were watching on the phone was worth the damage to your car and the ticket for failing to yield to a school bus."

"The kid was on the bus."

"I blocked your path, so you didn't hit the kid. If I hadn't, you'd be going to jail for hitting a child boarding a school bus. Instead of a fine, you'd have put the kid in the hospital and you'd be looking at jail time. You should thank me."

I heard the whine of the Port Aransas police siren.

"Who are you? You're not a local cop."

"I'm your worst enemy. I'm a federal cop."

The kid twisted around to look at my uniform. "You're a fucking park ranger. What the hell are you doing? This isn't a park."

"I took an oath to protect the laws of the United States. It didn't say *inside a park* anywhere. It's the same oath taken by the border patrol and U.S. marshals."

The Port Aransas police cruiser rolled to a stop behind the smashed car. I recognized the redheaded officer from an earlier interaction. Raymond Joseph (RJ) Smith put on his Stetson and swaggered up to us.

"Ranger Fletcher, what do we have here?"

"This fine upstanding young man was texting while racing toward a bus that was loading kids. I lit him up and blocked his path to protect the kids boarding the bus. When he looked up from his phone, he swerved into this mailbox to avoid hitting me."

"Let him up, Doug. He's the Baptist minister's son. I'll take him home, and I can guarantee that anything we, or the courts, could do to him would be minor compared to the fire and brimstone he's going to get at home. Isn't that right, Bobbie Joe?"

Bobbie Joe Bickell stood up, blood from his nose had puddled on the hood of his car and smeared his face. He sniffled and held his nose to staunch the bleeding. He glared at me and RJ. "My dad won't give a shit."

"Oh, Bobbie. The petty stuff your daddy has let pass is nothing compared to driving while you're texting and nearly running down a child boarding a bus. I'd be shocked if Reverend Bickell lets you drive again before you graduate high school." RJ looked at me. "Thanks, Doug. You might've prevented a nasty accident. I've got this if you need to get going."

"Do you need me to file a report?"

"Naw. Bobbie and I are going to handle this outside the county judicial system. I can assure you that Bobbie's pain will be greater than the slap on the wrist any juvenile judge would hand out."

Clarice and Danny were standing next to my pickup, watching the interaction between the

69

cop, the kid, and me. She pulled Danny to her hip and gave me a hug with her other arm. "Jill said you are special, and Ronnie is an angel. I can tell you're Ronnie's kin." Her Texas twang and homespun words touched me.

At a loss for words, I tousled Danny's hair. "When you start riding the bus, be sure to check for distracted drivers before you cross the street to board the bus. Okay?"

Danny nodded. Clarice looked at my bloodshot eyes and handed me a thermal cup she'd been holding in the hand hugging Danny. "I think you need this coffee more than I do."

"Thanks, but I'll get a cup at the convenience store."

Clarice jammed the covered stainless-steel cup into my hand. "Doug, I'm trying to thank you. Please indulge me."

Clarice was near tears. Between Charlie's close call and the incident with Allen boarding the bus, she was a mess, yet determined to make me understand the depth of her appreciation. "Thank you." I put my arm over her shoulder and gave her a hug.

I carefully drove away, sipping Clarice's coffee. I drink my coffee black. Clarice's coffee had at least three teaspoons of sugar and a cup of milk with a sprinkle of cinnamon. I stopped at the convenience store, poured Clarice's coffee into a garbage can, and filled the stainless-steel cup with hot black coffee. I was starting to feel human by the time I drove over the Packery Channel.

Chapter Eight

Rachel and I met in the Park Service parking lot, and I drove to the hospital. Rachel seemed tense, obviously on edge about viewing the autopsy, and our conversation was limited to the weather. We bypassed the hospital information desk, knowing where the morgue was located based on a previous trip. The medical examiner's assistant sat behind a desk outside the autopsy suite. He'd been introduced as Artie when we'd met earlier. His picture I.D. showed his name as Arthur Raymond. His skin was the color of mahogany, and he wore blue surgical scrubs. A pair of reading glasses hung on his chest, attached to a chain.

I offered my hand. "Hi, Artie. You probably remember my partner, Rachel."

Artie stood and shook my hand, then offered his hand to Rachel.

Rachel seemed pleased. "You're a gentleman, Artie. Most men don't bother shaking my hand."

Artie opened the door to a short hallway. "Ms. Randall, I don't judge people based on their sex. There are smart men and women, and there are dumb men and women." He pushed open the door to the suite where Dr. Rhonda Overgaard was examining Jane Doe's wet suit.

Artie leaned close and whispered to Rachel as he pulled a surgical mask out of a wall-mounted dispenser. "And I work for one of the smartest women I've ever met."

"Ah, the Park Service is here. Once again, we're safe from litterers and forest fires." The corners of the M.E.'s eyes crinkled. Although most of her face was covered, her smile was evident. Like Artie, Rhonda Overgaard wore blue hospital scrubs with a blue hair cover, a surgical mask, and a clear face shield.

I took a Tyvek coverall from a hanger and slipped it on. "Good morning, Doc. Have you found anything interesting during your external examination?"

"She's been dead long enough to start decomposition that darkened her skin and attracted scavengers."

I looked at the body, and the woman's face and hands had been shredded by birds, rats, and the coyotes we'd scared away. Her eye sockets were just dark cavities, although much of her blonde scalp survived. "There's sand ground into the back of her wetsuit where it was abraded by the beach, so she was dragged to where her body was found. I haven't found any evidence of defensive wounds. There's sand under the few fingernails the crime scene techs recovered, but no skin, blood, or hair to test."

"Cause of death?"

"Too soon to tell." The M.E. selected scissors from the tray next to her and opened the short neoprene wetsuit with two quick cuts. Artie helped her roll the woman's body to remove the wetsuit, and she continued her surface examination. The portion of the body covered by the wetsuit was turning dark, but the skin appeared pristine compared to the portions exposed to the elements and depredation of vermin.

"The CSI team found a gold coin tucked in her wetsuit when they searched for I.D." I said.

"That explains the somewhat rounded dark mark above her left breast. I take it the coin was slightly irregular because the mark isn't perfectly round, like a modern half dollar coin."

Rachel was eager to redeem herself for tossing her cookies at the last autopsy, so she threw out some history. "It was a Spanish coin, probably from one of the Padre Island shipwrecks."

Overgaard stopped and looked up. "There are Padre Island shipwrecks?"

Rachel took out her cellphone and scrolled through the photos while the doctor waited impatiently. "Here's a picture from the museum. These are coins recovered from the three 1554 shipwrecks."

"Not all of the coins have been recovered?" Overgaard asked.

Rachel shook her head as she tucked her phone away. "There are still tons of silver coins unaccounted for."

Overgaard went back to her examination of Jane Doe's body. Asking Arnie to help roll her over, then inspecting her backside. I was struck by how waxy and gray the woman's skin appeared except for her buttocks and back, which were dark bluish-brown due to the post-mortem pooling of blood after her heart stopped pumping.

"Come closer," Overgaard said. She pointed to the victim's neck. "Can you see the dark marks? She was strangled. Normally, there would be petechial hemorrhaging in her eyes, pointing to asphyxia as the cause of death if her face had been protected from the birds."

We stepped back as the doctor made the "Y" incision on the victim's chest and abdomen.

"I'd say your victim was a relatively young woman. Her body has good muscle tone, and we found no calluses from heavy labor on what's left of her hands. If I were to speculate, I'd say she worked out to stay in shape. There's no indication of sexual assault, nor has she ever had a child. The X-rays don't show any broken bones, nor are there tattoos or scars from surgical procedures."

While the doctor spoke, she cut through the ribs to expose the victim's internal organs. After cutting several ribs, she stopped and looked at Rachel. "Are you keeping it together, Ranger Randall?"

I glanced at Rachel, who was blushing. During her first autopsy, Rachel had rushed to the janitor's sink at this point. "I'm doing okay.

Doug suggested that coming to an autopsy on an empty stomach wasn't a good idea."

The doctor looked at me, and her eyes crinkled again like she was giving me a knowing smile. "Good call, Fletcher."

"The lungs are dry, and there's nothing remarkable about the victim's internal organs." Overgaard weighed and cut samples from the organs and placed them in specimen jars for later reference. She stepped back and set her scalpel on the tray.

"I hate to say this, but there's nothing remarkable about this young woman that'll help with her identification. Artie sent the one fingerprint we were able to recover to AFIS but didn't get a match, so she's never been arrested or fingerprinted for the military or federal security clearance."

I pulled off my mask. "Thanks, Doc."

"She was a young woman who was keeping herself in shape. Without a picture of her face or a fingerprint, you'll have to hope there's a missing-persons report stating her height, weight, and gross physical description. The best we can hope for is a dental or DNA match."

I threw my mask and the Tyvek suit into the garbage bin and was near the door when the doctor's voice stopped me.

"Fletcher, do you have a lot of treasure-hunters looking for coins?"

"Rachel's the expert on that."

Rachel looked like a daydreaming kid who'd been asked a question in class. She threw her

Tyvek overalls into the garbage and turned to the doctor. "It's always been an issue. The area around Padre Island is a protected archaeological site, so there are signs up saying it's illegal to dive to recover artifacts or to collect coins onshore. That said, Hurricane Harvey stirred up the bottom and exposed or washed up a bunch of buried debris including coins. That's triggered a new bunch of treasure-hunters. The internet has allowed people to spread the word more quickly through the treasure-hunter community, and that's sparked a new wave of people searching for coins and artifacts."

Overgaard nodded to Rachel, then looked at me. "Fletcher, try to get some sleep. You look like shit."

"Thanks for your concern, Doc."

Rachel led me to the elevators. "Time to drive the beach?"

"I'm going upstairs to see our neighbor. He ejected from his plane yesterday, and they rescued him from the ocean."

"Those planes cost like ten million dollars. I bet the Navy isn't happy to lose one."

The elevator arrived, and I punched the button for the third floor. Clarice had given me Charlie's room number when she'd handed me the coffee. "The Navy doesn't like losing pilots or planes. I think it costs more to train a pilot than the cost of a plane."

"Parachuting into the Gulf has to be scary," Rachel said as the elevator went up.

"I think the ejection from the plane would be scarier. There's an explosive charge under the seat that's meant to blow the canopy off, then shoot the pilot high enough into the air so his parachute can open even if he's sitting on the ground. They call it a zero-altitude ejection seat."

"That sounds terrible!"

"It beats the alternative of riding the plane into the ocean or ground, but it's a violent event and not without its own risk."

Rachel nodded. "I watched Top Gun with my brother. I remember what happened to Goose."

A Navy officer was speaking with a doctor at the nursing station, so we slipped past and walked into Charlie's room. The lights were dim, but I could see his bruised face. His eyes popped open when he heard our footsteps.

"More questions?" he asked.

I shook my head. "I'm Doug Fletcher, your neighbor. Clarice asked me to look in on you."

Charlie reached for the remote and turned on an overhead light. It made his bruises look worse, and the bright light seemed to bother his eyes. "You're the park ranger with the pickup and light bar."

I nodded. "This is my partner, Rachel Randall."

Charlie nodded but didn't try to shake hands. "If I remember correctly, Clarice said you offered to drive her to the hospital with lights and siren last night."

"I did. The Navy officer who drove out to tell her you'd been rescued said she didn't need to rush. You were bruised, but not in danger."

"I guess I'm not going to die, but I hurt everywhere, and I'm still cold. It took a while to find me, and the Gulf water isn't exactly warm."

"We heard your emergency beacon malfunctioned."

"Yeah. I was lucky because a Coast Guard helo decided to keep searching after sunset, and they saw the light on my vest. Otherwise, I'd still be floating out there." Charlie noticed our guns and cocked his head. "I didn't realize Park Rangers carried firearms."

"Rachel's a law enforcement ranger, and I'm a Park Service investigator."

"I remember reading about your shootout with the toxic waste dumper. I'd always thought of Park Rangers as guides, keeping people from getting lost or hurt. I didn't realize there was a police aspect to working in a park."

"That'll be a topic for some evening over a beer. I think we should let you get some rest."

Charlie put his left hand out, and I took it. "My head's a little messed up right now. But Clarice was here last night, and she told me about your wife dragging her over to your house after she saw the Navy officers at our door. I think she said something about you taking the boys out for burgers. I, ah . . . I can't thank you guys enough. We don't have any family nearby, and your wife really helped Clarice keep it together."

"Actually, Jill's my fiancé. And yes, she's a special person. I'm glad we could be there for you and Clarice."

"Clarice said something about a woman she called Ronnie. Is she another neighbor?"

"Ronnie's my mother. She's visiting from Minnesota."

"Doug, you're invited to our house for a barbecue when I get out. We owe Jill and Ronnie a lot. Rachel, you're welcome to come along too."

"We've got to let you rest. We can make plans after you get out of the hospital."

Charlie squeezed my hand. "Clarice said she was lost until Jill brought her to your house. From what Clarice said, Jill's a very special person."

"She has to be. She puts up with me. Get some rest."

Rachel was uncharacteristically quiet as we walked out of the hospital to the parking lot. She stopped in front of the pickup and crossed her arms. She left me standing with the keys dangling from my hand as cars passed.

"What?"

"No one says nice things like that about Toby."

I motioned for her to get into the pickup. "You're different people, at a different point in your lives."

"Toby will never be a giving person like Jill. He'll never offer to help the neighbors."

"He's trying to save babies from being born addicted to crack. That can be important."

"Toby's trying to get a degree so he can be a professor. He's only doing the crack baby thing because his advisor suggested it and so he can get his Ph.D. I don't think he really gives a damn about the women or babies except in the context of being test subjects."

"But you care for each other."

"He's getting more irritable and condescending. He doesn't value what I do and wants me to get a different job. I'm starting to feel like my only contribution to our relationship is money."

"I'm no relationship expert, but you need to talk to him about your concerns and needs."

"It's pretty hard to have a conversation when he spends the nights looking for pregnant crack whores to reform. He doesn't get home until I'm leaving for work some days."

"That doesn't leave a lot of time for a relationship."

"We haven't had sex in a month."

I knew we'd crossed a line with those words. If I'd been with a male partner, we'd have been talking through the ramifications of that situation. I wasn't sure what to say to Rachel, so I said nothing.

"You got very quiet."

"I was thinking," I lied.

"What should I do? I don't even see him enough to talk about this. And when I do, my feelings aren't important to him."

"Whose name is on the lease?"

"Toby didn't have a job or any income when we applied for the lease and set up the bank accounts, so everything is in my name."

"Go to a bank and open a checking account that's only in your name and have your salary deposit redirected to the new account. Then go to the old bank and close or remove your name from the old account. If you have any joint credit or debit cards, cancel them and cut up the cards."

Rachel twisted in the seat and looked at me. "You've been through this, haven't you?"

"Those are the things the divorce lawyer told me to do before I filed for divorce. He said I needed to separate our finances, so I wasn't left paying for my ex-wife's lifestyle. He was exactly right because I would've been on the hook for half of the credit card debt she ran up while we were waiting for the divorce, and she would've been writing checks for those payments from my salary. Once we were financially split, I changed the locks and put her stuff on the front steps."

"I don't think I can do that."

"Has Toby ever been physically abusive to you?"

"It's mostly mental. He demeans me with what I do or say."

"You evaded the question. Has he ever struck you?"

Rachel got quiet, and I peeked. Tears welled in her eyes.

I pulled off the highway and into a bank parking lot. "Let's go in here and open a new checking account in your name right now."

Chapter Nine

Rachel ate lunch with the young rangers in the break room.

I bought a Coke and a bag of chips from the vending machine and carried them into Matt's office. He was reading email on his computer while eating a sandwich and sipping an iced tea. He looked up and closed his email. "Looks like you're having the lunch of the ill-prepared again." He pushed half of his sandwich across the desk.

I lifted the bread and inspected the sprouts and brown meat. "What are we having for lunch?"

"Bologna and sprouts on whole wheat."

I took a bite, then scraped the sprouts onto the sandwich bag. I spun the bag of chips so Matt could grab some. "Things were a little crazy this morning, so there wasn't time to make a lunch."

Matt nodded. "Mandy's been at your house most of the morning. I got the whole blow-by-blow rundown of yesterday, last night, and this morning. It sounds like Mandy stepped in so your mom could get a nap. Mandy's been feeding Jill coffee to keep her awake while they watch Clarice and Charlie's younger son, Danny.

Clarice caught a cat nap then drove to the hospital."

I tried to stifle a yawn. "I could use a catnap myself. I'll let Rachel drive this afternoon, and I'll nap in the passenger seat."

"What did you find out at the autopsy?"

"Nothing earthshattering. The ME couldn't identify our Jane Doe. The main observations were that she was dragged across the sand in her wetsuit and was strangled. We don't know if she died on the shore or in a boat offshore and got dragged ashore."

"Strangulation was the cause of death?"

"Asphyxia due to strangulation."

Matt took a sip of tea to wash down the last of his sandwich. "Murder."

"Yes, she was murdered. A Spanish gold coin was inside her wetsuit, so I assume she was part of a treasure-hunting group and got crosswise with someone."

"Or, she was beachcombing alone, and someone killed her."

I mopped up breadcrumbs with my fingertip and sprinkled them into the wastebasket. "I hate to think about that possibility, but people do strange things when money is involved."

Matt considered my comment for a moment while sipping his tea. "I don't want Rachel patrolling alone."

"I won't argue that. We should be wearing vests while we're patrolling the beach, too."

"Shit. That's not the image of a ranger I want our visitors taking away."

"I've read that more rangers are injured in confrontations with visitors than in falls and wildlife attacks."

Matt shook his head. "It's a public relations nightmare, Doug. You guys were kidding about stringing razor wire on the beach, but putting you two in bulletproof vests is one more step in that direction."

"I don't want to call Rachel's next of kin to tell them she's been killed or wounded by a bullet that would've been stopped by a vest."

Matt put up his hands in surrender but never said yes. Instead, he changed the topic. "I made a few phone calls this morning, but I wasn't able to find much assistance for chasing down the treasure-hunters."

"But, you found some support?"

"I spoke with the Coast Guard lieutenant who commands the helicopter squadron. He agreed to have his pilots make a sweep up or down the island every time they pass over."

"That's it?"

Matt put up his hands defensively. "That'll probably quadruple the time anyone is watching the beach, and they'll be able to see our entire patrol area in two minutes."

"It doesn't get bodies onsite in time to arrest anyone or confiscate what they recover."

"I'd rather prevent the beachcombers from stealing stuff than arrest them."

"We've got a murderer out there, Matt. We're past the prevention stage."

Rachel stuck her head inside the door. "It smells like bologna in here."

I pushed the other guest chair toward her. "Matt spoke with the Coast Guard, and they're going to patrol the beach a little more."

"Sweet. Maybe they'll catch someone in the act."

Matt nodded. "Let's hope they have a deterrent effect." He paused and glanced at me. "Doug suggested that you guys wear vests while you're on patrol. I don't like the image that will create, but he argued that one person's been murdered, and he wants to err on the side of caution."

Rachel's eyes darted to me. "You think someone might shoot at us?"

"Someone killed Jane Doe."

"She was unarmed."

"People do irrational things when there's money involved. I'd like to be cautious."

Rachel looked at Matt, who nodded and then said, "We have to protect the Park Service resources, but I want you guys safe. I don't think you're expected to pay for vests out of your uniform allowance. I'll buy them out of Park Service funds somehow."

I got up and patted Rachel's shoulder. "C'mon, it's time to drive the beach."

Rachel fell in behind me as we left Matt's office. "It'll take Matt some time to requisition vests for us."

"I've got a pair of soft vests in my office. They're from my days as a St. Paul cop, so

85

they're black and say police rather than ranger, but they'll do until Matt comes up with Park Service vests for us." I opened a closet in the back of my office and took out the two black vests. "Adjust the Velcro straps to make it secure, but not so tight it's uncomfortable."

Rachel pulled the vest over her head and tightened the straps to fit her. I'd lost a few pounds since I'd quit drinking and gone to federal law enforcement training, so I also tightened the straps a bit.

Rachel tugged at the bottom of the vest and squirmed before making more adjustments. "This really isn't cut to accommodate a woman's body."

I shook my head. "It's one of my old vests, and I haven't ever had breasts. I'm sure there are enough women in law enforcement that some company is making women's vests."

"Yeah, there's probably a company run by a woman who's making them." Rachel readjusted the Velcro a couple times. "I'll have to leave the vest here when I go home. Toby would throw a fit if I came home in a bulletproof vest."

I led her out the door. "I thought you never saw him in the evenings."

"Odds are the night I wear a vest home is the night he'll be sitting on the couch, working on his dissertation or watching television, and he'll go ballistic."

"You know, someday you're going to have to sort out your job versus his opinions and bias."

Rachel climbed into the pickup without responding.

I chose to embrace the silence, leaned my head against the doorpost, and fell asleep before we passed the first mile marker.

I sensed the pickup slowing and lifted my head. The clock on the dash indicated that I'd been asleep for over half an hour. Ahead of us was a pair of tents pitched near the margin of the sea oats. An older pickup was parked next to the tents, and a pile of charred wood lay on the dunes midway between the tents, but there was no one in sight.

"Seems wrong," Rachel said. "I never see tents without people around."

We got out, and I walked to the campfire and put my fingers in the ashes. The charred wood was cool. "This wasn't burned recently."

Rachel knelt by an orange tent and looked in the flap. "Two sleeping bags and a cooler in here."

I pulled back the flap of the second tent. "Sleeping bags and a cooking kit. Footprints head into the dunes."

We followed the footprints, and I realized that we'd stopped at one of the wider spots on the island. We'd walked about a hundred yards before I heard voices. I signaled for Rachel to stop and listen. The breeze made it impossible to understand the conversation, but the only voices I heard were male. We moved ahead slowly until we walked through a break in the dunes and saw four men digging with their hands in the sea oats.

Our motion caught one man's eye, and he stood up abruptly, surprising his partners, who stopped to see what was going on.

I walked up to them trying to look professional but not accusatory. I wanted to see what they were doing before I put them on the defensive. "What's up, guys?"

A stocky tattooed man with sun-bleached hair stepped out of the knee-deep hole. He was bare-chested, and his denim shorts were caked with sand. He didn't have a weapon, nor did any of his partners, although a nylon duffle bag rested next to the hole they'd dug.

"What can we do for the police?" The man had a couple days growth of a mostly gray beard that made me think he was in his fifties. The others seemed to be younger and stayed back.

"We saw your gear on the beach with no one around. It's always good to be vigilant when you're in a remote area like this."

The tattooed man seemed too self-assured, and something about him made me uneasy. "We've been around since yesterday afternoon, and you're the only other people we've seen."

"That's quite a hole you've dug. Have you found anything interesting?"

"Mostly broken shells and sand dollars. Nothing much of interest."

I stepped forward, so I could see into the hole without being within reach of any of the men. Rachel hung back with her hand on the butt of her pistol. "We've had some treasure-hunters out here looking for coins from the shipwrecks. I don't suppose you guys have found any silver."

One of the men closed the flap of the duffle bag with his foot, trying to look nonchalant. "Why would people look for coins here?"

"The hurricane moved a lot of sand around, and things that've been buried for years have shown up on the surface. By the way, it's illegal to remove coins or artifacts from the National Seashore or the offshore marine archaeological area."

The stocky man smiled. "We'll keep that in mind if we happen to find any coins."

"It's also illegal to dig up sea oats or any rooted vegetation," Rachel added.

The man glanced at the sea oats they'd uprooted in their digging. "We didn't know that. We'll make sure to replant them."

I took a step toward the duffle bag, and a shaggy younger man stepped in front of me. I pointed at the nylon bag with my left hand, keeping my right hand free to pull the Sig or throw a punch, if necessary. "I'd like to take a look in your duffle bag."

The men looked at each other, but no one spoke or moved. The older man stepped closer to me. "That's private property, and I'm not inclined to let you search it without a warrant."

"A woman was killed near here a couple days ago. One of her earrings is missing. I'd like to make sure you didn't find it when you were digging."

"I can assure you we haven't found an earring, and we don't know anything about a woman who was killed."

I stepped around the shaggy man who blocked my approach to the duffle bag, carefully keeping him on the side away from my holster. I heard creaking leather and assumed Rachel had drawn her pistol. I bent down and reached for the duffle bag when the shaggy man grabbed my arm.

I used his forward momentum to pull him toward the ground. He released his grip to break his fall, and he hit the duffle bag, rolling it over. The other three men all reacted, moving to help him.

I spun left and kicked out with my right leg, taking out the knee of the closest man. I was about to grab the next man's foot when he let out a scream, and I ducked away as I caught a whiff of pepper spray. I scrambled away as the stocky man and his last upright partner clawed at their eyes. Rachel kept her canister of Mace aimed at them with her left hand while holding her pistol in her right hand.

I checked on the men, then realized Rachel's adrenaline was wearing off, and she was shaking. I took the can of Mace from her and motioned for the two men on the ground to join the others. "Open the duffle bag, Rachel."

She pulled the bag open, exposing clumps of black coins and a gold crucifix, still attached to a heavy crude gold chain.

She looked stunned, then she smiled. "It appears you men have just uncovered more exhibits for the museum."

"Bullshit! That's abandoned freight. It belongs to whoever finds it," the stocky man said.

I shook my head. "Not on Park Service land. The law says that anything identified on the National Seashore is to be pointed out to a ranger and not touched. If it's moved or removed from the site of its discovery, it's the property of the Park Service. We move it to the museum to be cataloged and put on display. However, since you illegally uprooted natural vegetation and assaulted a Park Service Ranger, you're going to be guests in the jail tonight." I pulled out my handcuffs, put them on the wrists of the shaggy man, who sat next to the duffle bag, and on the younger guy, who'd made a move on me.

Rachel stood and raised her pistol at the other two. "Both of you will face away from me and interlace your fingers behind your heads."

After cuffing the two guys who'd moved on me, I read them their Miranda rights and put them in the backseat of the Park Service pickup. Rachel gave water bottles to the two guys she'd maced, and they flushed their eyes. I lifted the duffle bag into the bed of the Park Service pickup and walked to the other two while Rachel radioed for backup to meet us at the parking lot.

I looked at the two men who were still rubbing their eyes after the water flush. "You're driving yourselves back to the Park Service building."

They shook their heads in disbelief. The stout guy glared at me. "And if we don't?"

"Where are you going if you don't drive the beach back? South, you hit the Port Mansfield Channel and the beach ends. If you cross the dunes, you'll hit Laguna Madre Sound. From there, you can swim across to the swamps on the other side and wade a few miles to solid ground. Or, you can follow us back."

The two guys looked like they'd swallowed a lemon. "Give us a few minutes to pack up our gear."

"Your gear is part of the crime scene." I waited for more protest, but the guys shut up. "Do you have any weapons, drugs, or valuables we should secure before we leave?"

They shook their heads just as I sensed the thumping of an approaching helicopter. I looked toward the Gulf and saw a speck that grew to an orange and white Coast Guard helicopter. The "Coasties" hovered south of our position, close enough so I could see the faces of the pilots and men in the back. The pilot, a young lieutenant J.G. named Marie, watched us. She gestured, asking if we were okay. I gave her a thumbs-up. The swimmer and petty officer in the back hung close to the side door. I had a sense they were close to weapons, but none were displayed. Marie nodded but continued to hover within sight until we were driving north.

Chapter Ten

There were two empty Corpus Christi police cars parked in front of the visitor center. A Nueces County Deputy leaned on the fender of his car talking on his cellphone, and an unmarked vehicle bristling with antennae was parked diagonally next to a handicapped parking spot. The sound of the helicopter rotors was still audible when I stepped out of the pickup, indicating that the Coast Guard had kept an eye on us our whole drive along the beach.

Rachel had been silent during the drive back and seemed oblivious to the helicopter following on the horizon when she climbed out of the pickup.

"Hey," I said to get her attention and then pointed toward the sky. "The Coast Guard followed us back."

Rachel turned and looked toward the speck on the horizon. "That's nice of them."

She obviously didn't feel the relief I'd felt knowing they'd backed us up. "The swimmer and his partner probably had access to firearms in the back of the helo and were trained to use them in an emergency."

Rachel nodded.

We opened the rear pickup doors and let out our handcuffed passengers as the camper's pickup slowed and parked behind us at the curb. "I'm happy to see our caravan showed up."

Rachel looked at me over the pickup bed. "You didn't expect them to follow us?"

"I always hope for the best but expect the worst."

The brown-shirted deputy, young, handsome, lanky, and looking cocky, closed his cellphone and trotted across to us. He wore a Stetson and cowboy boots. "We heard y'all caught yourselves some looters." He gave Rachel a smile that appeared more than professional courtesy.

I thought, *Toby, your open relationship may just bite you in the butt.*

The deputy put out his hand to me. "Ron Meland."

Rachel obviously knew the deputy because she introduced me. "This is my partner, Doug Fletcher."

I shook Meland's hand then let Rachel and the deputy guide the two handcuffed beachcombers into the building. I pulled the duffle bag out of the pickup bed, slung it over my shoulder, and gestured for the other two beachcombers to walk ahead of me.

Matt was in the breakroom with the two CCPD officers, so we gathered there, away from the prying eyes of our park visitors. I set the duffle bag on one of the Formica-topped tables with an audible clunk.

"We found these upstanding citizens digging in the dunes and throwing their recovered loot into this duffle bag." I pulled on a pair of purple gloves and lifted out a clump of black coins. "Unless I'm mistaken, these are Spanish silver coins."

The beachcombers attempted to look nonchalant, but Matt and the law enforcement officers leaned close to study the coins.

"They're black," observed one of the cops, garnering a sigh from the stocky beachcomber.

"They turn black as they oxidize," Rachel explained. "They also tend to fuse into chunks as they lie in the seawater."

Matt nodded. "Removing coins from the National Seashore and the Port Mansfield Underwater Archaeology Area is a federal crime. The CCPD officers are going to transport the suspects to the lockup at the courthouse until we can get a federal prosecutor to file charges."

The stocky beachcomber shook his head. "I want a lawyer. I don't intend to spend the night in jail."

The older CCPD officer smiled. "It's going to be damned inconvenient for you because I don't imagine there's a federal prosecutor available to file charges tonight, and without charges, you can't be arraigned. And all this has to happen in front of a federal magistrate, not a local judge. I expect you'll be eating bologna sandwiches for supper in the federal lockup and probably having powdered scrambled eggs and Spam for breakfast."

The three younger beachcombers looked at the stocky guy. He shook his head. "One call, and my lawyer will have us out of here."

I saw the corner of Matt's mouth curl into the faintest smile. "What I think you failed to understand is you're not petty thieves. You're being charged with federal crimes. Doug, what are the penalties for looting a federal archaeological site?"

"The guys I arrested in Arizona were facing ten years in federal prison and up to a half-million-dollar fine for stealing artifacts from the Wupatki National Monument."

The stocky man shook his head. "Don't worry. If we're stuck in jail overnight, it'll be plea-bargained down to time served."

"Your lawyer won't be negotiating with an overworked county prosecutor. Dealing with an Assistant U.S. Attorney with an army of investigators who are backed up by the U.S. Marshals is a whole different ballgame." I paused, then added, "I don't suppose any of you have open warrants or previous convictions. That complicates things."

I saw the stocky man's resolve waver as the CCPD officer recuffed him. "I might have some information you want about the woman you found in the dunes," the perp said.

I smiled. "Tell it to the prosecutor."

Rachel looked at me with surprise.

I shook my head and waited for the CCPD cops to escort the suspects out. "Don't let them think you're too interested. It ruins your bargaining position."

Meland nodded. "If they think they've got leverage, they'll try to walk all over you. If you look disinterested, sometimes they get desperate and start spilling information on the way to jail without getting a deal." He paused. "I think the older guy is too smart to fall for much. He looks like he's been through the system."

"He doesn't have jailhouse tattoos," I observed. "I suppose he might be a white-collar criminal. They tend to be smarter and spend their time in a minimum-security prison where tattoos aren't the status symbols you need to survive in a maximum-security lockup."

Matt stuck his head in the door and motioned for me to follow him. I left Rachel and Deputy Meland talking in the breakroom.

I sat in Matt's guest chair. "What's up?"

"You've got reports to write."

I rubbed my hand over my face. "I think Rachel's computer skills are better."

Matt pushed the duffle bag with his foot. "I assume this bag of coins is very valuable. The S.O.P. says it has to be cataloged by two people then locked in a secure location."

"Do you have a safe I haven't seen?"

"There's a small safe we use for the gift shop sales and entry fees. It's bolted to the floor behind the counter in the gift shop. These clusters of coins won't fit inside it."

"What do you suggest?"

Matt shrugged. "I hoped you had a suggestion."

I pointed to the back corner of his office. "Do you have room in your file cabinet?"

Matt turned and looked at the file cabinet meant for keeping secure files. It had heavy steel panels with a combination lock built into the face. "It's bolted to the floor and wall, and I lock it up every night, but it's not Fort Knox. The bottom drawer is empty."

I looked at my watch. "It's too late to put the bag in a bank safety deposit box, and the museum will be closed by the time we'd get there. The CCPD cops will be long gone by the time we catalog this stuff. Otherwise, we could've had them lock it in their property room."

Matt picked up the duffle bag and carried it to the file cabinet. "I'd feel better if we posted a guard at the door for the night." He dropped the bag into the bottom drawer. "It fits, but I'm not entirely comfortable with this option. I don't suppose you'd consider sitting in the hall tonight."

I snorted. "I got four hours of sleep last night. Pull the bag up here on your desk." I closed and locked his office door. "Take out your cellphone. We'll take pictures of all the pieces and make notes about the number and size of the clumps. Then we'll make out a custody tag, and both sign it."

I became increasingly concerned with the security of Matt's "secure" file cabinet as I considered the value of the coins and crucifix in the duffle bag. We made a rough estimate of the total coin count, and Matt calculated they were worth over a hundred thousand dollars. The crucifix and chain were priceless. Matt sent the pictures to the cloud while I locked the coins in the file cabinet. It wasn't your business-variety file cabinet. It was built to secure confidential files and personnel records, but as Matt said, it wasn't Fort Knox.

"While you were on patrol, I checked into the regulations about rangers wearing bulletproof vests. I get a dozen emails from the NPS a day, and I'd blown past this from 2015." He sat down at the computer and signed in, then clicked a file and spun the laptop around so I could read it. He'd opened reference manual RM-9 for law enforcement and security service. He'd opened chapter 29 section 2.3.2. I read it aloud. "The Service will provide appropriate fitting soft body armor to each commissioned employee. The following will apply..." It went on to explain options for fitted vs. off-the-shelf products and the tracking requirements, along with the protocol for transfer of the body armor if the ranger moved to a new posting.

I turned the computer back to Matt. "It appears you should find some fitted armor for us. Rachel commented that my SPPD vest wasn't tailored for her figure."

Matt nodded. "I'll call around and see what local options we have. Maybe I'll be able to get something that doesn't say 'POLICE' in a day or two."

A knock on the door had Matt nearly jumping out of his skin. I slipped out the Sig and opened the door a crack.

Rachel stood outside the door. "I'd hoped you two were still around."

I opened the door and let her in.

"What's up?" I asked.

She held out her phone, and I read the text message. "*Starbucks refused my card. What the hell?*"

I handed the phone back to her. "Toby doesn't know you closed the account."

Matt was curious. "Who's Toby, and what account is closed?"

"Toby's my roommate, and I closed our joint bank account this morning." Rachel looked at me. "What should I text him?"

I took the phone from her and started to enter a response.

"What are you doing, Doug?"

"I'm going to tell him the bank account is closed, and he needs a new meal ticket."

Rachel pulled the phone out of my hand. "No! I'm not ready to go there yet."

Matt asked, "What's going on?"

"Rachel's supporting a leech of a Ph.D. candidate who's suckling off her salary and emotions. She changed the bank account her paycheck goes into so he couldn't keep draining her. I suggested she put his clothes on the front step and change the locks."

Rachel didn't look as confident as she had when we met with the bank teller to close the one account and open a new one in her name only. "He's not going to deal with this well."

"Are you going to deal with it well when he finishes his Ph.D. and decides he doesn't need your paycheck anymore?"

Rachel gave me a sad look. "He might not dump me."

Matt sat on the edge of his desk. "He's not happy with your law enforcement career, right?"

Rachel ripped the Velcro bulletproof vest flaps loose and lifted it over her head. "I can't believe I'm getting relationship advice from two middle-aged guys."

Matt smiled. "Who better than us to give you advice? I'm happily married, and Doug's divorced. Between us, we've lived all the experiences you're going through."

"You guys are dinosaurs. You dated when you met people through friends or in bars. You made dates on the phone and probably showed up for your date with a dozen roses and a box of chocolates." Both of us were smiling because she was at least half-right. "You've probably never been on a dating website or even had a booty call."

"Does going home with a cop groupie count as a booty call?" As soon as the words were out of my mouth, I knew I'd said too much.

Rachel rolled her eyes. "That would be a hookup, not a booty call."

"You're missing the point," Matt said. "We've got a ton of relationship experience, and we're willing to help you through the relationship

101

minefield. Mandy and I are happily married, but I didn't get to this point without doing some stupid things, breaking up, getting dumped, and finally realizing I wanted to marry the pretty girl who was my best friend. How about you Doug?"

"The same story but throw in a divorce from a cheating gold digger who used me for my money until she finished school and thought she didn't need it anymore." I paused. "Like I said this morning, my story sounds eerily like what you're experiencing."

Rachel's eyes moistened. "You guys don't get it. I don't want to break up."

"Toby's playing you," I said softly. "You're in too deep to see it, but I've been there, Rachel. He'll suck you dry while making you feel guilty. You're doing all the giving and getting nothing in return but grief."

Matt took out his phone. "Do you need a place to stay tonight? Mandy and I have a spare bedroom. I can go with you to your place, so you can pick up some clothes and personal stuff. All I need to do is call Mandy and ask her to make up the spare bed."

Rachel shook her head. "I need to take care of a few things first."

"What are you going to do when Toby shows up ranting about the bank account we closed?"

Rachel shrugged as a tear ran down her face. She set the vest on Matt's guest chair and walked out the door.

"Do you think she'll be okay?"

I closed the door. "Eventually, but she'll have to hit the wall with Toby first. Lock up, and I'll go home and see how things are going with Jill and Mom. If they've got things under control with the neighbors, I'll drive over to Rachel's and see how she's doing."

"You need sleep. Go home. I'll call Mandy to let her know I'll be late. I'll drive over to Rachel's."

I opened the door. "I'm too tired to argue. I'll see you in the morning."

Chapter Eleven

The townhouse was empty when I got home. As inviting as a hot shower and crashing into bed sounded, I needed to go next door to find Jill and Mom. The boys weren't in the yard, and the door was open a crack. I smelled fried chicken from the doorstep. I knocked and walked in.

I recognized Jill's laugh. Clarice yelled, "Y'all c'mon in, whoever you are!"

Clarice, the boys, Jill, Mom, and Charlie were all seated around their dining room table that had been extended with the addition of a card table and folding chairs. The table was full of food, the centerpiece being a platter of fried chicken that must've included half of someone's chicken coop. Charlie, bruises getting darker but being gentlemanly, started to get up to shake my hand, but I waved him off. Jill had a silly grin, and I realized that all the adults had glasses with green liquid rimmed with salt. The boys gnawed on chicken legs and barely looked up when I came in.

Mandy Mattson emerged from the kitchen and handed me a Margarita. "We're celebrating Charlie's homecoming."

I accepted the Margarita, tipped it to Charlie, and touched it to my lips without taking a sip. I'd been avoiding hard liquor for several years and drinking a Margarita after getting only a few hours of sleep and having half a bologna sandwich for lunch would be a poor choice.

Jill realized my predicament and got up from her chair and picked up her empty glass. "Take my place. I was done anyway." She pulled the chair back and swapped our Margarita glasses as we passed. Mom pushed a bowl of mashed potatoes toward me, and Clarice handed me a bowl of gravy.

I dished up food and asked Charlie when he'd been released.

"The doctors wanted me to stay a few more days, but I told them I'd check in with the Navy flight surgeons in the morning, so they relented."

Jill leaned against me and slid a beer next to my plate. She pecked me on the cheek and whispered, "How are you holding up?"

I shrugged and picked up a chicken breast. Everyone was eating with their fingers, even Mom, who'd taught me to cut my chicken off the bone and eat it with a fork.

"Did you catch any litterers today?" Clarice asked, obviously feeling the effects of the tequila.

"Actually, we caught four guys who'd dug up a cache of Spanish coins."

Charlie stopped eating and wiped his hands and mouth on a paper napkin. "What's the status of Spanish coins if they're found on the National Seashore?"

I explained the protected status of the wrecks and their cargoes. "We arrested the beachcombers and seized the coins."

Mother wiped her mouth and daintily refolded her napkin. "Seems like you're overreacting, arresting guys for digging up a handful of coins."

"They had a duffle bag full of coins, and two of them assaulted me. Matt estimated that there was probably a hundred grand worth of coins in the bag."

Everyone but the boys stopped eating and stared at me. Mom wiped her mouth. "They assaulted you? You look okay."

"I'm quick for an old guy." I changed the topic as a phone chirped in the kitchen. "There were clumps of coins as large as bowling balls in the bag. We'll take them to the museum tomorrow so they can be cataloged, cleaned, and put on display."

Mandy refreshed the serving bowls, then slipped behind me and whispered in my ear. "Matt's at Rachel's house. I guess it's not going well. I'm going over to offer support."

I patted her hand and looked up. She always wore makeup, but it seemed like there was a little extra, maybe hiding the dark rings under her eyes. "Let me finish my chicken, and I'll drive you there."

Mandy smiled but was politely assertive. "Honey, you look like death warmed over. You finish your chicken, then take your momma and wife back to your house. Then y'all get some sleep."

"Yes, dear."

Mandy patted my shoulder. "I see you've discovered the magic words." She smiled at Jill. "You've taught him well."

Mother shook her head. "Oh, no. I was the one who housebroke him. Jill's just putting the final touches on his training."

Clarice was halfway through a swallow of Margarita, and she choked and started coughing. Charlie laughed, and that made the boys look up to see why everyone was laughing. We joked through the last of the meal, but I could see that everyone was winding down.

I took a swallow of beer and folded my napkin. "I do hate to eat and run, but I think all the adults could use a bit of sleep. Thanks for the nice dinner."

Clarice got up. "You've got Jill, Mandy, and your mother to thank for this supper. I'll have y'all over when Charlie gets on his feet, and we get some sleep."

I gave her a chaste hug and patted Charlie on the shoulder. "Don't rush back to the flight line."

"The flight surgeons won't let me in a plane until they're one-hundred percent sure I'm healthy enough to fly." Clarice stood behind him with a napkin over her mouth, shaking her head. She was obviously less enthused about seeing Charlie in a plane than he was.

Jill hugged Clarice, then took me by the hand. "I can't remember the last time I was this tired."

We walked out of Clarice's house and across the sidewalk. I put my arm around Jill's shoulders. "How about the night we slept under the stars with the coyotes howling?"

Jill pulled me close. "The night I grabbed your shirt, and you nearly had a heart attack?"

"Yes, that night."

"That was the night I realized you were my best friend."

Mother came up close behind us as I opened the townhouse door. "What are you lovebirds whispering about?"

"Just reminiscing about sleeping under the stars with the coyotes howling."

"That sounds terrible!"

"I'm terrified of coyotes," Jill explained. "I heard them howling and grabbed Doug's shirt when he was half asleep."

Mom nodded. "I remember waking Doug when he'd just come home from Iraq. He woke with a start and nearly ripped my arm off before he realized I wasn't an Iraqi trying to kill him. He scared me nearly to death."

"I grabbed his shirt, and Doug grabbed his gun. I wasn't sure if he planned to shoot the coyote or me."

They both looked at me. "It was a toss-up," I said.

Jill punched my arm. "You held my hand until the coyotes stopped howling. It was about the sweetest thing anyone has ever done."

Mom patted my arm as she passed, then started upstairs. "I suppose that's when you two realized you were in love."

Jill squeezed my hand and stood on her toes to give me a kiss. "I think that was the night I knew I always wanted you sleeping beside me."

I shooed Jill ahead of me up the stairs. "You didn't say anything at the time."

"I knew you were damaged by the divorce, and I didn't think you were ready to get into another relationship. And, I didn't think you'd want a tomboy like me even if you were past the divorce."

"Yet somehow, you convinced me."

Mom climbed the stairs ahead of us. "I think the kids call this TMI. I really don't need to know any more about your romance."

We walked into the bedroom, and Jill closed the door and leaned against it. "I still have a hard time believing how lucky I am."

I was going to kiss her when my cellphone rang. "Fletcher." I said, seeing Matt's name on the caller I.D.

"I hope I didn't get you out of bed."

"Not yet, Matt. We just walked into the house after eating supper with the neighbors. What's up?"

"I'm at Rachel's, and we've been talking for an hour. Then Toby came home and blew his top. They're in the bedroom. Rachel's crying, and

Toby sounds like he's ready to start throwing punches."

"Where's Rachel's pistol?"

"I don't know."

"See if you can find it, and when you do, unload it and put the shells in your pocket. Try to de-escalate the confrontation, but be careful. Domestic fights are dangerous, and if they see you as someone interfering, they might both turn on you. I'll be there in fifteen minutes. If things get ugly before I arrive, dial 911 and get out of the house."

"I'll try to get them quieted down."

"Protect yourself, Matt. Don't get between them."

"Mandy's on her way over. She's really good at settling people down."

I grabbed Jill's hand and pulled her out of the bedroom. "Jill and I are on the way. You're sitting on a powder keg. Back away if things start to go south. Okay?"

I grabbed my pistol off the closet shelf and trotted to the Park Service pickup with Jill on my heels. We jumped inside, and I peeled out of the parking lots with the lights flashing.

Jill was still buckling her seatbelt when I turned on the siren. "What's going on?"

"Rachel and Toby are at it." Then I explained the closed bank account, the deteriorating current situation, and what I'd told Matt.

We flew down the highway in silence, passing cars and pickups that were pulling off to the shoulder to let us by. Within minutes, we were crossing the Kennedy Bridge and were on the outskirts of Corpus Christi. I raced to the exit for Rachel's house and turned off the siren as we entered her street. We parked behind Mandy's Prius. From the sidewalk, I could hear Toby yelling. I picked up the radio mic and switched to the CCPD frequency, requesting backup for a domestic dispute.

Jill followed me up the steps, and we walked into the living room where Matt and Mandy were standing, looking helpless. Matt handed me the butt of Rachel's pistol. I made sure it was unloaded, then tucked it into my waistband.

The bedroom door was locked. I knocked once, and it didn't slow Toby's tirade. I leaned back and put my shoulder to the door, busting the latch.

Toby was in Rachel's face, and she was in tears. I stepped forward and put my hand up in front of Toby, not touching him, but prepared to pull his hand around behind his back. He stopped yelling and turned toward me, his face beet red.

"It's your fault," he hissed. "You filled her head with stupid ideas, and it's none of your business."

"Toby, you're leaving right now. The fight is over."

"I'm leaving? Bullshit! If anyone's going, it's her!"

I spoke softly. "The house is leased to Rachel. You're only living here because she's allowing you to be here. If there's something of yours here, come back and get it tomorrow."

I heard a siren wailing nearby, then it cut off as it turned the corner near the house. Toby was oblivious to the siren, focusing his rage on Rachel and me.

He raised his fist and pointed a finger at me. "I'm not leaving my house. I live here."

I grabbed his finger and twisted it, pulling his hand and his arm behind his back. "Either leave quietly or in handcuffs. Those are your two choices." I pulled up his arm until I knew his elbow and shoulder were in pain. I heard a knock on the front door, followed by Matt's voice and another male voice that I assumed to be a CCPD cop.

Jill pushed past me and wrapped her arms around Rachel. Jill slowly turned Rachel toward the corner away from Toby and spoke softly to her. I saw Rachel's head bobbing like she was agreeing with whatever Jill was saying.

The CCPD officer was young, blonde, and large. He quickly assessed the scene with Rachel and me in Park Service uniforms, and noting my badge and pistol. I nodded to him but kept upward pressure on Toby's arm.

"The young man and woman have been living together. They had a falling out tonight, and I just told Toby, the young man, that he was leaving for the night. The house is leased to Rachel, the young lady in the corner, and she wants him to leave. Isn't that right, Rachel?"

Rachel made a half-turn, and I saw the large bruise blossoming on her cheek. She nodded and wiped a smear of bloody snot from her upper lip with a tissue from Jill.

I looked at Jill, who glanced at Rachel's bruised face, bloody nose, and then nodded to me.

The cop's nameplate said Higgins.

"Officer Higgins, I've changed my mind. It appears this man has struck the lady during their argument, and I'd like you to place him under arrest for domestic assault. I can remove him to the other room while you speak with the young lady."

Officer Higgins looked again at my badge, the pistol stuck in my waistband, and my holstered pistol. "You've got all the weapons in the house under control?"

"I believe so. The Sig in my waistband belongs to Ranger Randall, the assault victim. It's unloaded and hasn't been discharged. You can inspect it if you'd like to."

Higgins shook his head. "You've got him under control?"

I took a deep breath. "I think it'd be in Toby's best interest if you'd handcuff him and put him in the back of your car...for his own safety."

I saw a hint of a smile on Higgins' face when he understood that I really, really wanted to hurt Toby, but was offering to release him into custody before something *unfortunate* happened

113

to him. Higgins took out his handcuffs and snapped them on Toby.

"You're not under arrest," Higgins said as he led Toby down the hallway. "You're being restrained pending my investigation. Tell me your version of what was happening."

I walked to Rachel and put my finger under her chin. "I'm so sorry." I looked at the bruise on her cheek that was spreading toward her nose and eye. She glared at me for a second, then she turned and hugged Jill.

Mandy and Matt sat on the only couch, looking lost, and out of place. "Toby punched Rachel. She's going to have one heck of a shiner. I think she should go to the emergency room to have her face X-rayed and to make sure she doesn't have some other injuries."

Mandy jumped up and trotted to the bedroom. Sobbing followed her arrival. I couldn't tell if it was Mandy or Rachel who was crying.

Matt shook his head. "I should've stepped in and broken up the argument."

"It wasn't your fight, Matt. And you might be the one with the shiner, or worse if you'd interrupted them."

Officer Higgins appeared at the door. "Our boy claims the girl closed his bank account and wouldn't give him his money. He also said Fletcher, you were the cause of all the friction, and if you'd just butt out, everything would've been fine."

"He's a grad student who doesn't make any money. Rachel's been supporting him with her salary, and she decided it was time for him to move on, financially and physically. My only role in this was to tell Rachel about my experience with a divorce, and to suggest that she move her money to an account in her name."

Higgins smiled and nodded. "I'll talk to the young woman and see what she's got to say. If the lease is in her name, and all the bank deposits are her paystubs, then it's pretty cut and dried."

"She needs an x-ray of her cheek and an exam to see if she has any other injuries."

"Do you think she needs an ambulance?"

"I don't think she has any acute injuries. I can drive her to the E. R. while you book Toby."

Higgins walked to the bedroom. Jill and Mandy came out—both looked like they'd been crying. Jill buried her face in my shoulder, and Mandy went to Matt.

"Does she have any injuries besides the bruised cheek?"

I felt Jill nod. "She needs to go to the ER. We'll drive her there as soon as Officer Higgins gets through interviewing her."

Matt shook his head again. "Mandy and I will take her to the hospital. You two go home and get some sleep."

I heard a woman shrieking outside, and I ran to the door. A pregnant Hispanic woman was yelling at Toby through the window and pounding on the roof of the patrol car. Jill and I walked over to her.

115

"What's wrong?" I asked.

"That shithead," she pointed at Toby, "promised to take care of me when I got out of treatment. He ain't provided shit, and I've got nothin' to eat and nowhere to stay."

I put up my hands. "I'll talk to the police officer, and maybe he can get you into a shelter."

"I'm not supposed to have to go to no shelter. Shithead was going to get me an apartment and groceries until the baby was born. That was the deal. Now it looks like he's going to jail. Who's going to take care of the baby and me if he's in jail?"

Jill stepped forward. "I'm sure we can find someone at the University to sort this out. We'll find Toby's advisor, and I'm sure he'll get something set up for you."

"I don't know nothin' about his advisor. It's him who got me into treatment and promised to take care of me. If I knew he wasn't going to take care of me after he got me pregnant, I would've stayed with my pimp."

Jill's head snapped around, and she looked dumbfounded. Then she realized that Rachel, Mandy, and Matt were standing right behind us. I turned and saw the recognition hit them all at the same time.

Rachel turned red, and Mandy grabbed her arm to restrain her. "You sonofabitch! You've been fucking the women you're supposedly helping with your graduate study? Is that where you found the pregnant women for the program?"

Toby turned away from the window, and Mandy directed Rachel toward the Prius. But Rachel wasn't done. "Don't bother coming inside when you come back. Your clothes will be on the steps and the locks will be changed!"

Chapter Twelve

I was the first person at the Park Service building. I unlocked the front door, got a cup of coffee from the vending machine and walked to Matt's office. The door was ajar, and the latch was broken out of the frame. I dropped my paper cup and pulled the Sig, then kicked the door open. I swung the pistol around the empty space.

His desk drawers had been rifled, and papers were strewn around the floor. The filing cabinet combination lock looked like it had been pounded with a sledgehammer. All the drawers had been pried open and the duffel bag of Spanish coins was gone. I backed out of the office and dialed 911 from the hallway. My second call was to detective Scott Dixon.

Dixon arrived a half-hour later with a crime scene investigation team. The four officers from two Corpus Christi cruisers had arrived within minutes of my call and had cleared the building, then strung crime scene tape around Matt's office. I was in the break room with them, looking at the video from the front gate, the only access point to the Park Service building.

The CCPD officers stopped talking when Dixon walked into the room. He wore western cut clothes, blue jeans, and cowboy boots, a bolo tie, and a Stetson. He shook his head. "Fletcher, what is it this time?" He reached out his hand.

I shook it, and said, "The men we arrested yesterday had a duffle bag full of Spanish coins. We'd locked the coins up in the superintendent's secure file cabinet for the night."

"Who was guarding them?"

I shook my head. "No one. The building was locked after the park closed. The file cabinet is bolted to the wall, and it's built like a safe with a combination lock."

Dixon nodded toward the video we were watching. "How much of the building has video surveillance?"

"Only the park entrance."

Dixon closed his eyes. "Did you catalog the coins you found?"

"We did in a gross sense. Most of the coins were fused together in lumps. We counted them, and Matt took pictures on his cellphone. He estimated that they were worth maybe a hundred thousand dollars."

Dixon whistled through his teeth. "That's a lot of silver."

"The silver isn't worth a lot if they melt it down, but a 1554 Spanish coin is worth a lot more than the value of the silver to a collector." I froze. "Shit, there was also a gold cross and chain in the bag too. It's probably worth more than the coins."

"Show us where you had them stored."

It was hard to miss the loop of yellow crime scene tape when we walked out of thc break room. Matt's office was only twenty feet away, and the area had been marked off by using two breakroom chairs to hold up the yellow tape. I walked to the tape with Dixon and the two techs. We stopped at the perimeter, and one of the techs unzipped a bag and took out two Tyvek suits, blue shoe covers, and purple gloves. He and his partner donned the protective gear and stepped over the yellow tape while Dixon and I hung back in the hallway.

"What made you think that a Park Service office was a good place to store an antique cross and a cache of rare coins?" Dixon's voice was teasing, but the message was serious.

Matt came through the front door and froze when he saw Dixon and me standing near the crime scene tape. "Oh shit."

Dixon looked over his shoulder at Matt. "Ah. The man in charge has arrived. I was just asking Fletcher why you guys thought your office was a good place to store valuables."

"It was late by the time we sent the suspects off to jail. Then Doug and I photographed and cataloged the coins. By then, the museum and banks were all closed for the night."

Dixon lifted off his Stetson and made a ceremony out of wiping his brow with a white handkerchief he'd pulled from his back pocket. He arranged the Stetson on his head, perfectly aligning it with the creases in his forehead where generations of previous Stetsons had rested. Then he looked at Matt. "One call, and you could've had my boys here, and they would've picked up your coins and put them in a secure evidence lockup for the night. One call."

Matt turned red and didn't have a word to say in our defense.

"Let's leave the Monday morning quarterbacking for now," I said, "and focus on finding out who did this."

Nearly on cue, one of the crime scene techs stuck his head out of Matt's door. "What time do your cleaners come through?"

Matt shrugged. "I'm not exactly sure. They come sometime after we close. They finish off the offices before seven, then they clean the campground bathrooms and showers from seven to nine. Why do you ask?"

Without answering, the tech asked, "Do they have keys to your office?"

"Their supervisor has a master key and . . ." Matt froze. "Shit. They open every door to clean."

"You need to check the gate video. Whoever was in here came through before the freshly mopped floor dried. I've got some great shoe prints if we get shoes for comparison."

I nodded toward the breakroom where we'd been watching the video on my laptop computer. I cued up the video for five o'clock when the ranger shut down the entry hut for the night.

Dixon leaned close to watch the computer images. "So, the park is closed from five until you reopen in the morning?"

121

"The park is open 24 hours a day, 365 days a year. We work off an honor system where campers entering after the hut closes come back to pay their entrance fee the next morning."

We watched a few cars slow at the entrance to read the rules, then drive in. A pickup and a car cruised through the exit without slowing down. Dixon turned to Matt. "I'd say your honor system isn't working very well."

"We're committed to providing access, not making sure we collect from everyone who drives in. We miss a few, but most people are honest, and it's not worth the cost of manning the gate 24/7 to collect from the people who decided to sneak by. Liz usually checks the campers each morning to see if they've got entrance permits. She doesn't catch many cheaters, and we've never had anyone vandalize or break into the headquarters buildings."

"You've been lulled into a false sense of security." Dixon looked at me. "Fletcher, you were a cop. You should've known better."

I put up my hands. "No one, but Matt, Rachel, and I knew the coins were in Matt's office."

"I always lock the file cabinet because that's where I keep personnel files and budgetary information. No one has ever tampered with the file cabinet or desk locks or even moved a pen on my desktop."

Dixon shook his head. "There were a lot of people who knew the coins were somewhere in the building, even if they didn't know exactly where." He ticked off groups on his fingers. "There were the three of you. There were the four guys you arrested. There were five or six cops and deputies here. I assume some visitors walked through when you were arresting the guys and digging through the coins. Each of your suspects made a phone call—only one of them needed to call a lawyer, and who knows who the other three called. And the phone tree goes out from each of those people. I'll bet that several hundred people knew about the coins by midnight."

Rachel stepped up behind us. She was moving slowly, and the makeup she'd applied did little to hide the dark bruise on her left cheek. "What's with the crime scene tape?"

I shook my head. "We put the coins in Matt's file cabinet after you left, and someone broke into it last night. Detective Dixon just counted off the number of people who might've known the coins were here."

Rachel took out lip balm and spread it over her cracked lip, below the bruise, while I spoke. Then she added, "I checked the treasure-hunter website this morning. The guys we arrested were posting pictures of the lumps of coins they were uncovering as they dug them up. They'd had over a thousand hits by the time I looked up the website this morning."

Dixon gave me an *I told you so* look.

Matt gently put his hand on Rachel's upper arm to steer her away from us to talk privately, but she winced with pain. He let go like he'd been

123

burned and gestured for her to follow him out of the break room.

Dixon watched silently until they were gone. "What's with your rookie's bruise? Did she piss off a litterer?"

"She was a victim of a domestic assault last night. Her significant other went to jail."

"Sorry about being flippant. I had no idea . . ."

"He was a leech, and she decided to end her generosity. As the CCPD cops were taking him away, a crack whore showed up and started berating him about getting her pregnant and not providing the apartment and food he'd promised."

"Ouch. I suppose your rookie would've been paying for all that."

"He was a college student without any means of support. I suppose that had been his plan until she closed the joint bank account. I hope she was late this morning because she had the locks changed and dumped all his stuff on the steps."

Dixon pulled out his cellphone. "What's her address?"

I gave him the street name and number. "Her ex-boyfriend is Toby Sanderson. It'd be nice to know if he's still locked up."

Dixon keyed information into his phone. "He's probably getting a jailhouse breakfast about now. He's got a bail hearing later this morning, although there's no record of a lawyer meeting with him. I suppose the judge will assign a public defender at the hearing if he hasn't arranged for someone before then."

"It would be good if you could have a CCPD car cruise past the house a few times this afternoon, just to make sure he doesn't let himself in through a window or something if he makes bail."

Dixon nodded as he keyed a phone number into his phone, then put up his hand. "Hi, Chelsea. Scott Dixon here with a request. Would you leave a note for your boss about Toby Sanderson? He's got a bail hearing coming up this morning, and she needs to know that Toby assaulted a federal officer last night during a domestic incident. I saw his victim this morning, and one side of her face is a big black bruise and she's walking like she's hurting in other places too. I'm guessing there are some photos of her injuries taken at the hospital." Dixon put his hand over the phone. "Do you know the name of the arresting officer?"

I closed my eyes for a second. "His name was Higgins. He was a big, young guy with an attitude. And my rookie's name is Rachel Randall. She was in uniform when she was assaulted."

"The arresting officer was Higgins, and the victim was Law Enforcement Ranger Rachel Randall. I hope Higgins got the pictures into the system, but if he didn't, would you follow up and make sure they're available for the hearing." Dixon listened for a moment, then smiled. "I'll bring you a Starbucks mocha the next time I'm coming to the courthouse. Thank you, darling."

Dixon shut down his cellphone and smiled. "Chelsea is going to follow up on the pictures and make sure her boss, the district attorney, has all the information about the assault and Rachel's injuries. Chelsea also offered to call the U.S. Attorney's office to notify them that there'd been an assault on a federal officer. This may move up the food chain pretty quickly because the Feds don't take an assault on one of their own lightly and moving this from the county to the federal system is going to make it much more unpleasant, and slow, for Mr. Toby Sanderson."

"Thank you."

"By the way, the medical examiner got a match on Jane Doe's fingerprint. Her name is Karla Johnson, and her prints are in the Texas system because she's a schoolteacher. The state does background checks on everyone who has contact with kids these days. She teaches fourth grade down in Kingsville."

"Where's that?"

"It's just south of Corpus Christi. It used to be the headquarters of the King Ranch. It's pretty much surrounded by the original ranch, which used to be the largest in the United States, but it's not just a company town anymore. I called a friend who's the KPD patrol lieutenant. He said Ms. Johnson was reported missing by the school on Monday. He was already checking to see where she's living, if she had a roommate, and who she hung around with. I should have that information this afternoon."

"Well, we know she was into treasure-hunting, so you could clue him into that. Maybe there's a local group who go out together, or maybe she linked up through some website he could find in her computer history."

Dixon smiled. "Fletcher, just because we live south of the Mason-Dixon line and talk slow doesn't mean we're backward or stupid. I'm sure Tom has all the resources of any city police department, and he's following all the leads you'd be following if you were back in Michigan."

I smiled. "My apologies. It's just that I'm really anxious to put the case to bed. And I'm from Minnesota, not Michigan."

Dixon gave me a wicked grin. "Really! I guess I lump all the Yankees from those northern 'M' states together. What are there, like five of them along the Canadian border? Minnesota. Maine. Michigan. Montana. Isn't there another one?"

"Massachusetts isn't on the Canadian border, but it's in New England."

Dixon was still intent on needling me about being from Minnesota. "I'm surprised you guys even speak English instead of Canadian."

I was about to offer up a smart retort about Canadians speaking better English than Texans, but Matt walked into the breakroom looking gloomy.

"Did Rachel go home?" I asked.

Matt shook his head. "She's hurting but is only taking Tylenol. She said she'd rather be here around people than sitting by herself. She's going back to her house at noon to get some things, then she's going to move into our guest bedroom for a couple nights."

I was surprised, considering Rachel's independence. "How'd you talk her into that?"

"Mandy can be very persuasive."

I nodded my understanding and explained it to Dixon. "Matt's wife, Mandy, is a force to be reckoned with. She comes on all sweet, smooth, and Southern. But there's no argument once she's made up her mind and notified you of the plan."

Dixon nodded. "They teach all the Southern girls that in debutante training. I'll bet she set her sights on you, Matt, and you never knew what was coming until she had you on one knee with a diamond ring in your hand."

"I'd like to think I had some say in the matter."

"That's the beauty of it. They learn how to 'give you' good ideas, so you think you're in charge, but the reality is that we never have a chance. I know. My wife went to the same training. I learned very early that 'yes dear' is the proper response to any suggestion."

Matt smiled at me. "What did you say last night when Jill suggested it was time to go home?" When I glared at him but didn't respond, he added. "Doug's engaged and has passed the stage of being housebroken and presentable to company. He's still working on the 'yes dear' part."

Dixon pointed at the laptop that had long since switched over to screensaver mode. "Let's focus on the hours after midnight and before your crew went over to clean at the campground."

I re-entered my password, and the dark image outside the ranger hut appeared. I struggled through the keys until the timer at the bottom of the screen was spinning, but the scene never changed until something flashed by as the timer passed four o'clock. While I struggled, using my limited computer skills, trying to stop and reverse the display, another vehicle flashed past.

Matt elbowed me aside, and the spinning timer stopped and started to slowly back up. He froze the frame at the second vehicle, which went past shortly before four. A pickup towed a pop-up trailer, and they stopped at the hut long enough to read the rules, then they pulled away. The angle of the camera showed grainy images of what appeared to be a man and woman in the pickup cab.

Matt started backing up the replay to view the first image. "I think we can discount the couple towing the camper. They're either very smooth, or they really are campers who were running late and searching for a place to park."

He stopped after another image flashed past. He backed up and slowed the replay down to real-time. Even at the slower speed, the vehicle was in view for barely a fraction of a second. "That guy was flying," Matt said as he went back and forth, trying to freeze the image long enough to identify the vehicle. He finally got a blurred image of a hatchback car, but the occupants were impossible to visualize.

Dixon leaned over Matt's shoulder. "That looks like one of the newer Nissan Rogue models. Is there any chance you can back that up like one frame so we can see the license plate?"

Matt toggled the controls until he got an image of the front of the car, blurred like the images of the occupants, but at least, it wasn't shaded from the light outside the hut.

"If you email a copy of that to me, I'll take it to our computer guy. He's had some luck enhancing video from other surveillance cameras."

Matt leaned back and gave me a sheepish look. I had a bad feeling about what he was about to say, whatever it was. "I think we should call the FBI. They might be interested in a theft of this magnitude. Officially, I'm obligated to report anything more than a misdemeanor to them, and they can choose whether to be involved or not."

I looked at Dixon, who was shaking his head and mouthing, "No."

"Matt, do you still have a record of your call from the FBI agent who tried to hijack the murder investigation?"

Matt scanned through his call history and stopped at the number identified as FBI. He was about to push the recall button when I took the phone from his hand. I pushed recall and waited three rings for an answer. The receptionist had a pleasant Texas twang and sounded like she really wanted to be helpful.

"I'd like to speak with Special Agent Mark Jones, please." I was put on hold and listened to classical music I didn't recognize. It made me wonder what played while people were on hold with the Park Service. I had a thought that maybe they heard the sound of the seashore. In reality, I assumed the federal government took bids for their *on-hold* music, and anyone awaiting a federal employee, regardless of the agency, probably heard the same classical selection I was listening to.

"This is Special Agent Jones. How can I help you?"

"Mark. Hi, this is Doug Fletcher from Padre Island National Seashore. How've you been?"

I could almost hear the gears grinding as Jones processed my information, then realized that I'd pulled a coup on his attempt to steal credit for a case I'd worked on with Scott Dixon, by using a reporter to release a story to the wire services ahead of the FBI's news conference where they were going to announce that they'd solved the case. Instead, they'd been forced to acknowledge assistance from the Park Service and the CCPD, which probably cost Jones a small part of his next raise and delayed

131

his next promotion. The FBI is highly political, and they don't get points for being good team players.

I turned on the speakerphone and signaled Matt and Scott to be quiet.

"Cut the social nicety crap and state your business, Fletcher."

"Someone broke into Matt Mattson's office last night. We're reporting the crime to you."

Jones let out a sigh. "Is this some kind of joke?"

"I'm serious. We had a break-in that needs investigation. I'm sure the resources you could bring to bear would solve the crime in no time."

"Let me guess. Someone stole Matt's lunch and some candy bars, and you need my help to recover them."

"Actually, there were a number of coins stolen."

"Did they take the money from the souvenir sales?" Jones asked.

"No. That cash is kept in a safe near the display counters. These coins were in Matt's file cabinet." There was a long pause. "Are you still there, Mark?"

"Tell you what, Fletcher. When you have a theft involving cash money, you understand that I mean currency, not coins, then you can call me, and we'll talk about how to investigate. I'll let you handle the coin theft yourselves."

I smiled at Matt, who was rolling his eyes. Dixon was about ready to start laughing. "Okay, Mark. But I wanted to make sure we'd notified you of the crime in case you wanted to investigate it."

"Thanks, Fletcher," he said, the sarcasm dripping from his voice. "By the way, you don't need to inform us when you ticket someone for sticking bubble gum to the underside of a picnic table, either."

"Got it, Mark." I cut the connection and handed the phone back to Matt. "Looks like we're free to investigate this crime without the involvement of the FBI."

Matt pocketed his phone. "You do realize that when they read about this in the newspaper, they're going to jump down my throat."

I put up my hands. "I'm not planning on telling the newspaper. Are you going to tell the newspaper, Scott?"

"Not me."

"Then I think we're clean on this. We told the FBI coins had been stolen, and they declined to investigate."

Matt frowned. "I think you've committed a sin of omission, Doug. You did technically tell them about the coin theft. He might've been more interested if you'd told him the coins were Spanish and were minted in 1554, or that they were worth somewhere in the neighborhood of a hundred grand and there was a gold cross and chain worth more than the coins."

"He didn't ask. I didn't offer. I think we're covered."

Matt turned back to the computer and sped up the play again. About five o'clock, another vehicle flashed past. Matt got to that one quickly and determined that it was the cleaning crew in their pickup with ladders for window washing strapped on top. Another image flashed past shortly after seven o'clock, this one leaving. Matt found the image and crept through the frames showing the passing vehicle, the same hatchback. This time with no view of the passengers, but a little better picture of the rear license plate came across. It had rocketed past as fast as it had gone by in the other direction.

Scott pointed at the rear of the hatchback. "I think our computer guy will have better luck with that view of the license plate."

Matt ran the images forward. Sunrise lit the image, followed by my pickup entering and the arrival of a ranger who opened the welcome hut. The CCPD cruisers shot past and the cleaners drove out shortly after the ranger arrived.

Dixon straightened up and stretched. "If you're paying the cleaning crew for eight hours of work, you're getting screwed."

Matt shut down the video after emailing a copy to Dixon. "It's an annual bid for service, not for the hours. They're the lowest bidders, and I've got no complaints about the job they do."

"I'll have my guy look at the video and see what he can pick up. I think you should talk with the cleaners, Fletcher. If they're not complicit in the crime, they may have seen the thieves."

I heard rapid footsteps in the hallway, and Rachel stepped in wearing the bulletproof vest with the police logo. "I've been trying to find Doug. The Coast Guard hailed us and said there's a boatful of beachcombers south of Shell Beach."

I put the laptop under my arm. "They might be picking up shells."

"Or they might be prospecting for coins," Rachel countered.

"I'll meet you at the pickup."

Chapter Thirteen

Rachel sat in the passenger seat. We'd been teamed up for several months, and she'd always driven the pickup on our twice-daily trips to Port Mansfield Channel and back. I set my bulletproof vest between us and buckled myself in.

"You must be really hurting if you're letting me drive."

She squirmed in her seat as if attempting to get comfortable. "I've been better."

"I can do this alone."

"Matt told us he didn't want us making this drive alone after the murder."

I drove out of the parking lot and accelerated down the short road to the hard-packed sand beach that took us the length of most of the island. "No, Matt said he didn't want you patrolling the beach alone."

"Same difference." Rachel grimaced when the pickup bounced as we left the paved road and drove onto the sand. "You're my partner, and we're patrolling together."

I was touched by her commitment but concerned about her body's tolerance of riding the several hours we were about to do, going over sometimes uneven sand to shell beach and back. "How badly are you banged up?"

"No stitches."

"That's not what I asked."

Rachel stared straight ahead and didn't answer. I let it slide, figuring she'd tell me in her own time if she wanted me to know.

She changed the topic. "What happened to your neighbor, the pilot we visited in the hospital?"

"He went home last night pretty banged up. He'll see the Navy flight surgeons for an idea of when they're going to let him start flying again."

"If he's badly bruised, they're not going to let him fly for a while." Rachel paused, and I thought she finished with the topic. "The doctors told me I shouldn't fly for a while. He said something about an embolism from the bruises."

I slowed the pickup.

"Why are you slowing down?"

"If the doctor's concerned about you flying, we shouldn't be bumping along the beach as fast as the pickup will go."

"I think it's more a matter of the pressure change when you fly."

"Just the same, you're grimacing every time I hit a bump, and there's no need to cause you undue pain."

"But the boat might leave."

"If they're just picking shells, they'll still be there when we arrive, and it's no big deal. If they're doing something illegal, they'll probably

137

see us coming from miles away and take off before we can talk to them, like last time."

"There's got to be some way to catch them without racing down the empty beach."

"Rachel, you and I are on the same page there, but short of swooping in by helicopter, I don't know how we'll ever sneak up on them."

Even at the slightly slower speed, we were still passing the mile markers every minute or so. The rough spots in the sand were becoming increasingly painful for Rachel, and I slowed down every time I saw a rough area approaching.

"Do you have any broken ribs?"

"They didn't do any x-rays. The doctor said it didn't make any difference because they treat bruised and broken ribs the same. Actually, having the vest tightened up around my chest makes it a little bit better than wrapping up with an elastic bandage."

"I tried to break up a bar fight one time and cracked a couple ribs. It hurt like hell for about ten days, then ached for another two weeks after that."

"Oh, goody. Now I know what to anticipate."

"What else did the doctor say?"

Rachel stared out the side window for a few minutes. "I was a few weeks pregnant, and I lost the baby."

I stepped on the brakes and stopped the truck. Rachel's forehead was against the side window, and she was crying. I walked around the vehicle and opened the door, taking her gently into my arms, wary of her sore ribs.

I had tears in my eyes. "I'm so sorry."

"It's okay. I'm not ready to be a mom, and now . . ."

"And now Toby's out of the picture." I let her lean on me and cry for a couple minutes. "Did you know you were pregnant?"

Rachel sniffed her nose, then dug in her pocket for a tissue. "I was late, but that sometimes happens."

"You and Toby weren't using birth control?"

"He didn't like using condoms, but because of our agreement, I didn't want him to infect me with something he picked up from someone else."

"That was wise." I thought about the pregnant prostitute berating Toby while she pounded on the top of the police car. "You must've had a slip up somewhere?"

Rachel shook her head. "Toby wasn't the only one in our open relationship."

That reality hit me like a brick. I'd had paternalistic feelings about poor naïve Rachel and had been ignoring the signals she'd been giving me about hook-ups, booty calls, and dating web sites. Then I realized she was an adult in a different world than I'd experienced. It made me want to rush home, hug Jill, and thank God for what I had.

Rachel peeled herself away from me, which made me realize that the hug was as much for me as it was for her. "We should get moving again."

I got behind the wheel and accelerated until the mile markers were going by once a minute.

Rachel was silent, and I wondered if I'd pried too much information out of her. "I talked to Scott Dixon, the CCPD detective. He asked the patrol sergeant to have a car go by your house a couple times a shift."

Rachel nodded. "It's not a big deal. I'm staying at Mandy and Matt's for a few days. Mandy was with me when the doctor talked to me, and she convinced me I should stay with them until I stop spotting."

My mind froze. Rachel had a miscarriage, I knew in a general sense what that meant, but not anything specific.

"Is it normal to spot for a while?"

"The doctor said it's usual for a few days and may last a little longer. If it lasts more than two weeks, I need to follow-up with an OB-GYN. I was so glad Mandy was there. She was just like a big sister, and she made it clear I was going to stay at their house until everything got settled with the miscarriage and with Toby."

"Scott Dixon checked on Toby's status this morning. He's supposed to have a bail hearing this morning, but Scott talked to a friend in the district attorney's office. Toby may be facing federal charges."

Rachel's head snapped around. "What federal charges?"

"Assaulting a federal officer is a serious offense."

"We were having an argument, that's all."

"He beat you badly enough to leave bruises and cause a miscarriage, and you were in uniform. That amounts to assaulting a federal officer. The district attorney's office is going to contact the U.S. Attorney to discuss who should take the lead in prosecuting him. Based on my experience, he may face charges in both federal and district court. Most times the local courts are pretty lenient with first-time offenders and put them on probation. With the pending federal charges, they may look at it differently." I stopped when a wave of revelation struck me. "This is Toby's first offense, isn't it?"

Rachel shook her head. "He's had some anger issues throughout his life. I think he's got a juvenile record back in his hometown and he was arrested in Corpus Christi for punching a guy in a bar. They let him off with a fine, but the judge warned him to get his anger under control or he'd be a guest of the county if he was arrested again."

"He's in it deep this time."

"He's going to kill me when he gets out. He blamed me for everything that was happening. Now he'll be kicked out of his Ph.D. program, and he'll be in jail. He's going to go ballistic."

"None of this is your fault. He has problems, and he was using you as his meal ticket and his excuse."

"It's okay for *you* to say that, but it's *him* who's going to kill me."

"Hold on. Remember the woman who was yelling at him in the police car? She's not your

141

fault. That's all on him, and I wonder how many other crack babies he's fathered to move his project along?"

"Do you really think so?"

"We know about her. Has he been tapping into your checking account to pay for an apartment for anyone else?"

"I don't know for sure. The money doesn't seem to go as far as it used to. We don't really keep track of our spending in a check book register or anything. Toby checks the balance once in a while when we get close to payday, and he tells me what we can afford for groceries and stuff."

I noticed a growing speck on the beach ahead of us. "There's the boat."

Rachel straightened up and composed herself. I thought briefly about my bulletproof vest sitting on the seat and the old police axiom *you don't need a gun until you need it immediately and badly.* There was certainly a corollary to that involving bulletproof vests.

Chapter Fourteen

The ant-sized people moving around on the beach got larger as we approached. The boat was bigger than the Zodiac-style boat we'd chased off the beach the other day. It appeared to be better suited for the rougher Gulf waters, with a deeper V-shaped hull and a solid cover over the forward cabin.

"They're not racing for the boat," Rachel said with noticeable relief.

"Maybe they haven't seen us yet. I've been staying closer to the fringe of sea oats, so we're not as obvious."

"Killjoy."

"You know, the point of doing this is to catch people doing illegal things, not to scare them away."

"My professor said that the purpose of having a police force is as much deterrence as it is enforcement."

"That's all well and good until you have a dead body. Then I want to catch, not deter, the bastards."

We closed in enough to see the faces of the people with the boat, and there was an equal number of children and adults. I eased off the gas and relaxed. I hadn't been aware of how firmly I'd gripped the steering wheel, and how tight my back muscles were. When I took a deep breath, the adrenaline seeped out of my system. I became aware of my target focus, the vision tunneling that occurred when the adrenaline coursed through your system and your sole focus became the target and nothing else. That primal response had cost many cops, soldiers, and pilots their lives.

"Looks like family playday," I said, slowing to near a walking pace as I eased the pickup to the fringe of the crowd and parked.

"Hello!" I said, addressing the nearest person, a heavyset woman in a black one-piece bathing suit who was herding children around like a mother hen. She wore a hat with an immense brim that flopped when she walked. She seemed surprised by our sudden appearance.

We climbed out of the Park Service truck.

One of the girls, who was maybe a second-grader, spied Rachel and ran up to her. "Are you really a policeman like it says on your shirt?"

Rachel knelt down to be eye-level with the blonde girl. "Actually, I'm a ranger, but sometimes I'm a policewoman, too. Are you finding any shells?"

The girl held up a pink plastic bucket. "Lots of shells and even a sand dollar!" The girl dug in the bucket and pulled out a sand dollar, which was the size of a silver dollar. "I thought they were bigger, but my dad says this is a real sand dollar."

"The ones in Florida are bigger, but the ones here in Texas only get that size."

The girl cocked her head at Rachel. "You're pretty smart about sand dollars for being a cop. Daddy got stopped for speeding, and he said the cop was as dumb as a stump."

I was talking to the mother and saw the wave of embarrassment sweep over her when she heard the dumb as a stump comment. "Ashley! Cops are as smart as anyone. Your father was just upset and said something he shouldn't have."

Ashley looked at Rachel. "Cops aren't as dumb as stumps?"

"Not all of us."

The mother excused herself and darted after a toddler who ran toward the surf. The man, apparently the father, who had missed the dumb as a stump discussion, came over to me and put out his hand. "I'm Brad Goetz. I didn't realize we were even in a park."

"This is the Padre Island National Seashore. It's part of the U.S. National Park system, and we patrol down here to the Port Mansfield Channel."

"Cool! At first, it seemed like such a treat to have a whole piece of beach all to ourselves. Then it seemed a little creepy like we were really exposed. My son asked if the pirates would come and kidnap us. I assured him they wouldn't, but it made me keep an eye on the ocean."

A young boy, just as blond as the little girl, came running up and wrapped his arms around Brad's leg. "You should ask this park ranger about the pirates, Mikey."

145

The boy was timid and peeked at me around his father's leg. I knelt down. "Hi, Mikey. There aren't any pirates around here. We chase them all away."

Mikey didn't seem concerned about the pirates as much as he was curious about the Sig in my holster. "Is that a real gun?"

"It is."

"Do you shoot many people?"

"I've never shot anyone with my pistol." What I said was true, but there was Iraq . . .

"Then why do you have it?"

"I have it just in case someone very bad shows up."

"Bobby was being bad." Dad seemed shocked and went speechless.

"Don't worry. I don't shoot kids for being bad. I just talk to them, and they usually stop being bad."

Mikey nodded like he understood. I straightened up, my bad knee screaming.

"Thank you," Brad said, again shaking my hand.

"It's our pleasure to visit with our guests."

Ashley ran off after Mikey and Rachel joined me. "This is my partner, Rachel. We haven't had any pirates, but we have had a problem with treasure-hunters digging up the dunes. Is this your first time here?"

"We're staying on Mustang Island, and we took this charter down a couple days ago."

"Did you see any other boats when you were coming and going?"

"There was only one group of folks, who looked like they were snorkelers. Other than them, I don't recall seeing anything else."

"Describe the boat, and what made you think they were snorkeling?"

"It was a black boat with an inflatable tube around it. There's a name for it, but I don't remember what they're called. Anyway, they were wearing wetsuits, like snorkelers."

"How many people were on the boat?"

Brad paused. "I guess there were like three or four people on each of the tubes, so maybe like seven people."

"Men and women?"

"We weren't close enough to tell. Wait, I remember one person had long blonde hair blowing in the wind, but I suppose it could've been a man. They were all kinda grouped closely together, so it's not like I could make out a woman's figure vs. a man's physique."

"Did you notice if they beached anywhere?"

"I think they were just pulling away from the beach when we approached. I can't tell distances here, but they might've been stopped a couple miles farther north."

"Which way did they go when they left? North or south?"

"Now that you mention it, I thought it was strange. They turned south, then it was like they changed their minds, and then looped way out, away from us, and headed back toward Mustang Island. Why all the interest?"

"Like I said, we've had some treasure-hunters. It's illegal to use metal detectors here, and we've had some destruction of the natural grass and bushes."

"You should talk to our charter captain. He's taking people out here all the time, and we've just been out twice."

Rachel tapped Brad's arm as he was turning to leave. "Have you found any black or gold coins on the beach?"

"Nothing gold, but one of the boys found an old tarnished lead plug or something. I told him to throw it into the weeds."

Rachel raised her eyebrows. "Could you show us where?"

"I'm not exactly sure where it went. Hang on. Joseph, come over here."

A taller boy, probably approaching his teens, raced over to us, more curious about us than obedient. "What?"

"Where'd you throw that lead thing?"

Joseph pointed in a general direction south of us.

Rachel smiled, and I could see the boy melting with a crush on her. "Please show me where you threw the black coin and help me find it."

"Sure! I'll bring everyone!"

Rachel and Joseph rounded up the kids and three parents, and they loped down the beach.

Brad and I watched, then he turned. "Why are you interested in a black plug. Is it some kind of pollution hazard?"

"Three Spanish ships sunk offshore here, and we occasionally get coins that wash up on the beach."

"The Spanish were shipping lead?"

"The silver coins tarnish and turn black in the seawater."

Brad's eyes went wide. "Joey threw a silver coin away?"

"Don't get your hopes up. This is an archaeological reserve, and you can't keep any of the coins or antiquities you find here. They have to be turned over to the Park Service, and they're placed in the museum."

"Oh." Brad digested that information, then realization swept over his face. "The people in the black boat were digging up coins."

"That's likely."

A sunburned older man with thinning gray hair climbed over the boat railing and threw a cigarette into the water. The Gulf breeze blew around his comb-over hair and tugged at the hem of his gaudy red Hawaiian shirt.

"Charter time's up. Gather up the kiddies so we can head back."

Brad nodded just as one of the children searching the dunes yelled, "I found it!"

The old captain looked me up and down. "Haven't seen you before. What happened to the woman? She's kind of cute."

"She's down in the dunes with the kids, looking for a silver coin."

The old guy looked down the beach where Rachel and the others were walking back. They

149

gathered around her while she was apparently telling them about the shipwrecks and lost coins.

"I don't tell my shell charter folks about the coins. I know you Park Service folks don't like people carrying them off, so I figure it's just better not to bring it up."

"We appreciate that. We've had a black Zodiac boat running the shore, and we suspect they're beachcombing for coins."

"Don't know nothin' 'bout that."

"But, you've seen them."

The man shrugged. "I seen lots of things that weren't my business, and I stay clear of all them. It's wiser when you get to my age."

"But you have seen them." I made it a statement, not a question.

"Yup."

"Do you see them every time you're out?"

"Nope."

"Often?"

He shrugged. "What's often?"

"Once a week?"

"I 'spose I seen 'em most weeks. They steer clear of us. Whatever they're up to, they don't want anyone nosing around it, and I respect that."

"Where do they beach their boat most often?"

"Couple miles up, most often."

Joseph raced up to me with the coin in his hand. "Rachel says this coin is like five hundred years old. It's off a treasure ship that sunk right out here."

I smiled. "I hope she also told you that we have to put it in the museum."

"She did, but she took down my name, and she said it'd be posted next to the coin when they put it on display."

I put on my best Park Service smile. "You'll be able to bring your kids here someday and show it to them."

Joseph handed me the coin and raced back to Rachel, who seemed to have rallied from her pain, but was still moving slowly. I showed the coin to the captain.

"Yeah, I seen 'em before." He gave me the slightest hint of a smile. "I might've even sold one or two of 'em over the years."

"But now you know better, and you'll turn any of them over to me."

The captain looked at the kids gathered around Rachel. "Not to you. But maybe her. She's kinda cute when you don't make her wear that stupid police vest."

"A woman was killed up the beach a few days ago. Until we find her killer, we're both wearing vests."

"A woman?"

"Yes."

The captain considered that for a while and looked at Rachel. "You're not in a vest."

"Mine's in the pickup."

The captain nodded. "I suppose it makes sense. You want to protect the cute ones. Old guys like you and me, we're not as important anymore."

151

I put out my hand. "I'm Doug Fletcher."

"They call me Captain Billy."

"Well, Captain Billy, people who don't think old guys like us are important don't know the value of experience and a diploma from the school of hard knocks."

Captain Billy studied my face for a second to make sure I wasn't making fun of him, then he put out his hand again. "The first time I shook your hand, I was being polite. This time I'm shaking it because you're smarter than you look." He winked at me and started loading kids onto his boat.

I walked over and helped the adults up the wobbly ladder. "If you happen to see that black boat or any other suspicious boats beached along here, hail us on sixteen and let us know about them."

Billy shook his head. "Can't do that."

"Why not?"

"Everyone listens to sixteen, and I might find a hole in my hull or my skull if I call you in on 'em."

"Do you have a cellphone?"

He patted his pocket. "Gotta have one these days, although sometimes the reception is spotty. It's pretty handy if you've got trouble, and your power's down."

I took a business card out of my wallet and wrote my cellphone number on the back of it. "Call me."

"This is you and not the cement blockhouse back there?"

"That's me." I patted my pocket.

"What's in it for me?"

I smiled. "I might have an emergency hundred-dollar bill folded in my wallet. But it only applies if I get to put the cuffs on somebody."

I could see that Captain Billy considered a hundred dollars a lot of money. He took out his cellphone and programmed my number into the memory. "I'm not saying I'll do it, but you got my attention." He climbed the ladder and pulled it up behind him.

He moved all his passengers to the back of the boat and waited for a bigger swell to lift the hull, then he hit reverse and eased the boat away from shore.

Chapter Fifteen

Rachel virtually threw herself into the passenger seat and then doubled over, resting her head on the dashboard. I started the pickup and turned the air conditioning to maximum. I put my hand on her back, not that she could feel it through the bullet-proof vest, but she reacted to the pressure by turning her flushed face toward me.

"Cramps?"

She straightened up but kept her hands on her abdomen. "Some cramps. Some sore muscles. Mostly I'm just hot and tired."

"Take off the vest and lean back."

She shot me a look. "You said, and I quote, 'You only need a vest when you need it immediately and badly.'"

I reached into the back seat and pulled a bottle of water out of our emergency gear. "Take off the vest and drink this. You're hurting, and it looks like you're overheated."

She pulled the Velcro straps apart and drew the vest over her head. "Where'd you learn all this stuff, Doug?"

I shifted the pickup into drive as she screwed the cap off the water. "The school of hard knocks."

"They should teach us stuff like this in school."

"Nah. Students don't pay attention to stuff like seeing a woman doubled over with cramps or someone's face redden as they approach heat stroke. You have to be at a teachable moment for things like that to stick with you."

"I wonder if I'll ever be a good cop."

"Every rookie asks that of himself. You get smarter with experience."

Rachel looked at me as she took a swallow of water. "Is that why Matt wanted you here? He knew I needed a mentor and some training?"

"Matt needed someone with experience to investigate the hazardous waste dumping last month. Being able to team us up was just the luck of the draw. He would've gotten someone else to help with your training if I hadn't been assigned here."

"You know I was pissed when you showed up."

"You kept it well hidden."

"I tried to be professional, but my guts were churning that they'd stick me with some middle-aged white guy who's been in the news."

"I had no idea."

"Yeah, well, you turned out to be a pretty good guy, and I got over my anger quickly. That, and Jill is just a sweetheart."

"Thanks. I feel lucky to be with Jill."

Rachel nodded, but then clutched her abdomen as another wave of cramps gripped her.

"Do I need to have an ambulance meet us at the visitor center?"

"The doctor said I might have cramps for a couple days, but they'd get better. If I start bleeding, he said I should come in immediately."

"And?"

"There's no way to know until I get to a bathroom."

I stepped on the brakes and eased the pickup to a stop. "I'll step around to the tailgate while you check."

"It can wait."

"No, it can't. If you're in trouble, I want to know now. I can rush the drive, have an ambulance meet us, or we can hail the Coast Guard. We need to know if you have a medical emergency."

I pulled open the door and walked to the back of the pickup. I stared at the southern horizon, and wispy clouds hung high in the sky. I heard a buzzing over the Gulf and shielded my eyes until I picked up the formation of Navy trainers flying low over the water. They crossed the coastline a couple miles south of us, then made a slow turn to the right, heading back to the naval air station.

"It's okay, Doug."

I got back in the cab as Rachel was tucking a fanny pack behind the seat. "Do we rush?"

"I'm spotting, not bleeding. We're okay."

I slipped the pickup into gear and accelerated down the beach. "You wouldn't lie to me just to ease my conscience?"

Rachel frowned. "I changed pads, but there were literally only spots. Do you want to see the pad?"

I put up my hand. "I'm only concerned about your wellbeing. If you're not concerned, I'm not concerned. I don't need to see the evidence."

"Thank you."

"For what?"

"For being concerned . . . and for trusting me."

"You're welcome."

We rode in silence for a couple miles while Rachel drank water, and her red face faded.

"Why didn't you defend yourself last night?"

"I guess I thought each punch was going to be his last. I didn't expect him to keep hitting me."

"You'd have been justified shooting him. Not a jury in Texas would convict you of defending yourself against a larger angry man."

Rachel sat in silence while she mulled my words. "I couldn't. There's a part of me that still cares for him. I didn't want him dead, I only wanted him to stop hitting me."

"Sometimes a bullet is the only way to stop the punches. On the other hand, you didn't know he was screwing the crack-addicted whores as part of his study at that point."

"I still couldn't have shot him, but I wanted to give him a piece of my mind. And, a kick in the nuts wouldn't have been out of the question."

I smiled. "A kick in the nuts would've been a fitting punishment."

"Gawd, did you see that whore? She was covered with tattoos, had needle tracks on her arms, and it looked like her teeth were going to fall out. I was afraid to get too close to her."

"Speaking of that, have you been checked for STIs or STDs lately. I know you made Toby use a condom, but they're not a hundred percent effective. It's likely that woman picked up something from a customer or sharing needles."

Rachel glared at me.

"Hey! Let's be frank. Toby got her pregnant, which means he *wasn't* using any protection when they were screwing."

"Oh, geez. I never thought of that."

"Call your doctor when you get back. If they didn't run a screening last night, go see her again."

Rachel pulled out her cellphone and checked for reception. I watched her punch in the numbers with shaking fingers. She turned away from me and kept her voice low as she had a discussion with a triage nurse at the doctor's office.

"They took like a gallon of blood last night. The nurse said the information I'd given them ranked me as a high-risk patient, and they tested everything. I'm fine." Rachel got the words out but then broke down. "That bastard! I'm a high-risk patient because he couldn't keep his pecker in his pants. Damn him!"

I waited for her to calm down, letting the singing of the tires on the sand fill the silence. Then I said, "You're okay, and Toby's in jail. You'll get your life together, and things will be better."

"That's what Mandy Mattson said last night. Do you really believe that? I mean, do things really get better, or is that just what people say to pull you back from the brink?"

"Were you suicidal last night?"

Rachel shook her head. "No, just messed up. Back from the brink is just a figure of speech."

"I'm not anyone's life coach, but having been through some pretty tough times, I can personally attest to the fact that there are second chances. They can be better than the first time around."

"Are you talking about finding Jill after your divorce?"

"I'm talking about getting divorced, crawling into a booze bottle, having my career messed up by a kick to the knee, and . . . Yes, and then meeting Jill. My life right now is better than it's ever been."

"Are you and Jill going to have kids?"

"Not unless there's an immaculate conception." I laughed. "Jill's biological clock ran out a couple years ago. It'll just be the two of us growing old together."

"Do you feel bad about that?"

"I don't know how to feel about that. I think it's just a fact. I'm focusing on a new life married to my best friend."

"Stop!"

I jammed on the brakes thinking that something had just changed with Rachel's medical condition. "What?"

Rachel pointed out the windshield. "Look at the footprints."

I'd stopped just short of an area of beach that was covered with footprints running from the breaking waves into the dunes. Rachel was out of the truck before I could warn her to put on her vest. I grabbed it off the seat, leaving mine behind, and dashed after her as she ran toward the sea oats on the edge of the dunes.

Rachel stopped at a high point in the sea oats and was staring down the backside of the dunes. I caught up with her and handed her the vest. She took the vest but didn't put it on. Instead, she pointed to a series of holes behind the dunes.

"Someone was digging behind us while we were talking to the families who were picking seashells."

I felt my phone vibrate. I opened a text from an unknown number. "Black Zodiac ahead. Went into state park boat launch. Billy."

"It was the black Zodiac." I showed the text to Rachel.

"Who's Billy?"

"He's the charter captain from the shell hunters. I gave him my cellphone number and offered him a bounty if we arrested someone stealing coins."

Rachel snatched the phone from my hand and punched in a number from memory. "Ron, it's Rachel. Are you anywhere near the Mustang Island State Park?"

She listened, then said, "Can you put out an announcement for any law enforcement? There's a black Zodiac that just pulled into the state park launch, and we think they've been digging up coins on the beach while we were patrolling farther south."

She ended the call and handed the phone back. "The county sheriff's department is asking any law enforcement in the area to check for the black Zodiac at the park launch."

"Who'd you call?"

"Ron Meland was the deputy who responded when we brought in the beachcombers and the coins."

"You know his number from memory?"

A blush crept up from Rachel's neck. I'd seen them talking while the CCPD cops had taken the beachcombers away but hadn't thought of their discussion as anything but professional courtesy. Rachel's reaction hinted at something more. She looked like she expected a question or a comment, but I shut down and pocketed my phone. "I hope there's someone near enough to at least get a description of their vehicle and maybe a license plate number."

Rachel's phone chirped as we pulled up to the visitor center. She answered, had a short discussion, then disconnected. "Nobody was close. Port Aransas PD sent a car, but there weren't any vehicles with a Zodiac in the lot or on their drive down."

Rachel retrieved her fanny pack, and we walked to Matt's office to update him on our day. The crime scene tape was gone, and he'd picked up the papers that had been strewn around the floor. The only remaining evidence of a crime was the bent file cabinet. Matt was on his phone. He gestured for us to sit in his guest chairs. His conversation seemed friendly, although hearing only his comments, mostly "uh-huh," really didn't clue us into the caller or the topic.

He hung up and leaned his elbows on the desk. "That was our local FBI agent. He wasn't pleased to learn from the Assistant U.S. Attorney that we had arrested four men for removing Spanish coins from the archaeological area. His greatest displeasure was learning the coins taken from my office were worth somewhere north of a hundred grand, and that Doug had omitted that tidbit when they'd spoken about the FBI entering the investigation."

I smiled. "What's going to happen?"

"Nothing. He vented. He still doesn't want anything to do with the investigation since we already have local resources working on it. He just wanted me to know how displeased he was."

I shook my head. "He's not done. He'll be back when the theft is solved."

Rachel suddenly caught on to the conversation. "You mean, to take credit for finding them and arresting the bad guys."

"Doug's cynicism is rubbing off on you, Rachel."

She nodded. "He's a good teacher."

Matt feigned shock. "You like Doug as a teacher!"

Rachel rolled her eyes. "I picked up another gem from his school of hard knocks today. If you keep him around long enough, I may become an investigative genius."

"Not to change the topic, but before Doug's head gets too big to fit in this office, how are you feeling?"

Rachel waggled her hand. "I've had better days, but I'm getting by."

I tried to discreetly shake my head, but Rachel caught it. "I'm doing okay, Doug. I'm not at the top of my game, but I dealt with the kids searching for seashells."

That reminded me of the beachcombers. I reached into my pocket and put the coin they'd found on Matt's desk. "You should lock this in your file cabinet to keep it safe."

"Ha, ha." Matt picked up the coin and examined it. "I think it'll go into the safe behind the gift counter for the night. I'll have someone take it to the museum in the morning.

Rachel pulled out a piece of paper and handed it to Matt. "Here's the name of the kid who found the coin. I told him his name would be displayed with the coin in the museum."

Matt took the paper and wrapped it around the coin. "I'm not sure how they handle the coins that get turned in, but it seems like that would be the least they could do to reward someone who turns in a valuable coin."

"We got a lead on a boat we think is ferrying the treasure-hunters on and off the island. A captain running a shell hunting ferry called me and said he'd followed in a black Zodiac boat that turned into the state park boat launch. Rachel contacted the county sheriff and Port Aransas PD, but the boat was gone by the time they got to the park."

"Do you think they might be our killers?"

"That boat, or one just like it, has been around here a lot the past couple weeks. I'd sure like to talk to them about what they're up to and about the dead woman."

Matt snapped his fingers. "The entrance shack called this afternoon. The campground is full."

I looked at Rachel, trying to discern the significance of Matt's comment. "It's not usually this busy except for spring break."

"Ah, treasure-hunters," I said.

Matt nodded. "Take a walk around and talk to the folks so they understand that removing coins and artifacts is a federal crime. Let's be proactive instead of arresting people."

Rachel explained, "I caught a few people with metal detectors lying outside their tents, campers, and vehicles just after the hurricane. They were unaware of the restrictions on metal detectors here. A few of them packed up and left. The others put them away like they weren't planning to use them once they understood the law."

"Rachel, get out of here. Go see Mandy and lay down for a while. I can drive through the campground and talk to a few folks. It's not like it'll take two of us to talk to anyone who looks like they're here to treasure hunt."

"Doug's right. Mandy's got supper in the oven, and she's called twice to check on you."

Chapter Sixteen

I drove the Park Service pickup through the campground and stopped next to people who had shovels or suspicious gear out. Each person I spoke to had no idea treasure-hunting on the national seashore was prohibited, and they promised to refrain from digging for coins or artifacts. In each case, my presence drew a crowd, and at least half-dozen more people nodded their heads with an understanding of the restrictions. It made me feel good about the outreach, but I spoke with fewer than a tenth of the people camped there, and I wasn't convinced that everyone who bobbed their heads was not going to dig for coins if we didn't watch them.

* * *

When I pulled into the townhouse road, I saw Charlie standing next to a charcoal grill in his yard. The boys played some game involving slapping cards, the quickest slapper got the pile. I reasoned that they were being quiet and not racing around screaming like they were being chased by banshees.

I parked next to my Isuzu, and Charlie waved me over with a spatula, his other hand held a plastic cup of iced tea. His bruises were fading, turning to yellows and greens, and he appeared like he felt well. "Supper's over here tonight. I'm grilling steaks as soon as the coals are hot, Clarice is fixing potatoes, and your ladies are whipping up a salad and dessert."

"No margaritas tonight?" I joked.

Charlie glanced at the boys and shook his head, apparently rethinking whatever he'd planned to say. "I think the ladies were over-served last night, and everyone's sticking to sweet tea." He held up his glass.

"Sounds like a plan."

"How do you like your steak done?"

"Medium-rare."

Charlie smiled. "It's overdone if it doesn't bleed when you cut into it."

I walked into the townhouse and put my holster on the closet shelf. "I smell cake!"

Mother stuck her head around the kitchen corner with a smile on her face. "It was no small feat. We had to dig through every cupboard to find a mixing bowl and cake pan." She had flour on her face, arms, and blouse. "I made it while Jill was on the phone."

Jill stuck her head around the corner. She was whisking something in a bowl and was less happy than Mom. "Get changed. We're supposed to be at Clarice's in five minutes."

"We've got time. Charlie says the coals aren't ready yet."

167

That got me a frown from Jill, so I hustled up the stairs and changed into shorts and a golf shirt.

Jill slipped into the bedroom and closed the door. "I called the university today to talk with Toby's advisor about the pregnant woman looking for the support Toby promised. The registrar said, Toby's not a student."

"Wow. That's quite a revelation. How'd you get them to talk to you?"

Jill looked sheepish. "They were willing to talk with a Park Service investigator."

"But what about his Ph.D. project?"

Jill shook her head. "The registrar referred me to the head of the sociology department. Dr. Pollock. He doesn't know who Toby is, and there are no advanced sociology degrees offered at the Texas A&M Corpus Christi campus."

I was speechless and gave Jill a hug. "You missed your calling. You should've been a cop."

"I appreciate the sentiment, but that's not my cup of tea."

I considered Jill's news again. "Rachel said he was gone every evening doing research. What was he up to? Was he just living off her money while trolling bars and picking up women?"

Jill shook her head. "Think about the pregnant hooker who showed up the night he was arrested. I think he was hanging out with the drug users and prostitutes in the dark alleys of Corpus Christi, using his cover story about the research study to get free sex from the hookers, and maybe getting some of them into county rehab programs. I doubt we'll ever know the real story."

"If that was what he was doing, this arrest might've saved him from a bullet in the back of the head from an angry pimp."

"Or an overdose," Jill added.

I closed my eyes. "I don't know how to tell Rachel. We knew Toby was using her. We just didn't understand the depth of his deception."

Jill hugged me. "I talked to Mandy and explained what had been happening. She's going to tell Rachel tonight."

I kissed Jill. "Thank you. That's not news Rachel should hear from me, and she told me today that Mandy treated her like a little sister. I think she'll take the news best from Mandy."

* * *

I came downstairs, barefooted. Jill was spreading frosting on a sheet cake, and Mom was sprinkling croutons on top of a salad.

I strapped on sandals. "I'm surprised we're having supper at Clarice and Charlie's house again."

Jill licked a glob of frosting before handing me the spatula covered with the last remnants of chocolate icing. "Clarice insisted that we come over for supper."

Mom spread Saran wrap over the salad while I licked the spatula. "I think she's a nervous wreck and having us around helps her through the day. She stopped and stared at me with a look of

169

wonderment. "Doug, I haven't seen you lick a spatula in thirty years."

I put the nearly clean spatula in the sink. "I suppose it's been that long since I've been around when you've baked a cake."

Mom looked away and busied herself, arranging the Saran wrap. "There didn't seem to be much reason to bake after your dad died. It's nice to bake for a family again."

Jill grinned and winked at me. "It's not much fun cooking for one."

"Neither is eating alone in a restaurant. You and Jill are lucky to have each other."

I wiped a smear of frosting off Jill's lower lip with my fingertip. I licked my finger clean and gave her a hug. "Yes, I am."

Jill pushed the cake pan into my hands. "Carry this over to Clarice while I clean up the kitchen."

I followed Mom across the yard, hardly garnering a look from the boys whose game had become louder and rowdier. Charlie was turning the steaks and nodded to me as we passed. Clarice was setting the table and waved us toward the kitchen counter. "Set your cake on the counter. Ronnie, the salad can go right on the table. Doug, would you grab the platter and help Charlie carry in the steaks?"

I looked in three cupboards before Clarice intervened and pointed me toward the farthest cabinet to fetch the platter. I carried it out to Charlie, who was spritzing water on the flaming coals.

"It'll be just another minute." He stepped back from the grill. "I hear you're having trouble with people boating in to pick coins out of the surf."

"Yeah. We're supposed to stop people from digging for coins because the whole island is an archaeological preservation area. It's frustrating because we drive down the beach in the pickup. The treasure-hunters beach their boats and see us coming for miles. All they have to do is jump into their boats and shove off, and we can't get near them. On top of that, we only drive the beach twice a day, so we get past each place four times as we drive back and forth. A cagey boat operator can pull offshore and wait for us to pass, then come in again behind us."

Charlie waved me over with the platter, and he started stacking steaks. "Seems like the Coast Guard would help."

"Their helicopters let us know when they fly over a beached treasure-hunter, but their priority is supporting your Navy flight operations and boaters who are having trouble. They occasionally spot treasure-hunters for us, but that's not their primary mission."

I carried the platter inside and set it on the table where everyone was already seated. Charlie pointed toward the end of the platter. "These are medium-rare, and the ones on the other end are medium-well. Pick what suits you."

Clarice stuck a fork in the middle of a steak and set it on Allen's plate. "You boys are splitting this one."

171

She stepped behind them, split the steak between the two boys, and cut it into bite-sized pieces. The rest of us passed the potato salad, lettuce salad, and steaks. Mother sat next to Clarice and put a scoop of each food on Clarice's plate as they came past.

Danny announced, "Mom, I want ketchup!"

Clarice took a deep breath, then smiled. "Would anyone else like ketchup or steak sauce? Oh, I'll just bring them both out."

Charlie dove into his food while Clarice looked for ketchup in the refrigerator. Mother politely waited for Clarice to sit down before eating, but Charlie waved his fork at her. "Ronnie, dig in while it's hot."

Clarice slid into her chair and tucked a loose strand of hair behind her ear while taking a deep breath. She seemed surprised to see a plateful of food in front of her. "Ronnie, did you dish-up for me?"

Mom cut into her steak now that Clarice was seated. "You seemed a little busy with the boys."

"I haven't eaten anything hot since Allen was born. I have to prep everything for the boys before I eat or they howl."

Charlie seemed oblivious to the conversation.

I looked at Charlie. "I suppose it'll really put all the load on Clarice when you finish flight training and deploy with the fleet."

"Yeah, we've talked about that. The pilot's wives are usually close-knit groups who help each other out. We'll have to move to San Diego or Norfolk, depending on which carrier I'm assigned to."

"The Park Service at least comes home every night," Jill said. "Although we seem to move around as often as military families if we're moving our careers ahead."

Clarice ate a bite of salad, checking to make sure the boys were okay. "Jill told me she's been in five parks since she joined the Park Service. She's excited about putting down roots here."

Mother perked up. "Jill took me on a tour of their house on the canal. You're closing soon. Right, Jill?"

"Actually, we're closing Friday."

Mom sounded excited. "She's got drawings of the inside, and she's got some construction people ready to start up. I just love the location on the canal. It reminds me of being on a lake in Minnesota."

"When are you getting married?" Charlie asked. The table went silent while everyone waited for Jill or me to answer.

Jill set her fork down. "We haven't set a date."

Mother waved her fork. "I think you should do it when Jill's parents are down here next week. Doug could reschedule my return flight, and we could all be here for the ceremony."

I expected Jill to panic, but when I looked across the table, she raised her eyebrows like she and Ronnie had discussed it, and the decision was up to me to endorse or veto.

I felt the room crushing me, and I stared at my plate. The engagement had been a big step, but somehow marriage seemed a monumental leap. "Um, we haven't talked about it. I don't even know where we'd have the ceremony or who we'd have to stand up for us."

Mother cocked her head. "Isn't it obvious. There are a couple of churches nearby. Who'd you have beside Matt and Mandy? Is there anyone you're closer to?"

Jill got up and stood behind me, leaning close to my ear. "Please."

Jill had never asked anything of me since telling me she wanted to make love to me, her best friend, when we'd been living in Arizona. She'd given so much and asked so little.

I put my hand up and pulled her head close to me and kissed her ear. "Yes, dear."

She gave me a sly smile and whispered, "You're going to eat those words one of these times."

I gave her an innocent look. "What?"

She stood up and pulled the cellphone out of her pocket and hit redial.

I twisted around to see what she was doing. "Who are you calling?"

"I have to see what days Matt and Mandy are available. You have to call the airline and rebook Ronnie's flight for later in the week."

A tiny voice at the other end of the table asked, "Are we going to a wedding?"

Jill stood in the kitchen, quietly talking with Mandy. I looked at Allen and smiled. "I guess you're going to a wedding."

Danny perked up. "Will there be cake?"

Mother nodded. "Yes, there'll be cake, even if I have to bake it."

* * *

Jill and I lay in bed, watching the news. She clicked off the television and rolled to face me. "You weren't listening to the news."

"Sure, I was."

"What's the forecast for tomorrow?"

"It doesn't matter. They're wrong half the time."

She poked me gently in the ribs. "You were checked out. What's going on in your head?"

"We're buying a house and getting married in the next week. It's . . . unreal."

"Are you getting cold feet?"

I turned my head and gazed into her eyes, seeing the concern she'd been hiding all evening. "Not at all." I kissed her gently. "It's just a lot of change for a middle-aged guy whose life's been in and out of the toilet for a decade. I'm excited and scared, all at the same time."

"Jamie Ballard told me you've been wandering a path leading nowhere since your divorce."

"When did he tell you that?"

"While we were hiking in Flagstaff, looking for the grave of the missing girl." Jill paused.

"You know, he's extremely perceptive. He had good reads on Liz and me too."

"What'd he say about you?"

Jill rolled onto her back. "He said I tried to be tougher than the men I'd competed with for Park Service jobs. He told me to look inside and open my heart to love."

"Is that why you came back to my Flagstaff townhouse after telling me you weren't into one-night stands?"

"That was part of it."

"What was the other part?"

She rolled toward me and put her arm across my chest, snuggling into my shoulder. "You are the kindest, most thoughtful, caring man I've ever met. I talked to you, knowing you weren't going to judge me or try to change me. I told you things no one else had ever heard, and all you did was listen and offer support." I thought she'd finished, but she added, "I walked to my truck that night and cried like a little girl, berating myself for not being willing to let my guard down around the one person I thought I could trust."

"And you came back and knocked on my door, not knowing if it was going to be a one-night stand."

"I decided I didn't care. I wanted to make love to my best friend, pretty sure it was going to happen only once, but praying it would be more. I never dreamt I would end up moving from Arizona and marrying you."

I patted her shoulder. "It'll all be okay."

"Only okay?"

"No, it's going to be heavenly. There are going to be bumps in the road, but I know we can handle them. We've already gotten over some pretty big ones to reach this point."

Jill stared into my eyes. "I've never felt like this. I guess I've never really been in love before. Are you feeling butterflies?"

"Some butterflies and the overwhelming realization that my world is changing. The aimless wandering Jamie talked about is coming to an end. You do realize I come with lots of nicks and bruises."

Jill embraced me. "We've both been bruised and hurt. That's what makes us fit together so well."

"Where are you going to find a wedding dress in a few days?"

Jill pushed herself away from me and sat up. "Damn you!"

"What?"

She hopped out of bed and snatched her cellphone off the nightstand. I watched her frantically punching numbers into her phone while she paced back and forth. "Mandy, I hope I didn't wake you. I just realized that I need something to wear to the wedding."

Jill listened to Mandy, and I could see her relaxing. "Yes, I can find clothes that fit off the rack at any store." She listened, making positive sounds, then shut down the phone.

"Mandy missed her calling. She should've been a therapist," Jill said as she slipped back into bed. "Mandy knows a woman who owns a wedding shop in Corpus Christi. She thought I could wear an off-the-rack gown if I buy some 'foundation garments' that'll help me fill out the bust and butt. She's calling her friend before the store opens in the morning, then she's picking Ronnie and me up at ten. She assured me we'd find something in my size tomorrow."

"I didn't know you wanted a wedding gown."

"Doug, this is my first, and only, wedding. I want a gown, like in my dreams."

"What am I wearing in your dreams?"

"I suppose you could wear your dress Park Service uniform since you don't own a tux or suit."

"No. I'm not getting married looking like Dudley Do-Right wearing a Smokey Bear hat. I'll find a suit and tie."

"Good answer."

I realized I'd just been finessed. "You suggested the uniform just to get me to buy a suit."

"It worked, didn't it?"

"Am I that transparent, or are you that cunning?"

She sat up again. "Can we afford a wedding dress? We're buying a house."

I pulled her to me. "My Park Service salary is more than I've ever made, and I'm still getting a St. Paul PD pension. I'm putting a thousand dollars a month into a savings account, and my checking account is overflowing. Buy any dress that you want. It'll be fine."

She relaxed. "You know I'm going to look like hell tomorrow."

"Why?"

"I'm too excited to sleep tonight. Maybe I should watch television downstairs for a while to unwind and let you get some sleep."

"Or we could pretend we're back in San Antonio again."

"Your mother is one wall away from us."

I slid my hand under her t-shirt. She closed her eyes, pressing her breast into my hand. "You're a devil," she purred.

"You pushed my buttons and got me to buy a suit. It's my turn to push your buttons."

"And you do that so well."

Chapter Seventeen

I was dressed, drinking coffee, munching toast, and watching the morning news when my mother walked down the stairs wrapped in a bathrobe she'd borrowed from Jill.

"I thought I smelled coffee." I started to get up to pour her a cup when she put her hand on my shoulder. "I know where the cups and the coffee pot are, dear."

"Jill has plans for you this morning."

I heard the cupboard creak and coffee pouring. "I know. Mandy's picking us up at ten to go wedding dress shopping."

Jill hadn't stirred when I showered and dressed, so I was surprised Mom was already aware of the plans. "You talked to Jill already?"

Mom sat in the chair across from me and gave me a sly smile while she sipped her coffee. "Jill's still asleep. Your walls are paper-thin."

I stopped with a bite of toast halfway to my mouth and didn't have a response.

"Do you think there's any chance you started a grandchild for me last night?"

I set the toast down and shook my head. "Jill's biological clock ran out a couple years ago."

Mother raised her eyebrows. "Miracles happen."

"Jill's a couple years older than she looks . . . or acts."

"I know Jill's age. I also know there are women older than Jill who've had children. She'd make a wonderful mother. You should see her with Allen and Danny."

I picked up my plate full of crumbs and the coffee cup and set them in the sink. "Don't get your hopes up. You'll only be disappointed."

"We'll see."

"Have fun picking out a wedding dress with the girls."

"We'll have a great time. Jill is wonderful, and Mandy's a hoot."

I kissed Mom on the forehead. "I can't tell you how happy I am that you and Jill are getting along. She was really nervous about meeting you."

"Had you told her I was a witch?"

"No, she just didn't know what to expect."

"I wish you'd met Jill the first time around."

I froze. "I thought you liked having a college professor for a daughter-in-law."

"I tolerated her, but I knew what she was doing to you. Jill is . . . good for you. She's grounded, interesting, fun, and mature. Those are all the things that were missing from your first marriage. That, and she loves you. She's not using you as a bank and meal ticket. On the other hand, you're finally mature enough to appreciate someone like Jill."

181

"Have a nice day, Mom."

"You're not using birth control, are you?"

"Mom, I'm not having this conversation with you."

"I'll ask Jill," she said as I closed the door.

"No!"

Chapter Eighteen

Matt was already in his office when I got to the visitor center.

I stuck my head in the door. "Is the Spanish coin still in the safe this morning?"

"Shit. I didn't check on it." He jumped up from his chair and pushed past me.

I had just logged into my computer when he sat in my guest chair. "That was cruel."

"Gotcha."

He shook his head. "You know, if you were a young ranger pulling stuff like that, I'd ream your behind."

"But, I'm not a young ranger, and you probably chuckled when you saw the coin was still in the safe."

He smiled. "What happened when you went through the campground last night?"

"I talked to several groups who had shovels and prospecting gear sitting out. They didn't know it was illegal to remove coins from the park. Quite a few people came over while I was talking to them, so I think the word has probably spread through the campground. I'm sure somebody will play ignorant, but everyone knows the rules."

"The ranger who opened the entrance hut said five groups had checked out overnight. I assume they may have been some of the people disappointed about the rules against recovering artifacts."

"Rachel and I will have to check with every group we see walking the beach today."

"Rachel's going to be late this morning."

"She wasn't feeling well yesterday."

Matt shook his head. "Toby's being arraigned in federal court. She asked for time off to go to the hearing."

"The arraignment is usually nothing. They state the charges, the defendant pleads not guilty, and the magistrate sets bail."

"The Assistant U.S. Attorney called Rachel and said Toby's public defender was trying to negotiate a plea deal. He wants to plead guilty to impeding a federal officer, which is a misdemeanor. The prosecutor said she laughed at the offer."

"What charge is she submitting?"

"The prosecutor wants to throw the book at him and go with assault of a federal officer using a weapon or causing great bodily harm. She looked at the pictures taken at the hospital and got the report of the miscarriage. She said that's a class C felony. I don't know what that means."

I whistled. "The statue ranks felonies A to D, with A being the most serious, which are kidnapping and murder. Class D is the least, and that's the simple assault of a federal officer, and Class C is assault with great bodily harm. I think the penalty for class C is seven to twenty-five years in prison. If they convict him and consider Toby's previous record, I think a judge will go for the high end of the range, and Toby will be an old man before he sees freedom again."

"Rachel told the prosecutor she didn't want to testify. It sounds like they don't need her testimony if they submit the pictures of her injuries and the medical reports as evidence, then you, Jill, Mandy, and I will have to testify about what we heard and saw."

I considered my experience with domestic assault victims. "Rachel would have a hard time testifying with Toby sitting there staring at her."

"Do you think so? Even after she knows he's been lying to her about being in school for years and milking her bank account so he can drink and hire prostitutes?"

"Love is a strange thing."

Matt shook his head and stood up. "Make another pass through the campground this morning, before you drive the beach, and see if you can prevent anyone else from prospecting."

"Anything you say, Boss."

Matt looked at me and shook his head before stopping at the door. "And wear your vest. Your nearest backup is going to be far away and slow to respond."

* * *

I drove through the campground and spoke to two gray-haired men who were unpacking a

185

metal detector from the camper on the back of a battered and dusty pickup. Based on their furtive attempt to jam the metal detector back into the truck when they saw me, I guessed they knew about the regulations.

I pulled on my hated Smokey Bear hat as I walked up to them. "Hi, guys."

The one with a tattered sweatshirt, dirty jeans, and a scruffy gray beard looked me over. The look in his eye said he was going to be trouble, but people from neighboring campsites migrated over to check me out. With the gathering crowd, he lowered his hackles a bit but was still unhappy.

"Lookie here, it's Smokey the Bear."

I forced a smile. "It's Smokey Bear. He doesn't have a middle name."

My sarcasm went over his head, and he just frowned.

"Using your metal detector on Padre Island or the surrounding waters is illegal."

"What metal detector?"

I walked to the back of the camper, opened the door, and pulled back a blue plastic tarp. "This metal detector."

"Hey! You can't just go into my camper without a warrant!"

"You need to bone up on the law. I saw you put the thing in the camper. That gives me probable cause to investigate."

A crowd was gathering, and I felt the need to be strong and defiant. "You can pack it up and leave, or I can seize it, and you can pick it up from the Federal Courthouse after filling out a receipt for the seizure of illegal contraband." I had no idea what the procedure was, but I was sure they knew less than I did.

"You can't throw us out. This is a public campground, and we paid our entry fee." The scruffy man did all the talking. His partner hung back and watched in a way that made my skin prickly. He appeared gaunt and wore a stained long underwear shirt and equally dirty jeans. His shaggy hair looked like he'd cut it himself, and he'd recently shaved so he only had stubble, not a beard.

"This is a part of the National Park Service system. I can throw you out for littering if I want to, and you're way past littering." Scruffy's partner edged toward the driver's door, and I kept him in my peripheral vision as I moved forward to get into Scruffy's face. "The metal detector is now federal property, and it's leaving with me. You pack up your gear while I watch, and I'll follow you to the entry hut."

The slender partner reached for the driver's door like maybe he was ready to leave, but I looked at their cookware and gear sitting around the campsite and knew they weren't going without packing up. I waited until he pulled the door open, then I threw my shoulder into Scruffy to keep him off balance and out of whatever was playing out with his partner. The unexpected move spun him around and one knee buckled, sending him tumbling.

187

His partner had his hand under the front pickup seat, and I had the Sig out of my holster when I grabbed his shoulder. "Just ease back and give me whatever is in your hand." I pushed the muzzle of the pistol into his ribs. I slipped off the safety but kept my finger outside the trigger guard to avoid an unfortunate accidental discharge.

The partner's eyes got wide when he felt the gun in his ribs, and he slowly backed up, exposing the butt of a gun in the palm of his hand. I wanted to look at Scruffy to make sure he wasn't going to do something regrettable, but my eyes were fixed on his partner's hand.

"Let go of the gun, then raise your hands over your head and face away from me." We were jammed into the small space between the pickup's door and the driver's seat. I could smell the man's body odor and the onions on his breath. Grabbing both of his hands in my left hand, I eased him away from the door.

I finally got a look a Scruffy, who was up and ready to rush me. I swung the pistol toward him. "Don't do anything stupid."

He stopped and decided to brush the dirt off his filthy jeans. I put the Sig back in the holster and clipped handcuffs on the partner, pushing him against the side of the pickup. I grabbed a purple glove out of my back pocket and used it to pull the gun from under the seat. I took a deep breath when I realized it was a double-barreled shotgun with a sawed-off barrel and the butt cut down to a pistol grip. I released the lever latching it shut and removed the two shotgun shells marked 00. Meaning double-ought buckshot. They were shells loaded with a dozen .32 caliber pellets. A load that was as deadly with one shot as me emptying my Sig into a suspect. My mind swam with the possibility that Rachel could've confronted these guys alone, and who knows what might've happened to her or the dozens of nearby campers. Then I realized I hadn't heeded Matt's request to wear the bulletproof vest.

"When did they let rangers start carrying guns?" Scruffy asked.

"When they started letting assholes bring guns into the park. Put your hands over your head and walk to the front fender of my pickup."

I cuffed Scruffy and put both of them in the backseat of my pickup after reading them their rights from a dog-eared Miranda card I had to dig out of my wallet. I took pictures of the shotgun and shells inside the pickup, then got the names and addresses of the people who'd been gawking. One of the male gawkers looked wide-eyed at the shotgun when I removed it from the pickup and placed it on the floor of the passenger side of my vehicle.

"They had that in their pickup?"

I nodded, then called Matt. "I need a couple rangers in the campground to pack up a pickup and have it towed to an impound lot."

"What?"

"I found two campers with a metal detector. One of them started to pull a sawed-off shotgun on me."

"In *our* campground?"

"Yes, our campground."

Matt paused while he digested the information. "Holy shit. Is everyone okay?"

"Yeah. I saw him going for the gun before he got it out, so we're all good here. But, I have to take two men to Corpus Christi and book them into the federal holding facility."

"You're going to have to fill out a pile of paperwork."

"Matt, it doesn't matter. I arrested two men who tried to assault me with a shotgun in the campground. Yes, there's going to be paperwork, but less than if there'd been a gunfight or if they'd shot a camper."

"I'm glad I told you to wear your vest this morning."

I shook my head and pulled the vest out of the pickup. "Yes, that was a good suggestion."

I shut down the call, took off my hat, and pulled the vest over my head before driving to the visitor center.

I locked the men in the back of the pickup and walked to Matt's office with the shotgun. "This is what they had in their truck."

"Man alive. I know we allow people to bring weapons into the park, but is that thing even legal?"

"I think federal law requires the barrel length to be at least eighteen inches. This looks like about eight inches." I paused. "Where is the federal holding facility?"

"It's on the backside of the courthouse, downtown, near the bayfront."

"I'll register my prisoners and maybe take a walk up to see what's going on with Toby's arraignment."

I turned to leave and Matt stopped me. "What would've happened if Rachel had confronted these guys alone?"

I shrugged. "I guess it might've gone either way. They might not have felt threatened by her and bullied her into leaving them alone. She might've been savvy enough to catch on to what was happening, or things could've gone south really fast, and someone would've gotten hurt."

Matt looked dazed. "Talk her through this when you're through filling out the reports. I want her to understand what you saw, how you reacted, and how you controlled the situation so no one got hurt."

I nodded.

Chapter Nineteen

The Federal Courthouse wasn't far into Corpus Christi and only a block from the FBI building where I'd gone for a news conference a couple weeks earlier. It looked like most federal buildings, but with a stunning view of the bay from the upper floors. I assumed the offices with those views were reserved for the Assistant U.S. Attorney and the senior magistrates.

I got my disgruntled prisoners booked into the holding cells where they would be processed for arraignment, and then I filled out the most basic of information, promising to submit the full report as soon as I got access to my computer.

I parked in *a Law Enforcement Only* spot and went through the front entrance. I had to join the line at the metal detector, then put my weapon, handcuffs, spare clips, cellphone, and keys in a bin while I went through the detector. I was taken aside by a uniformed officer who scrutinized me and my credentials carefully before handing me the bin with my gear.

He smiled, told me to turn off my cellphone, and directed me to the elevators. "You're the second Park Ranger here today. I can't say I've ever seen one of you guys in your Smokey the Bear hats before."

I smiled and chose not to point out that he was Smokey Bear, and his middle name wasn't *THE*. I found the courtroom where the arraignments were taking place, and I showed my I.D. to the uniformed U.S. Marshal before slipping through the doors. There was a rush of air as the doors swept open, and the few people inside, including the judge, looked back to see who had entered. Mandy and Rachel were in the second row behind the prosecutor. I saw Toby, wearing an orange jumpsuit and flipflops, in a holding cell with a half-dozen other prisoners. Toby glared at me, but I ignored him and slipped into a chair next to Mandy. I reached across Mandy's lap and squeezed Rachel's hand. She jumped like she'd been jolted with electricity. Her head jerked toward my hand, my hat then to my face. She took a breath and gave me a weak smile.

I leaned close to Mandy and whispered, "Have I missed anything?"

Mandy shook her head and put her finger to her lips, signaling me to be quiet.

The bailiff called a case, and a haggard-looking young lawyer flipped through sheaves of files as a marshal brought a manacled prisoner to the defense table. The lawyer chatted briefly with his client, then nodded to the bailiff.

"Robert Chandler is charged with three counts of bank robbery, use of a firearm in the course of the felony, and resisting arrest."

The judge looked over the top of her reading glasses, assessing the defendant. "How do you plead, Mr. Chandler?" Her voice sounded tired, and she looked like she'd heard a thousand hard-luck stories.

Chandler whispered in his public defender's ear, and the judge stopped him. "Do you speak English, Mr. Chandler?"

"Um, yes, ma'am."

"What's your plea?"

"I was asking my lawyer if I had an option."

"Of course, you have an option. You can plead guilty, and you'll be sentenced. Or you can plead not guilty, and your lawyer will request bail. If you can put up the bail money, you'll be released until the trial. If not, you'll be jailed until the trial."

Chandler whispered to his lawyer again, and the judge was about to interrupt when the public defender put up his hand. "My client has some dental problems, and he wants to know if he'll get a better dentist in prison if he pleads guilty." I could tell that neither the lawyer nor the judge wanted to deal with Chandler's question.

The judge took off her glasses and leaned forward. "Your dental care shouldn't be the deciding factor in your plea. You should either plead guilty or not guilty upon your conference with your lawyer."

Chandler whispered in the lawyer's ear again, and the judge erupted. "Mister Bosner, will you please enter a plea for your client if he's incapable of making the decision for himself."

"Your honor, my client has put me in an uncomfortable position."

The judge cut him off before he could continue. "This is a simple, yes, or no question. I have people patiently waiting. I want an answer. Guilty or not guilty? And before you start another grade school secret exchange, let me be clear. If you start whispering, I may hold you both in contempt."

"My client wishes to plead, not guilty."

"Not yet! I need to know about the dentist. If I wait until I'm convicted, will I have to wait longer or should I plead guilty now and get right to prison?"

The judge closed her eyes. "I think your client just pled guilty."

"Well, I am guilty. I just want to know . . ."

"Bailiff, enter a guilty plea, and if the defendant changes his mind, he can appeal. The public defender will prepare a pre-sentencing proposal. Who's next?"

"Toby Sanderson. Mr. Sanderson is charged with assault of a uniformed federal officer and doing great bodily harm."

A marshal brought Toby shuffling forward while the public defender rifled through his files. Toby glared at Rachel as he passed the prosecutor's table. The judge didn't miss the move.

"Mr. Sanderson, how do you plead?"

"Not guilty, your honor."

"Does the government have a bail recommendation?"

The Assistant U.S. Attorney, Jane Pruett, stood. "May I approach the bench, your honor?"

The judge waved her forward. Jane picked up a file folder and walked to the bench. She opened the folder in front of the judge and spread something. The judge put on her reading glasses and looked at Jane's offering. After a second, the judge picked up one sheet of paper and read it carefully. She set the paper in the folder and searched the courtroom, locking eyes with Rachel, then looking back at the offering in front of her. Jane took the folder back to the prosecution table and set the file on top of her briefcase.

"Based on the brutal nature of the attack on Ranger Randall and the defendant's criminal record, we ask for bail of one million dollars."

The judge looked at the defense table. "And does the defense have a counter proposal?"

The public defender rifled through the two sheets in his file folder to understand why the government was asking for such an immense amount of bail for an assault. Jane reached across the aisle and handed her file to the public defender. He flipped through photos, his eyes going wide, then he read two sheets of paper. He showed the pictures to Toby, and they whispered.

Toby's head twisted around while he tried to see Rachel. He mouthed, "Miscarriage?"

Rachel looked away, then Toby looked at me. I nodded.

"Is there a counter-proposal for bail?"

"Your honor, there's material I've never seen here, and it's beyond the scope of the discussion I've had with my client. I'd like to . . ."

The judge had reached the end of her fuse, and she banged her gavel. "You can discuss those matters with the prosecution during discovery. Bail is one million dollars."

Toby looked like he'd been slapped. "I don't have that kind of money!"

Rather than rapping her gavel and silencing him, the magistrate leaned forward. "Then you'll sit in a cell until your trial date. Bailiff, the next defendant, please."

"Wait! I'm not done!" Toby complained as a marshal pulled his arm, attempting to guide him toward the holding cage in the courtroom.

The judge put down her glasses and glared at him. "I suggest you shut up before you're held in contempt and lose what few privileges you might have in the jail."

"But, she egged me on!"

I looked at Rachel, who was shaking like a leaf. The judge noticed Rachel's reaction, too. "Marshal, remove that man from the courtroom immediately!"

"She faked all those bruises!" Toby yelled as a second marshal grabbed his other arm and lifted him.

The judge glared at the public defender. "Silence your client and get him out of here."

Toby searched for Rachel, but the marshals were hustling him away so he couldn't see her shrinking behind Mandy and me. Jane Pruett reached back and patted Rachel's hand. She whispered, "He's going away for a long time."

Rachel broke into tears.

I touched Mandy's arm and motioned toward the door. She nodded and helped Rachel to her feet. The judge had been moving things along quickly, but she waved her hand at me, signaling that we didn't need to rush. The next shackled defendant moved slowly to the defense table.

Rachel fell into Mandy's hug in the corridor, and I wrapped them both in my arms. I kept an eye on the people moving in the hallway, and everyone gave us a wide berth. Jane Pruett came out the door with her briefcase, looking harried. She slowed and put her hand on Rachel's arm.

"Are you okay, honey?"

Rachel shook her head. "What did you show the judge?"

"The pictures from the hospital and your medical report."

"Isn't that private?"

"My investigator got a subpoena and picked them up. They're evidence of your assault."

"But the defense attorney told Toby I had a miscarriage."

"I'm legally obligated to share all my file information with the defense. I think it'll work to our advantage. I suspect I'll get a call from the public defender this afternoon with a plea offer. He'll try to get me to drop the charges to a misdemeanor. I might accept a reduction to a class D felony, but I'll demand the maximum sentence. Toby won't be out of prison until he's forty, no matter what happens."

Pruett rushed off, leaving us standing in the hallway.

I looked at my watch. "Can I buy coffee?"

Mandy put her arm around Rachel's shoulders and shook her head. We walked to the elevator together. When we reached the ground floor, Rachel had pulled herself together.

"Mandy said Jill picked out a wedding gown this morning."

I'd been so caught up in the arrests and bail hearing that I'd forgotten about the dress. "What's it look like?"

Mandy smiled. "It's white and that's all you'll hear about it until you see it at the wedding."

"She found one off the rack?"

Mandy shook her head. "Jill's a slender little thing. They're going to have to take it in a little bit in a few places."

"Can they get that done before whatever date you and Jill decided on?"

Mandy patted my arm. "I have people, Doug. Jill's going back tomorrow to try it on after the alterations. By the way, the wedding is Monday."

"Monday? That's only four days from now!"

"Jill's parents will be here tomorrow and the minister made time for us Monday afternoon."

Rachel looked at me and shook her head. "Suck it up, Fletcher. You're the luckiest guy in Texas."

I put up my hands in surrender.

"Did you catch any coin thieves this morning?"

"I never made it to the beach. We had an incident in the campground and it kept me busy."

Mandy cocked her head. "What kind of incident did you have that took your whole morning?"

"I caught two guys trying to hide a metal detector. One of them pulled a sawed-off shotgun on me when I confronted them."

Rachel's eyes got wide. "Did anyone get hurt?"

"I disarmed him before he got it all the way out of his pickup."

"I should've been there to back you up."

"It all turned out okay. Nobody got hurt, and the bad guys are in jail."

"Had they been around long?"

"Matt's checking. Their pickup is in the impound lot. I talked to Scott Dixon, and he's getting a search warrant for it. I'm curious if they've got more arsenal packed in the camper. They refused to give me their names, so I suspect they have criminal records. I don't think they thought a park ranger would have access to the criminal databases. They were long-faced when I booked them into the federal lockup. I imagine we'll know who they are in a couple hours. They were being fingerprinted when I left."

Mandy pulled Rachel close. "I think you need a nap."

"I'm okay. I could go back with Doug for an afternoon beach drive."

"It's pretty late. I'll just cruise the campground and call it a day. You and Mandy go home. I'll see you in the morning."

Chapter Twenty

The boys played some variety of tag in the yard. Allen, almost two years older, was always able to outrun and taunt Danny, who gamely tried to catch him. Clarice sat on the steps, staring at her shoes like she'd lost her last friend. I parked in the driveway and walked over.

She didn't even notice me until I sat down next to her.

"You look like your puppy died."

She turned her head, and I could see that she'd been crying. "The flight surgeon cleared Charlie. He called and said he was flying again today."

"I bet he was excited."

She looked about ready to cry again but held it in and watched the boys tearing around the yard. "At least one of us is."

My Minnesota lifetime training to maintain large personal boundaries made me hesitate, but I slid closer and put my arm over her shoulders. She pressed her head against me and sobbed. I pulled her tight, not knowing what to say, and finally deciding, there was nothing I could say that would comfort her. She just needed a shoulder to cry on for a bit.

It took a few minutes for her to cry herself out, then she eased herself away from me, pulled a tissue from her pocket, and wiped her nose.

"Thanks," she said, gazing out at the boys.

"What happens now?"

"When Charlie graduates, we'll move somewhere close to a Navy base where he'll be assigned to a carrier."

"That could be exciting."

Clarice glanced at me. "I'm not big on being a single mom six months a year. The boys are a handful, and Charlie thinks we should try to have a girl, too."

"I think Ronnie and Jill were looking at wedding dresses today. I'm sure they'd like to show you what they looked at and tried on."

"That's okay. I don't want to be around anyone that happy right now. I'd just be a Debbie Downer."

When I walked into the townhouse, Jill and Mom were huddled at the kitchen table. I put my holster on the closet shelf and caught them closing a catalog of wedding dresses.

"Do I get a preview?"

Jill was ready to open the catalog, but Mother snatched it out of her hand. "Not until the wedding."

Jill smiled but didn't try to take the catalog back from Mom. She made a quick segue. "Mandy said she was going to the arraignment with Rachel. I wonder how that went?"

"I was in CC for something else and dropped in. The U.S attorney suggested a million-dollar bail for Toby, and the magistrate agreed. He stays in jail until the trial. The prosecutor told us she expects a plea bargain proposal that would avoid a trial, but still keep Toby in prison for maybe fifteen years."

"Isn't that steep for a first offense?" Mother asked.

"It's not his first offense and the severity of the beating factors into the amount of prison time he has to serve. The judge saw the pictures of Rachel taken in the E.R., and she read the medical report that says Rachel had a miscarriage because of the beating. I think the judge would've been willing to convict him at the hearing solely based on those items if it'd been within her discretion."

Jill digested that information. "Is Rachel going to be okay? I mean mentally and physically."

"I think she's messed up in both departments, and it's going to take some time for her to compartmentalize them and move on. She had some real trauma. I imagine she might be dealing with some PTSD."

After a pause, Jill went on. "The house closing is tomorrow. The realtor says the papers are ready, and we can go to the closing company and sign at one o'clock. Will that work? Otherwise, she said you could pre-sign in the morning, and I'll just show up with the check and sign at one."

I felt stupid about forgetting the closing. "Do you have the check?"

"I'll go to the bank in the morning."

"I'll get half out of my savings. We're going to own it together, right?"

Jill shook her head. "I offered to pay for all of it out of my savings account when I suggested buying the house."

"I want it to be *our* house. I'll hit the bank in the morning. End of discussion."

Jill reached out and squeezed my hand. "There are going to be a few more wedding expenses than I expected. You said you'd pay for the dress, but we've got to pay the minister, and Mandy reserved the VFW hall for a reception. We'll have to pay for the hall and the food."

Ronnie stood. "I'm paying for the reception. I put aside some money for a rainy day, and I'd like to give it to you now rather than waiting for Doug to inherit it sometime when I'm dead. This way, I actually get to enjoy it."

Jill was surprised but smiled and nodded. "Thank you. Doug, you did remember to rebook Ronnie's flight, so she's not flying out tomorrow."

I got up and pulled out my cellphone. "I didn't know when the wedding was going to be, then things got crazy. When's a good time for your return, Mom?"

"I don't want to hang around and be in the way after the wedding. How about flying me home Tuesday?"

I called the airline and paid the rebooking fee and an additional cost for getting one of the last seats. "It all worked out for the best," I said, walking back into the kitchen. "You're rebooked, and all they had left were first-class seats. You'll be flying in style."

"Oh, dear. That must've cost you as much as the wedding."

I waved off Mom's concerns about the extra money. "What are we doing for supper?"

Jill gave me a sly smile. "I thought we'd let Ronnie experience Peg Leg Pete's."

Ronnie looked apprehensive. "That sounds like a sleazy bar."

Jill smiled. "It is! That's part of the ambiance. It's got fishing nets hanging from the ceiling, and there's a kind of pirate feel, but they serve the best shrimp on the island."

"Oh, I don't know if I'm up for any more shrimp. Is there someplace we can get barbecue?"

"Rudy's!" Jill and I said in unison.

Then I thought of Clarice. "Let's see if Clarice and the boys will join us."

Jill's look turned somber. "She told me Charlie's flying again. Clarice isn't pleased with the news."

"I just talked to her before I walked into the house. She's not happy, but there's nothing we can do about it except be supportive."

Jill slipped on sandals. "I'll ask if they'd like to come along to Rudy's."

I cornered Mom before she could go upstairs. "Is the wedding dress going to cost a month's salary?"

Mom stared at me for a second. "Does it matter? This is the only wedding gown she's ever going to buy."

"I just thought . . ."

"You just thought you were going to be a cheapskate. This is your last marriage, Doug. This is the love you've both been waiting for all your lives. A couple thousand dollars is irrelevant." Mom went upstairs before I could come up with a reply.

A couple thousand dollars! Holy shit! I thought to myself.

Jill came back inside, looking less than perky. "Charlie just came home. We're all meeting at Rudy's." She looked into the kitchen for Ronnie. "Where's Mom?"

"You're calling Ronnie 'Mom?'"

Jill smiled. "She asked me if I would. I think that means I'm part of the family."

I shook my head. "I'll take you back to Minnesota for a reunion sometime. You might not be as excited about being *part of the family* after you meet some of them."

"I met El and Todd in Flagstaff. They were nice."

"They're two of the sane ones. I have two dozen crazy first cousins."

"Two dozen?"

"Yes, two dozen, and most of them are nuts."

There was a gentle knock on the door. Clarice had put on a little makeup and a summery dress. "We've got the boys in the car, and we'll meet you at Rudy's."

Jill leaned around me. "We'll load up as soon as Mom gets changed."

Clarice looked into my eyes. "Mom?"

"Jill's been adopted."

Clarice smiled and patted my arm. "Jill's a prize, and you're the winner."

Jill was right behind me when I closed the door. She grinned. "How many times have you been told that you're a winner?"

I hugged her as I heard Mom's footsteps on the stairs. "I've been a winner since I met you."

"Will you two quit acting like lovebirds. I heard Clarice say they were leaving for Rudy's."

"You were upstairs," I said.

"Your walls are paper-thin. You keep forgetting that, Mr. Winner."

Chapter Twenty-One

Rudy's was busy and loud. Clarice and Charlie were already in the dining room when we got in line. Jill explained the menu and side dishes to Mom while I collected our soda pop, potato salad, and coleslaw from the coolers along the wall. When we got to the counter, I recognized the same guy who'd waited on us when Jill and I had stopped once before. He had been amused with our lack of knowledge for Rudy's menu and their unusual dining arrangement that involved ordering meat, then carrying it to the tables covered with butcher paper.

Jill was pointing to the menu when the clerk's eyes met mine. He broke into a big grin and leaned his elbows on the counter. "You must've liked the food. I see you came back with your older sister."

Mom smiled but shook her head. "My future daughter-in-law suggested this as the best place in Corpus Christi for barbeque."

"Ma'am, this is the best place in the world for barbeque. What would you like?"

Jill gave the man a dazzling smile. "We'd like half-pounds of both dry and wet."

The man rang up our choice and put a ticket on the window behind him. He helped me set the sodas and side dishes on the counter and rang them up, occasionally glancing at me and shaking his head. He told me the total and I handed him my VISA card.

"The lady paid last time."

I nodded. "You have quite a memory."

He leaned closer. "That's one classy lady, and I don't see a lot of women who carry themselves with confidence like she does. She said you were on a blind date last time. Since you're here with your Momma, you must've grabbed the brass ring."

"I guess I did."

Jill picked up the platters of sliced brisket, and Mom grabbed the side dishes. I found a bottle opener screwed into a support beam and brought our open soda bottles to a table next to Clarice, Charlie, and the boys.

Jill was explaining the sauces to Ronnie when Charlie leaned close. "Did you hear I got cleared for flight duty?" He beamed.

"Clarice told me."

"I talked to the major, and I'll be able to graduate with my class."

"Great!"

"I told him about your problem catching the boats that are bringing in treasure-hunters. We've got flights going out over the ocean about eight times a day, and we contact the Coast Guard every time we fly, so they've got the helo in the area. The Major says he'll talk to the flight leaders and have them scan the island for beached boats. We don't have a frequency to reach you directly, but we can relay information through the Coast Guard."

"That'd be great! Thanks."

Allen placed a greasy hand, dripping with sauce, on Charlie's arm to get his attention. I turned back to Jill and Mom, who were already eating. Mom had just taken a bite from a sandwich she'd made from the family-style loaf of bread filled with a few slices of brisket. She was oblivious to the sauce dripping out the opposite end of the bread because the look on her face told me she thought she'd died and gone to heaven.

"Doug, you have to move back to Minnesota and open a chain of Rudy's restaurants. You'd be a millionaire."

Clarice and Charlie were both damp by the time they got the boys and themselves washed up after supper. The boys thought the long wash trough was a great splash game, and I was glad we'd hung back when they cleaned up.

Clarice came up behind Jill and hugged her. "Thanks for inviting us. We needed the break."

Jill patted her arm. "I know."

Charlie shook my hand. "We'll see if the Navy/Coast Guard link works tomorrow."

* * *

Mom chatted the whole way home. She was taken with Rudy's, the rowdy boys, and life in

211

general. I parked the Isuzu in the driveway. We'd barely got the lights on when Jill's phone chimed. She checked the caller I.D., and her eyes lit up.

"Hi, Mom." She listened, with many 'uh-huhs,' and then said, "Tomorrow?"

She disconnected the call as Ronnie and I waited for her to tell us what was happening tomorrow.

Jill took a deep breath as she pocketed the phone. "Mom says they're making better time than they thought. They stopped when it got dark in San Marcos. They get up when the roosters crow, so they'll be on the road early and should arrive here before lunch."

Ronnie broke into a big grin. "They'll be here a couple days before the wedding. Your mother can come along when we go for the dress fitting."

I could see the apprehension in Jill's eyes.

I tried to be reassuring. "It'll be okay. We all have to meet at some point."

"I guess, but tomorrow is so soon."

Mom read the situation. "I think I'll get ready for bed." She took a few steps up the stairs then leaned over the railing. "Remember, the walls are paper-thin. If you're going to talk about me, whisper."

Jill looked into my eyes. "Will you be okay with this?"

"What?"

"With another man under the roof."

"It might be a relief from all the estrogen of the past week."

"I heard that," Ronnie yelled from upstairs.

I pulled Jill close and whispered, "It'll be fine. You've been telling everyone I'm housebroken and trainable."

"I know, but Daddy's a rancher, and he's used to running a string of cattle and a rotating bunch of hired cowboys. He can be 'salty,' and he doesn't filter his thoughts much."

"I've heard people swear, and I'm accustomed to standing up for myself. We'll do fine."

"Crap! I have to call Mandy to find out where we can find a room for them. Most of the motels and condos on this side of the bay are still shuttered or under repair."

Jill pulled out her phone, and I went upstairs and turned on the bedroom television. I heard the shower running in the guest bathroom and took the opportunity to call Scott Dixon without Mom listening through the paper-thin walls.

"Hey, Scott. Did your guys find anything when they searched the truck?"

"Well, let me put it this way, those two characters you arrested were a traveling crime wave. Let me start with their history. When their fingerprints were run through IAFIS, we got a call from the federal lockup because we'd picked up their prints at a couple of local home burglaries. Then, the identities went into the NCIC, and those guys have been in and out of prison nearly all their adult lives. One of them is from Iowa, and the other is from Nebraska. Their names won't mean anything to you, but there are

213

pages of petty crimes, then felonies all across the Midwest. The last time they were arrested was during a home burglary in Enid, Oklahoma, and they took a shot at the local cop. They'd be dead if they didn't give up before the Oklahoma State Police made it to the scene. You were fortunate because they don't have much respect for small-town cops, and I imagine a park ranger is pretty far down their list of fearsome cops."

"That's quite a history. What'd you find in the pickup?"

"An arsenal and a bucket of Spanish coins. From what we've been able to determine, most of the guns were stolen in home burglaries. The serial numbers have been ground off, and our expert is trying to coax the serial numbers out of the deeper metal. He's having some success, but we're never going to be able to tie all the guns we found to specific robberies. The shotgun you took from the guy was from southern Missouri. I talked to the gun's owner, who was nearly in tears because it was an old Browning worth over ten-grand. I hated telling him they'd cut off the barrel and stock."

"I assume the coins were taken from the national seashore."

"We have no way to know, and they're not talking."

"How many coins were recovered?"

"They had a 5-gallon pail half-full. At least a hundred, although we can't tell exactly how many because some of the coins are fused in lumps."

"I wonder if they're the ones stolen from Matt's file cabinet?"

"If you've got pictures, we can compare them. Otherwise, they may have been prospecting the area beaches for a while and just found these on their own."

"That's probably it. We had that car buzzing past the entrance surveillance camera right before and after the cleaning people entered. I think these two are more pickup-camper types."

"I've got some bad news. Because you turned them in to the lockup at the Federal Courthouse, the fingerprint identification went to the FBI, and the interstate aspect of the crimes has their interest."

"Shit," I said as Jill walked into the room.

"I can hold them at arm's length for a while because we have the pickup, guns, and coins, but they know you brought the two guys in from the Park Service campground, and the FBI can smell a news conference."

"Thanks, Scott. Keep me posted."

I flipped the phone on the bed and peeled off my clothes, putting them in the hamper.

Jill walked out of the bathroom as I ended the call. "The FBI must be involved. That's the only time I see you this angry."

"The guys I arrested at the campground . . ."

"Whoa, cowboy. What guys did you arrest at the campground?"

I waved Jill back into the bathroom, which was three walls away from Mom and told her the whole story, starting with spotting the metal

215

detector to the guy reaching for the shotgun. And then I shared Scott's information about the two guys I'd delivered to the Federal Courthouse.

"You disarmed a guy with a shotgun?"

"I anticipated his plans, and he never got it out from under the seat."

"But still."

"I'm just relieved that Rachel didn't try to confront those guys. It could've gone south really fast, and I doubt she'd have had the confidence to face them down alone."

"That's why she's your partner. She's learning from you."

My mind wandered, and I had a terrible thought. "I wonder how long those guys have been checked into the campground?"

"What?"

"The two guys with the long records. I wonder if they were in the campground when the woman was murdered?"

"You've been after the people in the black Zodiac."

"I may have been barking up the wrong tree."

I grabbed the phone off the bed and hit redial. "Hey, Scott. It's Doug again. "Talk to your crime scene guys and see if there's anything in the pickup that'd tie those guys to the woman we found murdered on the beach."

"Sure, Doug. But if they killed her, how'd she get on the island in a wetsuit?"

"Let's cross that bridge later. For now, have them look at the forensics and see if there's a link."

Jill was already in bed when I got off the call to Scott Dixon. I climbed under the sheet and spooned with her. "You're not going to sleep tonight after your talk with your mother, are you."

"Probably not."

"It'll be okay. Really, it will. I'll be on my best behavior, and everyone will get along."

"I think Ronnie and my mom will get along just fine. My dad's a wild card, and like I said a long time ago, I'm not sure how he's going to react to me sharing a bed with you before we're married."

"He knew about your South Dakota fiancé and must've suspected you two were being intimate."

Jill rolled over. "Dad ran him off the ranch with a shotgun when he found my birth control pills."

"Oh."

"Exactly."

"Do you think he's got a shotgun in the pickup?"

"I doubt it, but I know he's got a South Dakota concealed carry permit, and he carries a pistol on his belt when he goes into town."

"It'll be okay. A lot has changed since you were a kid having a fling with a cowboy. I've got to believe he understands that you're a strong woman, and he'll respect your decisions."

"Doug, I'm still his little girl, and I'll always be his little girl. He'll be excited about the wedding, but he's going to size you up to make sure you're worthy of his trust and respect."

I kissed her gently and closed my eyes.

She rolled over and our noses were touching. "You know I can't sleep, and you're going to just nod off?"

"What did you expect me to do?"

"Turn on a movie, or we can go downstairs and play cards."

I slid my hand down her back, and she grabbed it before I got to her buttocks. "Not now that I know the walls are paper-thin."

I pulled my hand back. "Do you know how to play cribbage?"

Jill pushed herself up and rolled out of bed. "That's what we played over lunch every day when I worked at Mammoth Cave."

"I didn't know you'd worked at Mammoth Cave."

"I guess it never came up. I might be full of secrets that might come out while playing cribbage until the wee hours of the morning."

Chapter Twenty-Two

I beat Matt and all the rangers into the park visitor center on Friday morning and called the Corpus Christi Coast Guard station. I got transferred to the officer of the day, Lieutenant Rivard. After introducing myself, I asked him to speculate on how someone might've come ashore in a short wetsuit, been murdered, and not have any of her boating or diving party report her missing.

"Is that the woman found on Padre Island. I read about that in the newspaper."

"Yes, we recovered her body, but we haven't found a clue that would lead us to her murderers, except a black Zodiac boat that keeps showing up every day or two."

"Our helo pilots have reported seeing that vessel, but we've been busy with more pressing things most of the time."

"So, let's say the Zodiac has nothing to do with this. How would a woman dressed like that show up on our dunes without transport?"

"I suppose she might've fallen overboard in the Gulf and washed ashore."

"Her body was much higher in the dunes than the high surf line. I assume you'd get a man-overboard call if a boat had lost a passenger or crew member."

"We would unless she was with some drug smugglers. They sometimes run up the coast from Mexico and dump loads on South Padre, but they rarely go as far north as you guys."

"Here's another tidbit, we found a Spanish coin tucked inside her wet suit."

"Hmm. You don't suppose she was snorkeling offshore looking for the Spanish shipwrecks?"

"We didn't find any snorkeling gear. No mask or fins were with the body, and a forensics team searched the area."

"Hang on." Rivard left me listening to canned Barry Manilow songs that were close to putting me asleep after my long night of cribbage. It struck me that the Coast Guard must've hand a different low bidder for their 'on hold' music than the FBI. "When did you find the dead woman?"

I counted back the days. "Saturday. We spotted a bunch of coyotes acting like they'd found an easy meal, so we checked to see if a dead porpoise, or something, had washed ashore. We found her in the dunes."

"So, you think she'd been dead for a while."

"The medical examiner thought she'd probably been dead for three days when we found her, so she probably died Wednesday or Thursday last week."

"We found an unmanned sea kayak a couple miles out in the Gulf off Port Mansfield Channel on Friday. We put out a general alert to the boat captains and dispatched our own boats and the helo, but we never found a body. We speculated that it had washed off a passing boat or floated off a beach with the tide, and no one reported it lost."

"Did you recover the kayak?"

"A weekend fisherman did. He towed it back to the marina under the Kennedy bridge."

"Is it still in your possession?"

"I think I saw it in a corner of the hangar. Do you want it?"

"I'll call the CCPD and ask their forensics people to inspect it. Maybe there's some touch DNA somewhere on the floor or sides."

Rivard chuckled. "That would be the deck or gunwales. You must be a flatlander."

"Minnesota."

"Go Vikings! The kayak will be ready whenever you get someone over here to collect it."

I called Scott Dixon's number and left a message about the kayak. Then I went to Matt's office. I knocked on the door, and he looked up. "Rachel's coming, but you'll have to drive. She's still pretty sore, but she doesn't want to sit around either."

"That's great, but I've got another agenda item. The guys I arrested yesterday were a two-man crime wave. They had an arsenal of stolen guns and a bucket of Spanish coins."

Matt whistled. "Wow. We were lucky you arrested them without anyone getting hurt. So, you think they're the ones who stole the coins from my office."

"Probably not, but if you email the pictures you took to Scott Dixon, he'll compare them to the coins they recovered from the pickup." I wrote Scott's cellphone number on a notepad and pushed it to Matt.

"I've got another wild hare to chase, Matt. I want to know when those two came to the campground and if they stayed here the whole time. If they were here a week ago, they could be suspects in the murder of the woman in the dunes."

"I thought you were after the people in the black boat."

"Let's keep our minds open. The black boat is a possibility, but the Coast Guard spotted an unmanned sea kayak adrift a couple miles off the Port Mansfield Channel. They haven't been able to locate the kayaker, nor have they had any reports of one being lost."

Matt leaned back and considered my comments. "That would explain how she got here. But why wouldn't someone report her missing?"

I picked up Matt's phone and dialed Scott Dixon. He didn't answer, so I left a voicemail. "Hey, Scott. Here's another question. What did KPD find out about the missing teacher?"

Rachel walked in and sat in the other guest chair. "Who are you calling?"

I explained the theory that the two criminals from the campground might've killed a kayaker.

Rachel nodded. "That kinda makes more sense than people on a boat killing her and leaving her body behind."

Rachel's bruises had turned from black to dark blue with greens and yellows spreading below them. If anything, she looked worse than the day after her beating.

"I need someone to review the campground logs and the entry hut video to find out when the two criminals arrived at the campground. Could you do that today?"

Rachel got up, shaking her head. "You don't need to give me made-up work. I'm ready to drive the beach. Have the campground manager do that. He's got all the records and knows how to access them quickly. I'd just be sitting there watching him pull the information off his computer. I'll grab us a couple coffees for the drive, Doug."

I looked at Matt, who shrugged. "She has spoken. Have a nice drive."

We were a mile down the beach before Rachel said anything. "Jill called Mandy late. I guess you're going to meet the future in-laws tonight."

"Jill's pretty uptight."

"Why? You're a nice enough guy. A little old for my tastes, but friendly and conversant."

"She's uptight about her dad seeing her clothes hanging in my closet and only one bed in the bedroom."

"Oh, gawd. That is so old fashioned. He should be glad she's not knocked up and marrying a drunk who's been sleeping around."

"Her dad ran off her ex-fiancé with a shotgun when he found her birth control pills."

"When was that, 1890?"

"Birth control pills weren't invented until the 1960s."

"You know what I mean. It's ancient history. I'm sure they have a television in South Dakota. They know what life's like today. Besides, Jill's bright and mature. He's got to respect that."

"That's what I told her, but she said, in daddy's eyes, she's still his little girl."

Rachel got very quiet and sipped her coffee.

"What's the matter?"

"If my dad was around, he'd kill Toby." She sighed.

"You said Jill's dad should be happy she's not marrying a drunk who's sleeping around. That sounded like it came from close to home."

"I can't believe I was so stupid. Mandy and I have had a lot of time to talk, and she says I was 'love stupid.'"

"I've heard that love is blind. I think it's more than visually blind, but it's trusting, naïve, and stupid, all at once. I had told Jill I loved her for a month before she admitted that she'd heard that too many times from guys who only wanted to get into her pants. Her issue wasn't the word, love, but the reality of having someone she could trust."

"I trusted Toby."

"It took Jill a long time to get to that point, and I had to earn her trust."

"Naïve is a cool word. I like it better than Mandy's 'love stupid.' I'd like to believe I wasn't worldly enough to understand what was happening."

"Are you there now?"

Rachel adjusted the Velcro straps on her vest, pretending they weren't quite right.

"Who was the baby's father?"

Rachel looked at me. "There's just no foreplay with you, is there? You just throw the bombshell out there."

"Mandy asked, didn't she?"

"Yeah, but she's like my big sister. You're like . . . I don't know. You're more like my dad."

I could see she wasn't ready to share that with me. "Where is your dad?"

"I don't know. Mom filed for divorce when I left for college. He moved out, and we haven't stayed in touch. Mom made it clear that contacting him would be betraying her, so I haven't even done an internet search to try to find him."

"You're an adult now. I think you could look him up without betraying your mother. Besides, those divorce scars heal."

"Really? Are you inviting your ex to the wedding?"

"I said they heal. I don't intend to rip them open again."

Rachel nodded. "Touché."

225

"Let's stop at the tent ahead. I waved at the guys yesterday, but we should check in with them like good Park Service ambassadors."

Rachel pulled at her Velcro again like a batter adjusting his batting glove between pitches.

The red nylon tent was faded to an ugly pink. An ancient Subaru pickup was parked next to it and a charred pile of driftwood from the previous night's campfire. We walked up to the empty campsite and looked around. The tent fly flapped open, revealing clothes and rumpled blankets inside along with some food wrappers.

Rachel shielded her eyes and looked inside the truck cab. "They must be hiking."

Footprints were all around the tent and trekked a path into the dunes. I nodded toward the trail. "Let's see where this goes."

We walked for a couple minutes then saw sand flying into the air. I put my hand up to slow Rachel, and we crept up on two young men digging into the side of a dune like two dogs digging up a bone.

"What'd you find?" I asked as Rachel stayed back a pace and stepped to the side, so she could see the men or take a shot without hitting me.

The closest man twisted around so fast he flipped onto his butt. He slammed his hand on his chest like he experienced a heart attack. Dark-haired and skinny, he wore only cut-off jeans. Another man, blonde and slightly heavier, reacted less violently, but also jumped when I spoke. Neither had seen their twentieth birthday.

The dark-haired guy stood up and brushed the sand off his arms and shorts. "Man, you scared the shit outta me."

The blond just rose slowly. Neither displayed a weapon or any animosity.

"What are you digging up?" I repeated.

"We found this black thing sticking out of the dune when we were hiking. I tried to pull it out, but it's stuck." He pointed to a black crescent hidden behind him.

Rachel approached the men slowly and looked at their dig. "I think it's a Spanish silver coin."

The blonde looked surprised. "No way!"

Rachel nodded. "Three Spanish treasure ships sunk off the island, and some of the coins washed ashore with the hurricanes over the years."

The dark-haired kid studied Rachel's bruise. "Looks like someone hit you with a baseball bat."

Rachel grimaced but turned it into a smile. "Fell down the stairs in the dark."

"That must've hurt like hell."

Rachel knelt down and examined the cluster of coins the men had started to unearth. "Not my greatest moment." She brushed aside some of the sand. "This is one of the largest coin clusters I've ever seen."

"Cool!"

I stepped to the side to see it better and could tell it was at least the size of a basketball. "I hate to be your joy-killer, but this is an archaeological preservation area. Any coins or artifacts that are discovered have to be turned over to the Park Service."

The guys went from elated to deflated.

"If you can get that loose, I'd appreciate it if you could carry it over to our pickup. My partner, Rachel, will take your names and when the coins go on display, we'll put your names next to them."

The guys freed the cluster after another minute of digging with their hands. Bigger than a basketball, the two of them struggled to carry the coin-cluster through the loose sand. I lowered the tailgate and pulled out a tarp for them to set it on. Rachel chatted with them, getting their information, while I called Matt to report the find.

"A call just came in for you, Doug. The Coast guard got a call from the Navy flight controller. They said there's a black Zodiac coming north about a hundred yards offshore." I shielded my eyes and looked out into the Gulf but saw nothing.

"Did they say how far down the island they were?"

"They can't see our mile markers, but they said they were still south of your pickup."

"Thanks. We'll secure this clump of coins, and then I'll head toward the county boat launch. That's where they launched the Zodiac the other day."

Rachel was a great PR person for the Park Service. She explained the history of the shipwrecks and the two guys were smiling, apparently happy about finding the clump of coins and turning them over to us. I hated to drag her away, but I started the pickup and waved to get her away from the campers.

Chapter Twenty-Three

Rachel buckled her seatbelt as I turned the pickup around. "Why aren't we driving the rest of the beach?"

"The Coast Guard reported that the black Zodiac is just offshore, motoring toward the county boat launch. I'm going to try and cut them off before they get it on a trailer and drive away."

Rachel turned her head and searched the Gulf. "I don't see a Zodiac or the Coast Guard helicopter."

"The information got relayed from Navy flight operations."

"Whoa. What?"

"I talked to one of the flight cadets and explained our problem tracking the boats that are coming off the Gulf to look for Spanish artifacts. He talked to his commander. They're on different radio frequencies than we have, but they communicate with the Coast Guard, so they asked their training flights to watch for boats on Padre Island, and they relay that to us through the Coast Guard."

"Man, that's convoluted. So, some Navy cadet spotted the Zodiac we've been chasing, and it's going toward the channel between Padre and Mustang Islands?"

Rachel picked up the mic and switched frequencies. She asked CCPD to give us backup at the county boat launch. Then she contacted the county and made the same request. CCPD didn't have a car in the area, but the sheriff's department had a car near Port Aransas and directed their deputy to the county park.

I raced down the sand, bouncing over the ridges and steering around the soft spots. I could see Rachel grimace each time I hit a large bump.

"You're in pain. Do I need to slow down?"

Rachel wrapped her arms around herself and shook her head. "We need to get those bastards. Go!"

I slowed through the visitor center parking lot, then turned on my flashing light bar and raced past the entrance hut. We were near the Packery channel, the waterway that separates Mustang and North Padre Islands, when the county announced that their car was at Mustang Island County Park.

"Tell them we're less than five minutes out, and we'll meet them at the first condo building north of the park."

Rachel made the request but looked at me with a question in her eyes.

"If we're sitting at the boat launch, they'll see us, and they may turn away. Ideally, I'd like

231

to catch them just as they're pulling the Zodiac onto the trailer."

I killed the flashers when we pulled onto Highway 361, the main route down Mustang Island. I saw the turn for the county park and saw more than half a dozen trucks with trailers parked at the boat launch. We drove past the entrance without slowing and met the county cruiser behind a condo that was still undergoing rehab but within sight of the park.

I pulled next to the driver's side of the county car and rolled down my window. I recognized the young deputy I'd met the day we brought in the big silver haul.

"You're Deputy Meland, right?"

"Ron is fine. You're Fletcher, right?" He looked past me at Rachel, who waved rather than introducing herself.

Meland looked at the boat launch. "What's up?"

"The Coast Guard reported that a black Zodiac boat was coming this way. We've seen them beached down the island, but they always push off before we can get to them. Yesterday they put the Zodiac on a trailer at the park and left before we could get there. I'd like to catch them just as they're getting ready to pull it out of the water so we can get the number off the boat and the license number of the truck. Then I'd like to talk to the operators and see what they're doing. Best case, I hope we can tie them to the woman who was killed and left on the dunes. Worst case, they're just gathering seashells."

Rachel had binoculars out, watching the park. "I can't see any boats. They're too low in the water. But I see a guy climbing onto the launch pier and pulling a trailer around. He's backing it down the ramp. I see several heads now, and they're winching the boat onto a trailer. It's the Zodiac! Go!"

Ron peeled out of the parking lot, and I made a three-point turn to follow him. Meland drove into the parking lot with lights and siren screaming. Rachel and I were a minute behind. I stole a glance at Rachel—she was focused and tight, like a good cop would be going into an unknown situation. I saw no fear or apprehension, just a hint of an adrenaline rush, and I felt a little pride. She'd turned a corner.

Meland locked up his brakes and slid to a stop on the sandy boat ramp, blocking the black extended cab pickup. He was out of the cruiser with his gun drawn when I pulled alongside him and jammed the transmission into park.

Rachel and I were alongside him. Rachel held a gun on the driver whose hands were in the air. I took the left side of the boat and trailer while Meland yelled commands from the right. There were five people around the boat, four men and two women. All looked confused and were compliant with Meland's demand to lean forward with their hands on the side of the boat. They were wearing either short wetsuits or swimsuits with rash guards protecting their upper bodies. One of the men had a dive knife strapped to his calf. Otherwise, there was no obvious place for any of the others to hide a weapon.

I held my Sig low and yelled, "Rachel, get the driver out and check him for weapons."

"What's going on?" The guy with the dive knife asked.

I walked behind him and took off his drive knife. "You've been evading us and acting guilty for a week. We decided it was time to find out why."

The man with the knife was obviously the leader. He had sun-bleached hair and wore a skin-tight rash guard shirt with a curling wave logo and surfer swim trunks that hung to his knees. He was about six-two and muscular. "Do you have any other weapons?"

"Do you have a warrant?"

"I don't need a warrant. I'm detaining because you're impeding a federal investigation. You have an open boat that I can inspect, and I can look in the pickup. Do you have any other weapons?"

"Where would I put a weapon?"

"I asked if you have another weapon. If you're lying to me, I can arrest you."

"No one has a weapon. I carry the dive knife in case we get tangled in a net or something."

Meland frisked the men on his side of the boat, then switched places with Rachel, who checked the one woman. "No weapons here."

I ran my hand over the blond guy, then checked a dark-haired guy in a wetsuit. "No weapons here, either."

"Okay, Blondie, you go stand by my tailgate." I put my hand on the dark-haired guy's back. "You stand next to the front fender of the pickup."

Rachel and Meland split up the others so they couldn't talk to each other, then Meland jumped into the boat. He moved some gear that looked like tackle boxes, then lifted a tarp and smiled.

"I've got a pail of black coins." He checked the other nooks and storage spaces of the boat, then jumped down, pulling the pail behind him. He showed the bucket to Rachel. "There are two metal detectors tucked under one of the tubes."

I walked up to the blond guy. "Do you have any I.D.?"

"My gear's in the truck. I've got a driver's license in my wallet."

"Are you the leader?"

"Leader of what? It's my boat, and I'm out with a bunch of friends for an ocean ride."

I nodded. "The silver coins were floating on the surface, and you plucked them out of the water on your ocean ride?"

"We walked the shore for a while and saw some black coins in the sand. So what?"

"Padre Island is an archaeological protection zone. Any coins recovered there have to be turned over to the Park Service. It's illegal to possess a metal detector on the national seashore."

"That's news to me."

"If it's news to you, why do you push off and run away every time you see the Park Service pickup coming down the shore?"

"I have no idea what you're talking about. Today's the first time we've been out in a month."

"Turn around."

"What?"

"Turn around and put your hands behind your back. I'm going to handcuff you and put you into the pickup while I talk with your friends."

"This is bullshit! You have no right to cuff me or . . ."

"Shut up and put your hands behind your back. I've caught you with illegal metal detectors and coins removed from a protected area."

He turned and put his hands behind his back. "What's the penalty? The same as littering in the park?"

"It's a federal crime with up to six months in jail and a ten thousand dollar fine. Step into the pickup and watch your head."

The rest of the group was watching and listening intently.

"Rachel, escort the young lady over to the picnic table and see what she has to say."

Meland stood by the other two men from the boat and the pickup driver, frowning and looking like the meanest sonofabitch in the valley. I knew that was the secret to keeping people under control. If you look like you could rip their arms off, people didn't challenge you.

I took the other man to the fender of the boat trailer. "Tell me what's going on."

He looked at the blond guy, and his hands trembled. "I contacted Rick's website and agreed to go on one of his Padre Island treasure-hunts. He's got pictures of silver coins and gold chains that he claims were recovered from the sand. We each pay a hundred bucks for a half-day trip, and he guarantees that we'll each find at least one silver coin."

"How many did you find?"

"I've got four in the bucket."

"Did you know it was illegal to search for coins on the national seashore?"

"I had no idea we were on anything but an uninhabited island. He warned us that the owners didn't like beachcombers, and if we saw a pickup coming, we should jump in the boat so we could get offshore before we got in a confrontation."

"Thank you for being honest with me. Do you have any I.D.?"

"I've got a wallet in a dry bag stashed in the pickup bed."

"Please stay right here."

I walked over to Rachel and the woman, who was now crying. "What's her story?" I asked.

"She paid for a half-day treasure-hunting trip. She's never done it before, and she was told they were beachcombing on an uninhabited island."

I sat next to the woman who looked at me with teary eyes. She appeared to be close to forty, with quite a few gray strands in her hair. "What do you do for a living?"

"I'm a teacher. I'm supposed to be in training today. If you arrest me and the school finds out, I'll be fired." I glanced at Rachel, who nodded.

"Who's the pickup driver?"

"He's Ed, the helper guy. He made sure our gear was stowed, and he jumped out and pulled the boat ashore. Rick ran the motor and did all the talking."

"Did you ever see any weapons?"

The woman shook her head.

"Did Rick or Ed ever show any anger or threaten you?"

The woman looked shocked. "No. They've been nothing but pleasant and gentlemanly."

I separated the last two passengers and got substantially the same story. One of the men had been on two other trips with Rick. We'd interrupted one of his trips with our beach drive, but Rick had pulled offshore until we'd gone by, and they went back to their treasure hunt.

"Did you find coins on all your trips?"

"The second time I was using the metal detector and found a clump of maybe a dozen coins."

"They're Park Service property. Do you still have them?"

"I've been showing them to my friends. A couple of them have gone out with Rick because they were so excited about my find."

"Did they find coins too?"

"Everyone finds coins. Rick guarantees it."

I walked to Deputy Meland. "This is one big mess. They all admit picking coins off the island, and say they paid the blond guy, Rick, for a half-day treasure-hunting trip. One guy says he's done this before, and he has a clump of coins he's been showing his buddies. Rick guarantees they'll find coins."

Meland nodded. "You've opened a can of worms. Who's going to track down all Rick's customers and recover all those coins?"

I glanced at Rachel. "I'm not sure, but I think Rachel might be making a lot of threatening phone calls over the next weeks. I'm going to arrest Rick and hope that will motivate him to give us his client list."

"How does he fit with your dead woman?"

I ran my hand over my face. "I don't know. Everyone says he's a pussycat and treats them well. He's surly with me, but I just don't see him strangling a woman out of a boatload of treasure-hunters and not having one of the others report it. I suppose we'll have to call all the female clients on his customer list to make sure they're all still alive."

Meland smiled. "Rachel's making those calls?"

"I'll retire before spending the next month calling people and threatening to arrest them if they don't return the coins they found."

Meland smiled. "Being a cop isn't all that glamorous. This is the most exciting thing I've done in over a month." He paused and looked at

Rachel, who was comforting the schoolteacher. "I've got a lot of downtime when I've got radar out checking for speeders or doing surveillance. If you gave me part of the list, I could make some calls."

A wave of revelation swept me. "How long have you and Rachel been dating?"

Meland stared at me for a second before answering. "I guess it's been a couple months now."

"She had a miscarriage after her roommate beat her up."

I could see surprise turn to anger. He looked at Rachel and the teacher, and he softened. "She hadn't told me she was pregnant."

I put my hand on his arm, and he looked at me. "We never had this conversation."

Meland nodded.

"And don't do anything stupid about Toby. I talked to the federal prosecutor, and Toby's going to be in a federal prison for many years."

Meland nodded. "Yeah, I'm not going to risk my job and pension over some shithead. Rachel's going to recover, and it'll be okay."

"I think she needs to move out of her rental place. It's kind of a pit, and I'm sure she doesn't want to go back to the site of her attack. Do you know of any place she can stay for a while?"

"I don't know if she's ready for anything steady yet, but I've got an empty half of a king-sized mattress."

Rachel was watching Ron and I talk. I realized I'd crossed a line with what I'd told

Meland and had probably violated some privacy laws. I decided to change the topic before digging myself any deeper.

"We've got a cluster of coins in the truck, and then there's this pail. Have you got time to catalog them and take them to your evidence room until we make arrangements for secure transport to the museum?"

"It's pretty quiet this morning. That shouldn't be a problem."

"Rachel can help you list them and take pictures while I talk with Rick."

I opened the back door of the pickup. Rick wasn't happy, but he didn't explode. "I've got the stories from your clients. Tell me about your business."

"I want a lawyer."

"That's certainly our right, but you're not under arrest. I'm planning to give you a ticket for removing artifacts from a national park, but that's a misdemeanor." I let that sink in, and Rick relaxed.

"I need some help from you if I'm going to overlook the egregiousness of your daily treasure-hunting trips."

"What are you talking about?"

I counted off on my fingers. "You're out of business as of today. We're taking all the coins in your bucket. I'm seizing your metal detectors. You're going to give me your client list, so I can recover the coins they removed from the island."

"What's in it for me?"

"I let you keep the truck, trailer, and boat."

"You can't take my truck and boat!"

"They were used in the commission of a crime. Once the boat was on the trailer, the truck is part of the package."

Rick looked at the truck and boat. "Shit. There are going to be a lot of unhappy customers. They're going to sue me."

"They can't. They're all co-conspirators in a crime. It'd be like the driver suing a bank robber who promised him a thousand bucks if he drove the getaway car."

"The clients are on my home computer. You'll have to come to my apartment, and I'll print it out."

"One other question. We found a dead woman in a shorty wetsuit. Do you know anything about that?"

"Hell no! All my clients left alive and happy. I didn't kill anyone."

"I didn't say you killed her. I was asking if you knew anything about her or where she came from?"

"When was that?"

"Somewhere in the Wednesday or Thursday time frame."

"The Coast Guard hailed all local boats to look for a missing kayaker on Friday. We cruised the shore, but never saw anyone in the water."

"Did you see someone in a kayak that day or the day before?"

"I don't remember what day it was, but a woman was cruising the shore in a sea kayak. I guess I never connected that with the Coast Guard message."

"Can you describe her?"

"Ah man, that was over a week ago, and we just kinda waved as we passed. I slowed down, so we didn't swamp her with our wake, but that's really the only reason I remember her at all."

"Close your eyes for a second and think back. What color was her hair?"

"I don't know. She wore a cap, and it covered her hair."

"How about her clothing? Life jacket? Swimsuit?"

"No life jacket. Wait! She wore a kinda greenish-blue short-sleeve wetsuit."

"Where were you when you saw her, and which way was she going?"

"We were like halfway to the Devil's Knuckle, and she was paddling north."

"Step out of the truck and let me take my cuffs off of you."

Rick slid out, and I unlocked the cuffs. He shook his wrists.

"My partner and the deputy will follow you back to your apartment. We're done if you give them your client list."

"Done, done? No arrest. No ticket. Nothing?"

"You forfeit the coins and metal detectors, and I think today's clients might want a refund since they didn't get any coins."

"You're an okay guy, for a cop."

"It's easy when you cooperate. If you'd been an asshole, you'd be in the federal lockup before lunch." I smiled and watched him gathering his deckhand and clients.

Rachel and Meland were taking photos of the coins when I met them at the trunk of the cruiser. I told them the plan and said I had to run to a bank and get a check for a house closing.

Chapter Twenty-Four

There was a dirty pickup with a topper parked in the townhouse driveway. It had a ladder strapped to the top, and the body looked like it'd been used for work, not driving around town as a second car. The license plates were from South Dakota.

I walked into a silent house with six people around the dining room table. All looked up, but only Mandy Mattson smiled, and it wasn't a happy smile. Jill jumped up and walked to me, wrapping her arms around my neck.

"Why all the sad faces?"

"Daddy checked the house this morning. The house is filled with mold."

"I thought the remediation people sprayed it."

The slender weathered-faced older man studied me and the uniform. The top of his forehead was white but deeply tanned from the middle down. His resemblance to Jill was evident. He stood up and reached out his hand but didn't smile. "I guess my daughter forgot the manners we taught her. I'm Al Rickowski, and this is my wife, Molly."

Molly was heavier than her husband but looked solid. She smiled at me with her mouth, but not her eyes.

We shook hands. "I'm Doug Fletcher. Where's the mold?"

"Under the siding. In the vents. In the attic. Almost everywhere but the inside of the walls where they sprayed. I'm sorry to say it, but the house has to be demolished. The first time the air conditioner kicked in, there'd be mold spewed all over the place, and it'd be seeping into the insulation as soon as you put up the sheetrock."

I looked at Jill, who nodded. "I called the realtor and told her we're backing out. She cancelled the closing."

Mandy put up her finger as if asking permission to speak. "Actually, the realtor is making a counteroffer to buy the lot, less the cost of the house demo. We're waiting for a phone call."

I hugged Jill close, and Al's eyes flared. "Is this what you want to do?" I asked.

"I love the location," Jill said into my shoulder. "But Daddy's right. It's just not livable."

"I thought we paid a house inspector to check it out."

Al shook his head. "That guy must've been checking by Braille. He never looked under the siding, and it doesn't look like he opened the furnace or vents. You should sue him."

"I appreciate you stepping in and helping us out, Al. We could've really been stuck with a mess if you hadn't shown up when you did. Can we buy you a nice dinner tonight as thanks?"

Al looked prepared for me to confront him and question his opinion. My olive branch caught him off guard, and he glanced at Molly. Jill's mom was also taken aback by my offer of thanks.

Mandy broke the ice. "You'll do no such thing. Matt's grilling shrimp and I've got all the makings for Texas slaw in the car. Y'all are coming to our house for supper, and I won't take no for an answer."

Al was equally surprised by Mandy's offer. "We've got to check into our hotel and take a shower. Is it far from here?"

Mandy shook her head. "Al, it's about fifty steps from our back door. The owners are friends, and your room is ready any time you want it. You're getting the Park Service discount too."

"Your husband is a ranger too, Mandy?"

"He's the superintendent."

Al looked at me. "Mandy's husband is your boss?"

"Yes. He's the second-best boss I've ever had." Al looked confused. "Jill was the best."

Mandy jumped back in. "Let me clear that up a bit. Doug is a Park Service investigator and reports administratively to Matt. But Doug runs the law enforcement part of the national seashore and is at a higher level than Matt."

Al studied my badge for a moment. "That's not the kind of badge Jill wears."

"This is more like a policeman's badge. It helps people understand what I do when they see me carrying a sidearm."

"You can shoot?"

"Daddy, the last time Doug qualified with the St. Paul Police, he shot a smiley face on the silhouette target." I glared at Jill. I'd been trying to outlive that legend.

"I've done that with a rifle. You did it with a pistol?"

Jill cut me off. "He did it in a ten-second, seven-shot speed trial at seven yards."

Al considered that for a moment. "How long have you known Jill?"

Molly interrupted. "Al, this isn't an interrogation or a job interview. Behave yourself."

I put my hand up. "Jill and I worked together for about a year. At some point, we discovered we were best friends, and that quickly turned into love. I've been married and divorced, and I've never had as deep a love as I feel for your daughter." I grabbed Jill's hand and squeezed it. "It took a while to convince Jill how much I loved her."

Al's eyes darted to Jill. "Daddy . . ." Her eyes filled with tears, and she pulled out a tissue. She blew her nose and stared in her father's eyes with tears streaming down her face. "I waited fifty-one years to meet someone who deserved my love. And he's standing next to me."

Mom reached across the table and took Molly's hand. "This is the real thing, Al. Doug's not perfect, but Jill fills in the holes. They are just beautiful together."

Al looked unconvinced. "She's living in sin with you."

Jill stepped between us and placed her hands over Al's chest. "I went to Doug's house and told him I wanted to be with him. He held me and suggested that we snuggle up on the couch and watch a movie. I was the one who took him by the hand and led him into the bedroom. If we're living in sin, it's because I chose that path, and I'm not ashamed of falling in love with my best friend. Can you accept that?"

I looked at Molly and Mom and saw first the surprise, then the tenderness in their expressions.

Al was grinding his jaw. "I can't say I'm pleased about it, you throwing yourself at him and all. It sounds kinda desperate."

Jill leaned her head against Al's chest. "Daddy, this is the love I've dreamt about since I was a little girl. I'm head over heels in love, and I feel butterflies in my stomach every time he walks in the door. Is that how you felt about Mom before you married her?"

Al wrapped his arms around Jill. "That was a long time ago, honey. I guess I had butterflies."

Molly got up and slid past Al. She stood on her toes and kissed my cheek. "I've never seen Jill like this. You've got to be someone special."

Jill tipped her head back. "Daddy, there's going to be a wedding Monday. You can give him my hand, or you can stay in the motel room and sulk. Either get on board or get out of the way."

Al's eyes went wide. I assumed he wasn't unaccustomed to anyone giving him an ultimatum, and certainly not Jill. He stared at me without saying a word.

Mom leaned on the table. "Al, they're in love. It's real, and I've been watching them together for a week. There's nothing phony, juvenile, or insincere in anything I've seen. Jill's part of my family, and I'd love to have them spend holidays and vacations with me if you can't accept their situation. She's a lovely woman, and Doug's lucky to have met her."

Al looked into Jill's eyes. "This is it? This is your dream?"

Jill held up the ring on her finger and wiggled it. "I've had dozens of men who've flirted with me, dated me, or tried to get me into their beds. Doug did the one thing none of them ever tried—Doug wanted to be my friend. Then he became my best friend."

"When I said I loved her, she refused to accept it. I had to earn her trust, her complete trust. Then she let me put a ring on her finger."

Al didn't know where to look. He stared at the floor, then at the staircase. He finally released his grip on Jill and stuck out his hand to me. "I guess I always wanted a son-in-law who could shoot. Can you ride a horse?"

I shook his hand. "I'm scared to death of horses."

"I guess that's something you and I can work on when you come for Christmas." He looked at Mom. "Ronnie, you're invited too. We'll put on a real ranch spread and invite all the neighbors. I guess we'll call it a wedding reception."

I looked at Mandy. "What time is supper?"

"I guess six would be good."

I pulled the cashier's check out of my wallet and handed it to Jill. "Put this someplace safe for the time being. I've got to get back to the park."

"You could take the afternoon off and hang around."

"I've got two murderers in jail who don't know that I'm on to them yet. I've got to get them into an interview room and see if I can make them stumble."

"You caught the guys in the Zodiac boat?"

"Yes, but they're just treasure-hunters. I think the killers are looking forward to a plea agreement on a couple burglaries. I might be able to blind-side them before they get a chance to make up a good story."

Al overheard me and cocked his head. "You had a murder in a National Park?"

"We found her body being eaten by coyotes in a sand dune. I've spent the last week chasing the wrong people, but I think we've got the killers in custody."

"So, you investigate real crimes? Like a real cop?"

"Daddy, Doug was a St. Paul detective before I hired him as a Park Service investigator. He's been on the podium with the FBI when they

251

had a news conference to announce the success of his last two investigations. The newspaper clippings are upstairs if you'd like to see them."

"I'm unaccustomed to eating crow," Al said, staring at the floor. He looked me in the eye. "Maybe you are good enough to marry my little girl."

"I'm not sure of that myself, but it's nice to hear that you think so."

Mandy was beaming.

Molly, Mandy, and Mom huddled around the table, all smiles as I opened the door.

I heard the refrigerator open. "Jill, I don't suppose you have a beer in here. I need to get the flavor of my boot out of my mouth."

"On the door, Daddy. The opener is in the first drawer on your right."

Chapter Twenty-Five

I called Scott Dixon from the driveway and left another message on his voicemail, offering to meet him at the CCPD building if he was available.

I looked through my phone history and found my earlier call to the Coast Guard and hit redial. Lieutenant Rivard was off-duty, but still on base, so I asked to have him paged. It took several minutes of Manilow and Elton John music before he answered, and he sounded unhappy to be paged while he wasn't working.

"This is Fletcher, from the Park Service. We talked this morning about the radio call you relayed from Navy flight operations."

"Yeah. I remember. You were looking for a black Zodiac boat."

"I wanted to thank you. We caught them at the state park boat launch before they could get the boat trailered."

"Really? That's great. Were they what you thought?"

"In part. They were treasure-hunters, and we seized a bucketful of silver coins and two metal detectors that are illegal on the national seashore. We thought they might be involved in a murder.

They weren't, but they provided some information that will help both of us. They saw a woman paddling the abandoned kayak you recovered in the Gulf. She was just off Padre Island and paddling north. I suspect she may be our murder victim. Did the CCPD crime scene techs pick up the kayak?"

"I'm not sure. I told a petty officer to pull it out of storage, but I didn't hear if anyone came for it. Hang on." I heard him yell at someone, followed by a muffled response. "Fletcher. Yeah. A policeman picked it up a couple hours ago. I hope it does you some good."

"I may know in a couple hours. Even if it doesn't give us what we're hoping for, I really appreciate your follow up and the connection with the Navy."

There was a pause, and I wondered if he'd hung up. A female voice came on the line. "Ranger Fletcher?"

"Yes, ma'am. I'm here."

"The lieutenant just asked me to speak with you. He said you had some feedback on our interactions." Her tone sounded defensive.

"I just thanked the lieutenant for his assist this morning. Because of a link we'd set up with Navy flight operations and the Coast Guard, we were able to apprehend some criminals who'd been evading our shore patrols by pushing offshore and motoring away. We used Rivard's link to catch the criminals when they were pulling their boat out at the county park on Mustang Island this morning. We recovered several thousand dollars worth of contraband Spanish coins and other treasure-hunting materials. We've been trying to catch these guys for over a week, and we nailed them today."

"Your name was Fletcher?"

"Yes, ma'am."

"I'm Commander Isley. When Rivard handed me the phone, I expected to have my butt chewed again. Your feedback is refreshing and much appreciated. I'm pleased we could assist. If you have the chance, could you email me your feedback? I like to pass this kind of thing up my chain of command. They hear all the complaints, but sometimes it's nice to let them know that people appreciate what we do. It's especially nice to hear it from another federal agency."

"Commander, I'll draft a letter for the national seashore superintendent and ask him to sign it and send it to you and the lieutenant. It'd be a nice and well-deserved addition to his personnel file. This is far outside the scope of his responsibilities, and it really made a difference."

"You're not a run of the mill ranger, are you Fletcher?"

"I'm a Park Service investigator assigned to the national seashore."

"You sound more, um, seasoned than most of the rangers I've encountered."

I chuckled. "I've been around the block a few times."

"It takes a couple times around the block for someone to realize how much appreciated feedback like yours is to others. Thank you." I thought she was going to hang up when I heard more discussion in the background. "Are you still there?"

"Yes, Commander."

"Rivard just handed me his cellphone with a video of an FBI news conference. Are you the ranger with the sunburned face next to the FBI spokesman?"

I sighed. "That would be me."

There was a pause while I heard the news conference playing in the background. "I'm speechless. We've worked with the FBI on numerous occasions, and I've never heard them mention the Coast Guard in their news conference. You must've done one hell of a job on the investigation of that floating body our helo directed you to."

"It was a big team. You guys. The sheriff's department. CCPD Detective Dixon and his forensics people. Everyone played a role."

"You didn't mention the FBI."

"Their role was to announce that they'd solved the crime at the news conference."

Isley laughed out loud. "I bet your boss just loves your tactful description of the FBI."

"My boss is a great guy, and he's stood behind me through everything I've done. He's a little naïve about the FBI, but we're working past that."

"Fletcher, I hope we cross paths some time. I'd like to buy you a beer and share war stories."

"I'd like that a lot, Commander."

My phone had been buzzing during my Coast Guard conversation, and I pulled over to see if it was Dixon returning my call, or Jill calling to update me on the counteroffer on the house. The caller I.D. said RRandall. I hit redial, and Rachel picked up on the first ring.

"You rotten bastard!"

"Rachel, this is Doug."

"I have caller I.D. I know damned well who this is. How could you do this to me?"

My mind swam with scenarios of Toby, his arrest, his plea bargain, and more. "I'm sorry. What happened?"

"You stuck me with twenty pages of people to call. How in hell am I supposed to call all these people and convince them to send back the silver coins they uncovered with the treasure-hunter charters?"

I let out a deep breath. I could deal with anger over making phone calls. I wasn't sure if I could deal with whatever shitstorm was brewing with Toby. "It's okay. Ron Meland offered to call half the list. For now, focus on the female customers. We need to make sure that none of them are the Jane Doe we discovered in the dunes."

"Great! That's only about fifty calls. That makes it so much better."

"Rachel, take a deep breath and listen to me. Police work is boring, mostly fruitless, phone calls. If you want to be an effective law enforcement officer, whether a ranger or a cop, you've got to get good at making calls and

257

listening. Make sure you catch the things people tell you but also catch the nuances of their speech that may make you suspicious or lead you to other questions."

"I'd rather lie naked on a fire ant hill."

I laughed.

"That wasn't meant to be funny." She waited a beat, then asked, "Did you close on the house?"

"No. My future father-in-law checked under the siding and in the vents and found out it's full of mold. Jill told the realtor to cancel the contract, and they put in a counteroffer for the value of the lot minus the cost to demolish the house."

"Oh, no. Jill was so excited about that house and the redrawn interior plans."

"Maybe it'll work out. Otherwise, we'll move on. We're just lucky her dad is savvy and showed up before the closing."

"Maybe it's karma."

"I'm not much of a karma guy. I'm more of a dumb-luck guy."

"Jill's dad didn't shoot you on sight for taking his daughter's virtue?"

"Her virtue?"

"You know what I mean. You said he'd shot at some cowboy after he found her birth control pills, so you weren't the one who popped her cherry."

"He didn't shoot me. He didn't punch me. He wasn't too pleased that we were *living in sin*, but by the time I left, he was accepting of our living situation and was cooling down."

"Are you coming back for the afternoon beach drive?"

"Blow it off. Tell Matt that I asked you to meet me at the lockup in the Federal Courthouse. I'm going to try to ambush the two geezers I arrested with the sawed-off shotgun and bucketful of coins."

"Why do you want *me* there? It's not like I can add anything to the mix."

"I think you should sit behind the one-way glass and watch the process. If I'm not mistaken, these guys might be conceited enough to think they've gotten by with a murder, and that we're too dumb to know it. It will be educational and possibly entertaining."

"Cool. I'll tell Matt."

I was signaling to turn onto the road over the Kennedy Bridge when my phone rang again. I pulled into the gas station and just before it rolled over to voicemail, I answered, "Fletcher."

"Scott Dixon. You've filled my mailbox with voicemails. I quit listening to them and decided to erase the rest and call you. What's up?"

I explained the incident with the Zodiac and my theory that the person missing from the kayak was Jane Doe. "I'm going to sweat the two geezers I arrested with the sawed-off shotgun."

"I'm skeptical. They're burglars, not killers. They're looking good for a half-dozen home burglaries. The bottom line is that they're carrion feeders, and they steal anything that's not nailed or chained down. They don't like to confront people, choosing mostly homes where they know the owners are at work. However, they fight like cornered raccoons if someone walks in while they're burglarizing a house. They've plea-bargained down a couple of assault charges, but it's not because they didn't do the deed. The prosecutor just decided to be lazy and take the easy plea and move on since the burglary was going to put them into prison anyway."

I digested Scott's information. "Here's my theory. They're scum-sucking leeches. They find a pretty woman who happened upon a cluster of coins. She won't give them the coins she's found and argues with them. One of them chokes her to death, either by accident or on purpose, and they take off with the loot, maybe throwing some sand on top of her body. It's hidden until the coyotes smell the rotting flesh and dig her up."

"I'd say that's pure speculation. You don't have a shred of evidence, do you?"

"I think you should put your guys to work on checking for the woman's DNA on the coins you pulled out of their truck."

"That's a long shot, but it's a thought. What else do you have?"

"She probably pulled her kayak onshore, and possibly the incoming tide floated it out. Or, maybe the geezers pushed it out to dispose of it."

"There's nothing on the kayak. The guys in the crime lab looked at it, but too many days awash in the Gulf with the sun beating on it pretty much wiped out any recoverable DNA. I mean, there are skin cells there, but they're baked, cooked, UV sterilized and washed with seawater. They're not going to be able to make a meaningful DNA comparison."

"How about the woman's wetsuit. Can they pull touch DNA off the neck where she was strangled?"

"Let me ask. That might be our best shot at tying them to the body."

"I called Rachel, and she's meeting me at the federal lockup. I'm going to put each of the geezers into an interview room and see what I can do with them."

"They've already lawyered up."

"It doesn't matter. Neither they nor their lawyers think we're interested in anything more than tying them to the stolen guns and the silver. I may be able to use their notion that I'm only a hick park ranger to my advantage."

"Doug, they've been in and out of prison all their lives. They're not smart, but they're cagey. They're not going to talk to you."

"What've I got to lose but a little time?"

"There's an old southern saying. 'Never wrestle with a pig. You both get dirty, and the pig enjoys it."

"I'm not going to waste a lot of time with them. They're either going to clam up, or they're going to think they can play me. If I get them talking, I just might get one of them to trip up."

"You have a good time, but I'm going to pass. Let me know if something breaks, and I'll talk to the crime lab about the wetsuit."

Chapter Twenty-Six

It took five minutes to locate street parking by the Federal Courthouse after finding all the police vehicle spots occupied. I parked at a meter and hoped no self-respecting cop would ticket a Park Service pickup with a light bar on top. On the other hand, an underpaid, pissed-off meter maid might delight in ticketing me. I didn't have a quarter and didn't want to stick my federal charge card into a parking meter.

I started walking to the courthouse and saw a cop ticketing a car a half-block away. I walked back to the meter and plugged in my charge card for a two-hour stay, figuring Matt would rather take the heat over a dollar charge than listen to me complain about having to pay for a $30 parking ticket out of my own pocket.

The entry to the jail portion of the courthouse was in the rear, and I went through the metal detector routine again, but this time had to lock the Sig and my cellphone in a cubbyhole. No weapons or phones were allowed inside except for those carried by the federal guards, and only when there was an emergency.

I found an officer sitting behind a Plexiglass plate that looked like it could stop a rocket-propelled grenade. "I'd like to interview two suspects I arrested yesterday."

A tinny voice asked, "Their names?"

"They wouldn't tell me their names when they were booked in."

The very patient officer smiled. "Everyone here is listed by name, sir. If you don't have their names, I'm not sure how to determine if we still have them in custody."

"Can you cross-reference the prisoners by arresting officer?"

"No."

"Do you have pictures of them? They were old grizzly guys."

"I don't have prisoner's pictures. Is there someone you could call to get their names?"

I patted my pocket for my cellphone and remembered it was in the locker. "I had to lock up my cellphone when I entered."

"I can call a number for you and ask someone. Do you have a number?"

"Scott Dixon, with the CCPD."

"What's his number, sir."

"I have it on speed dial. Don't you have a CCPD directory?"

"No, sir. I have access to the FBI phone list. Is there someone there I could contact for you?"

I saw Rachel going through the metal detectors on the other side of the access-controlled door. "My partner is going through the metal detector. Let me back out, and I'll have her get the prisoner's names."

I heard the solenoid click open, and I walked out, catching Rachel before she'd locked away her weapon and phone. "What are the names of the guys I arrested yesterday?"

"Senior moment, Doug?"

I shook my head. "They wouldn't give me their names when I booked them. They were identified from their fingerprints later in the day."

"And their names were?"

"I don't know! Call Scott Dixon on your cellphone. He told me they'd been identified and had long rap sheets."

Rachel pulled up Dixon's number and hit the call button. "Didn't Scott tell you who they were when he told you they'd been identified?"

"He probably did, but I don't recall their names."

"Like I said, senior moment." Rachel put up her finger. "Hi, Scott. This is Rachel Randall. I'm in the federal lockup, and Doug can't remember the names of the prisoners he booked yesterday. Do you have them?" She waited a second then repeated the names back to Scott. "Leroy Quarls and Frances Xavier Pickel. Got it. Thanks."

"He never told me. I swear. I would've remembered a name like Pickel."

We went through the security door, and Rachel gave the officer behind the Plexiglass the two names. He nodded and directed us to a row of vinyl chairs with a rail behind them for attaching handcuffs. It took about five minutes, but a solenoid clicked and a black-clad officer with a complexion as black as his shirt opened the door. His badge was a sewn emblem, and his name, Jackson, was also embroidered on.

"You two Randall and Fletcher?"

We got up. "That's us."

"I put Quarls in room four and Pickel in room three." He shook his head. "If my last name was Pickel, I think I'd change it." He walked us to room three. "You both going in, or is one of you watching?"

I nodded toward Rachel. "My partner will watch through the mirror."

"The observation room says 3-A. You can come and go out of there. The interview room only opens from the outside. I'll stand by the door until you knock, or I hear screaming." He smiled. "I usually open it quicker for a knock. It sometimes gets messy if there's screaming."

"Quarls is in three?"

"Pickel. I thought you'd want to talk to the colorful one first." Jackson opened the door, and I walked into a beige room that looked like most every interview room I'd ever been in. Pickel wore an orange jumpsuit and flip flops like Toby and the other prisoners had worn to their arraignments. Pickel was the one I'd called Scruffy. He was the one who'd done all the talking while his partner had attempted to slip out the hidden shotgun.

"Mr. Pickel. That's an odd name. No wonder you wouldn't tell me who you were when I arrested you."

Pickel stared at me for a second, then looked at the mirror. "Who's back there?"

"I brought a trainee along to see how an interview goes."

"You can tell him it ain't going nowhere. I want my lawyer. He said not to talk to anyone unless he was here."

"You probably don't need to bother him. I'm here about something other than your case."

Pickel's eyes narrowed. "Something else? Like what?"

"We've been watching a black Zodiac boat pull ashore every day. We haven't been able to catch them because they see us driving down the beach and pull offshore before we get close enough to catch them or to even get the registration numbers off the boat. I thought since you've been up and down the beach a lot you could tell me more about them and maybe describe the people operating the Zodiac."

"I don't know what a Zodiac boat is."

"It's got like a big inflatable black tube around it with an outboard motor on the back."

"Yeah, I seen it, but I didn't see no numbers on it."

"Can you tell me what the skipper looks like?"

"Why you want them? They been picking up coins, too."

Gotcha! You just admitted that you were illegally taking coins.

"We think they're doing that, but I'm more interested in where they might've been seen last week."

"Last week was a long time ago. I don't know exactly when I saw them."

"They might've been around when a blonde girl was kayaking along the shore. Do you remember seeing her at the same time or place you saw them?"

"Why?"

"We found her body, and we suspect they killed her."

"I don't remember a woman in a kayak."

"It was bright yellow. You don't remember a girl in a bright yellow kayak?"

Pickel shook his head.

"That's too bad because we might be able to do something about your sentencing if we could tie the black Zodiac boat to the area where the girl was killed."

I saw a flicker in Pickel's eyes. "Still nothing?"

He shook his head. "Nothin' comes to mind."

I knocked on the door, and Jackson opened it right up. I pulled it shut. "Leave him for a bit and let me talk to the Quarls."

Rachel came out of the adjacent room and let her eyes adjust to the lighter hallway. "That didn't seem helpful."

"We're not done yet. Take me to room four, Officer Jackson."

Quarls looked tired and haggard like he hadn't slept well. "Do you remember me?"

"You're that ranger that ran us out of the park."

"I've got a problem, and I was hoping you could help."

Quarls shook his head. "I ain't helping anyone wearing a badge."

"Even if it meant shaving some time off your upcoming sentence?"

"Whatcha offering?"

"It depends on what you know. I'm looking for information about a black Zodiac boat that's been running up and down offshore."

"That's one of them with the inner tube?"

"That's the one. Pickel says you guys had seen it a few times."

"That's a lie. Pickel don't talk to a cop without his lawyer."

"I'm not talking about your burglaries or even picking coins off the island. I just want to know about the black Zodiac. Pickel says you'd seen it a few times, but he couldn't remember if you'd seen it last Thursday."

"What day's today?"

"It's Friday. So, we're talking about a week ago yesterday."

Quarls shook his head. "I don't remember nothing that long ago."

"There was a girl kayaking that day, and we think the black Zodiac boat stopped where she beached her kayak."

"So what?"

"I think the guys in the Zodiac killed her and pulled her kayak offshore."

"If I remembered that, what would it mean on my sentence?"

"It depends on what you can tell me, and whether you tell me before or after Pickel. He's taking a piss right now, but when he's done, the guard's going to knock on the door, and I'm going back to see him."

"I saw a kayak. It was a yellow one. And that black innertube boat came along right after her."

"Did you see what happened?"

"They kinda followed her into the dunes."

"Then what?"

"It's like you said. They left, and she didn't come back to the kayak."

"Did the kayak float off, or did they pull it out with them?"

"They pulled it out a little bit, and it just floated off."

"Did you hear a struggle in the dunes?"

"Something happened."

"But you don't know what? Didn't you go check on her to see if she was okay?"

"What'd Pickel tell you?"

"He said she was dead."

"Yeah."

"Yeah, she was dead?"

Quarls looked at the mirror. "If I'm the first one to help you, then I get more time off?"

"That's the deal."

"Yeah. She was dead. Those guys strangled her and took the coins she found. The guys in the innertube boat."

"They strangled her and left her in the dunes after they stole her coins. Right?"

"Yeah."

"You didn't touch the body or anything, did you?"

"Naw, we left her just like we found her and went off."

"Was she face up or face down?"

Quarls stopped and gazed at the mirror like he was visualizing it. "Her eyes were all red. She was looking at the sky with those red eyes."

"Why didn't you call the cops?"

Quarls looked at me. "We're cons. We never call the cops. We just picked up the coins and left."

"You picked up coins? Did the Zodiac boat guys leave some of her coins behind after they killed her?"

Quarls froze. "No. There weren't no coins left. We picked up our coins and left."

"Did you spill your coins, so you had to pick them up?"

"Yeah. We spilled some coins when we saw her there dead."

"Did she die fast, or did it take a long time to choke her?"

"What?"

"She was strangled. There must've been a struggle, and it must've taken a couple minutes for her to die."

"I wouldn't know. It wasn't like I was right there. She was up in the dunes digging, and we were walking the beach. I couldn't have heard nothin'."

"Somebody strong must've done that. It can't be easy to strangle someone."

"I suppose so."

"Pickel's a lot stronger than you. Isn't he? He must've been the one who was carrying the bucket and spilled the coins?"

"Yeah. Sure."

"Did he find her body first, or did you?"

"I was . . . um, Pickel was checking on the dunes, and I was on the beach looking there. So Pickel found her first."

"Then, he called you up to the dunes to see her dead body."

Quarls didn't know what to say, so I waited, but he just stared at the table.

"Have you ever killed anyone?"

"I'm a burglar, not a killer."

"How about Pickel?"

"I wouldn't know."

"Wouldn't she give up her coins? Did she fight back?"

"I think I need my lawyer?"

"Why? We're not talking about anything you did, we're talking about the innertube boat guys, aren't we?"

Quarls stared at me with his mouth open. He licked his dry lips.

"Or were you on the beach so you couldn't see into the dunes when Pickel strangled her?"

"I didn't have nothin' to do with it. I heard her arguing, and then they was fighting."

"You were scared and didn't want to see what was happening in the dunes."

Quarls shook his head. "I didn't see. It got quiet, and then I snuck up there. Pickel was

271

picking up the spilled coins, and she was just a staring at the sky. I thought maybe she was just stunned, but her eyes were all red like a demon had done something to her."

"And Pickel told you to leave."

"We left together after we picked up her coins." Quarls let out a sob. "It weren't worth it, killing some pretty girl because she didn't want to give up her coins. He could've just slugged her or hit her over the head. There's no reason he had to kill her. No reason at all."

I looked at the blinking red light on the camera in the corner to make sure everything had been recorded, then I nodded at the mirror and knocked on the door. Jackson opened the door and looked at Quarls, who was face down on the table like he was asleep.

"Is he okay?"

"He'll want to talk to the prosecutor."

"She's in court."

"Can you page or text her?"

Jackson looked at Quarls again. "Did he confess or something?"

"He just told me about witnessing his partner kill a woman."

Jackson's eyes got wide. "No, shit?"

Rachel edged out of the observation room. Her eyes were red, and she was wiping her nose with a tissue.

"No, shit. We got it on camera."

Jackson closed the door. "I can get a message to the bailiff."

"Do it. And keep Quarls in segregation. He'll be killed if anyone finds out what he just told me."

Jackson hustled further into the secure unit.

I took Rachel's elbow and steered her toward the security door. "Get out of here and call Scott Dixon. Tell him what Quarls said and tell him to leak it to whoever he has as a contact in the local newspaper. Tell him to do it tonight, so it hits the wire services before the morning news."

"Why?"

"The Assistant U.S. Attorney will be down here shortly. I'll have her watch the recording of the interview, and she'll want to talk to Quarls herself. But I'll bet my next paycheck the FBI will know about the interview before she leaves the building, and they'll have an army of interviewers grilling Pickel and Quarls. I guarantee they'll have a news conference tomorrow morning, in time to make the noon news broadcasts, announcing that they've solved the murder. They'll look pretty silly if it's already in the newspaper that the Park Service and CCPD solved the case, and they'll have to cancel their dog and pony show."

"Why don't you . . ."

"Because I'm going to stall. Get out of here and make the call. If Dixon isn't available, have him paged, or radioed. If that fails, call the newspaper yourself and spill the story. It'll be better from Dixon because he'll have the forensics, but you witnessed the interview, and your word is golden. Now get!"

I waved at the camera, and the solenoid clicked, releasing the door. Rachel walked through, looking over her shoulder. I nodded and pulled the door closed.

Jackson was back five minutes later. "I got a note to the bailiff. He said they usually don't break until four unless one of the lawyers asks for an early recess. Ms. Pruett might not be here for over an hour."

I nodded. "Can I buy you a cup of coffee, Officer Jackson?"

"Folks call me Jack, and the coffee is bad but full of caffeine."

I reached out my hand and shook his. "I'm Doug. I take my coffee any way I can get it."

"The security booth watched while you interviewed that guy. Sharona said she's never seen anyone as smooth as you. Not even the bigshot FBI interview specialists. And that's a big compliment."

"Thank Sharona for me." I stopped. "Can Sharona make a copy of the interview for me?"

"Sure. We email copies to prosecutors and the FBI all the time. C'mon up to the booth, and I'll introduce you."

Five minutes later, email copies were out to Matt, Rachel, Scott Dixon, Sarah Hawkins (my contact at *The Santa Fe Journal)*, and me. Sarah would be lost without the context, so the cellphone voicemail would be backed up with messages when I got through with Jane Pruett, but Sarah was enough of a bulldog reporter I knew she would be scouring the internet for background would hang around until I called her. I also knew she'd put the story on AP and Reuters wire services long before the FBI knew there was a story to be had. If Scott came through with his newspaper contact, the wires would have two stories, and the FBI would be reeling and there would be calls flying all over their hierarchy trying to figure out how to put the right spin on a story they couldn't control.

Chapter Twenty-Seven

Jane Pruett didn't get out of the courtroom until after four. She came through the security door, looking like a charging elephant.

She waved a piece of paper at me. "Fletcher, what the hell is this?"

"What is that in your hand?"

"It says, 'Murder solved. See Fletcher in the federal lockup.'"

"That's it. I interviewed the guys I arrested for pulling a gun on me in the park and stealing Spanish coins. One spilled that he witnessed the other kill the girl we found murdered on Padre Island this week."

"What made you even suspect they'd been involved?"

"It's complicated. Why don't we go up and watch the interview, and it'll be more clear. I'm sure you'll want to talk to the witness yourself and probably have a transcript of the interview made and have him sign it."

"I feel like I'm being railroaded."

I pointed the way to the security booth. "Sharona, can you cue up that interview for Ms. Pruett?"

"Certainly, honey."

Pruett looked at me. "Honey?"

"I bought her coffee."

"I wouldn't call you honey if you bought me a bottle of Johnnie Walker Blue."

"Now we know your weakness and your price," I said with a smile.

We watched the video twice, and Jane Pruett couldn't stop shaking her head. "You didn't entrap him, but you sure walked close to the ledge."

"He's not the murderer, so we have much more latitude with his questioning."

"Are you certain that if we asked the same questions of Pickel that he wouldn't say Quarls did it?"

"Sharona, can you cue up the Pickel interview?"

"Certainly, honey." Pruett rolled her eyes.

At the end of the Pickel interview, Pruett leaned back and stared at me. "How did you know to interview Pickel first?"

"Quarls wasn't strong enough to strangle a young woman, and I needed to see the look in Pickel's eyes when I tried leading him down the trail. He was smarter, but I could tell he was holding a lot back."

"Do we have any other evidence that Pickel is our man?"

"The CCPD crime lab is looking at touch evidence on the neck of the wetsuit to see if they can match that DNA to Pickel. We're also looking at DNA on the coins. Some of them will likely have DNA from both the victim and the killer. If they work some magic, we might even get some of Pickel's DNA off the kayak from when he pushed it off."

"We should use the FBI DNA lab. They have world-class analysts and the latest equipment and techniques."

"It's up to you, prosecutor. You do whatever you think is best. Perhaps you'll want to bring in an expert interrogator from Washington to take a crack at Pickel."

Pruett stared at me. "I've heard about you. You don't like the FBI, yet here you agree to use FBI resources and personnel. I don't think your tiger stripes have changed. What's up?"

"I'm getting married Monday and I've turned over a new leaf."

"You're joking. You're not getting married Monday."

"My future in-laws drove in from South Dakota and tonight we're eating shrimp on the barbie to celebrate the union of two families."

"Who's the lucky woman?"

"Jill Rickowski, my former Flagstaff boss."

"Office romances can be awkward."

"I didn't kiss her until she was no longer my boss. At that point, we were best friends, and that drifted into romance. I'm happier than I've ever been in my life."

"Congratulations. And excuse my comment about the Johnnie Walker. I was being a smartass."

"I should get going. It'd be poor to be late for my first dinner with my father-in-law."

"Are your in-laws really from South Dakota?"

"Ranchers from Spearfish in the Black Hills."

"They're kind of rugged individualists, I hear."

"Jill said her father ran off a suitor with a shotgun in her younger days."

"And he's not running you off?"

"Jill told him I shot a smiley face on a silhouette during a timed firing. He was impressed and happy about having a son-in-law who can shoot. He's going to try and overcome my fear of horses when we go home for Christmas."

"I'm happy for you, Doug. Good luck."

"I've used up my share of good luck when I met Jill, and she agreed to marry me."

Pruett looked at her watch. "Damn. The main FBI offices are closed. I hate to bother the evening duty officer with non-emergencies. I'll call them in the morning."

I walked Pruett to her car, then called Scott Dixon while I walked the blocks to my pickup. He answered his cellphone on the second ring. "Scott, did Rachel talk to you?"

"Yeah, like an hour ago. She had a crazy story about a witness to the Padre Island murder. Then a video showed up in my email, and I put the pieces together."

"I stalled the federal prosecutor until the FBI went home. Did you get your information to someone you trust?"

"It'll be on the front-page tomorrow and will probably hit the wire services tonight."

"Perfect. The Special Agent in Charge will read it with his morning coffee, and it'll ruin his day. It'll be in the evening papers before they can even decide how to spin it."

"Doug, thanks for letting us be a part of this. We have resources and good people. We get run over roughshod sometimes, and you've worked very hard to make sure we're partners. I appreciate that and so does the chief."

"We are partners, Scott. And unlike the FBI, we respect each other."

"Hey, there's one other thing. We've got a guy who trolls the pawnshops and internet for stolen stuff. I told him to watch for Spanish coins and a gold cross on a chain. He got a call from a pawnshop on the south side. A guy walked in with a clump of silver coins and tried to sell it to him. He got suspicious and low-balled the guy an offer based on the discounted value of the silver, and the guy thought about it but walked away. We've got the video, and we're trying to match the face to somebody in our database."

"Thanks, Scott. Let me know if you get a hit."

I dialed Sarah Hawkins at the New Mexico newspaper from the pickup as I was driving toward Port Aransas. "Okay, Fletcher. What's this about?"

I explained as I drove. Her keyboard was clicking like a machine gun. By the time I got to Mandy and Matt's, Sarah had the story roughed out and had her intern trying to catch Scott and Rachel to corroborate the story,

I pulled in Matt's driveway, tucked the gun under the seat, and locked the pickup. I heard laughter from the driveway and knew Mandy had worked her magic again. Either that or the margaritas were flowing. When I got inside, I knew both were in play.

Jill jumped up and met me outside the dining room with a kiss.

"I've been waiting for your call or text with an update on the counteroffer."

She shook her head. "We haven't heard back. The realtor said they may be mulling it overnight, and maybe we'll hear something tomorrow."

"How did the gown fitting go?"

"I'm really glad Mom got to come along and see it before the wedding. She had tears in her eyes. I think she thought she'd never see me in a wedding gown after I'd spent thirty years wearing a uniform."

Matt came out of the kitchen and handed me a beer. "Can I steal Doug for a minute?"

"He's all yours," Jill said as Matt steered me to the door.

Matt closed the door behind us. "You've had a hell of a day."

"I guess it's been a little crazy, but no more than usual."

Matt shook his head. "I got three calls as I was trying to get out the door. One from *The Santa Fe Journal,* one from *The Corpus Christi*

281

Times, and one from the Secretary of the Interior."

"Oh, oh."

"Sarah Hawkins called the Secretary from Santa Fe and asked for his comments on the arrest of the man who killed the Padre Island visitor. He hadn't heard about it, so she filled him in. I guess he gave her vague supportive comments, then he called and reamed me for not warning my chain of command there'd been a breakthrough and an arrest."

"Sorry. I was rushing around trying to get the story out before the FBI . . ."

Matt waved off my apology. "After reaming me, he told me that you're the best thing that's ever happened for Park Service recruiting. The application website has been jammed with candidates who want to be rangers, and the numbers show an increasing number of experienced law enforcement people applying who didn't even know there were law enforcement rangers."

I didn't know what to say. "I guess that's great."

"We had another development today. I had one of the rangers paint a sign that we posted at the entrance. It says that using a metal detector or removing coins or artifacts from Padre Island National Seashore was a federal crime punishable by up to six months in jail and a ten thousand dollar fine. The guard at the entrance told me that about one of three vehicles read the sign and turn around before coming to the gate."

"That'll help quiet things down."

"The two new law enforcement rangers the secretary is assigning will also help."

"You got two additional rangers?"

"Yes. The secretary said he didn't realize how hard it was to protect this resource, and he bumped my budget and added two rangers. They'll be here in two to three weeks. He said he'll get me some seasoned, not seasonal, help."

"Wow."

Matt stuck out his hand. "Good work. I was told to write a commendation and forward it to him for a signature."

"Write two of them and put Rachel's name on one. Oh, and send a letter to the Coast Guard commander thanking Lieutenant Rivard and his crew for their assistance with capturing the treasure-hunters in the Zodiac boat. I spoke with the commander, and she was amazed they were being thanked for assistance. It sounded like she gets beaten up all the time for problems, and my call was a breath of fresh air."

"Write up something when you come back next week, and I'll sign it."

"But . . ."

"I've already been delegated enough from above. I don't need you dumping any monkeys on my back."

I shook my head. "No good deed goes unpunished."

Matt steered me back into the house, where we found the women huddled around the table. Jill's dad was sitting in a recliner with his feet up

283

and a beer in his hand. "It's about time you two got back in here. I was about to go deaf from all the women talking in here."

Al appeared to have enjoyed at least a couple beers, and it took him three attempts to get out of the recliner. He joined Matt and me in the hallway. "You got a computer on your phone, Doug?"

"I've got a smartphone with Wi-Fi."

"Jill said you should look up the Reuters wire service."

I handed my beer to Matt and keyed in Reuters, and the website opened. The day's headlines scrolled down. "What am I looking for?"

"Matt said there'll be a story about someone getting arrested for killing a girl in your park."

I looked at Matt, who handed my beer back and took my phone. He scrolled down and touched the story he wanted, then watched it open.

"Here's the one," he said, handing the phone to Al.

Al read slowly, asking Matt to scroll down when he finished each page. When he finished, he handed the phone back to me and nodded. "That Sarah makes you sound like the Lone Ranger of the Park Service."

I shut the phone down and put it in my pocket. "I haven't read the story."

"Open that back up and let me show it to Molly."

"I'd rather not, Mr. Rickowski."

Al shook his head. "Jill showed me the newspaper clippings this afternoon. She said you were humble, but the clippings with you standing behind the FBI didn't look like you were hiding from the limelight."

"Sir, it was not my choice to be at those news conferences. I'd rather have been a million miles away than standing there."

"My name is Aleksander. My banker calls me Mr. Rickowski. My hired hands call me boss. Molly calls me honey. Jill calls me Daddy. My friends call me Al. No one calls me, sir, and I'd appreciate it if you'd knock that off." He punctuated his comments by tapping the neck of his beer bottle against my chest. "If you're in for the long haul, we gotta come up with an agreement on what you're going to call me."

I caught myself before I said, yes, sir.

"Al would be fine with me, but if you'd prefer something else, you let me know. But it's not going to be 'sir.'"

"Is Dad okay?"

Al's eyes opened wide, brows furrowed as if stunned by the question. "Jill's always called me Daddy."

"I heard that."

Al looked me in the eye. He had the same deep brown eyes as Jill, and it seemed like he was trying to read something inside me. "Your father died a while ago."

"I was in high school when he passed away."

"Ronnie said he never got to see you play football."

"No, sir ... Mr. Rickowski...Al."

"I never had a grown son who called me dad." He took a swig of beer. "Open up that story again for me."

"I'd rather not."

The conversation at the table stopped, and every eye was glued on us. Mandy started to get up, but I waved her back.

I saw a flare in his eyes for just one second. "I'm not accustomed to hearing, 'no.'"

"I'm not accustomed to taking orders, at least, not since I left the National Guard."

Al put out his open palm. "I'd like to read that article again, *please.*"

I opened the phone and entered my password. I found the article about the murder investigation and handed it to him. Molly got up and stood at his shoulder, so she could read it too. I looked at Jill, who looked like she was waiting for one of us to throw a punch. When they were through, Molly took the phone to Mom and let her read.

Al's face was somber. He stood so close I could see every leathery crease and valley from his years in the sun. "It takes balls to stand up to a man who's used to giving orders."

"I've been a cop a long time, and I've had to stand up to a lot of people in some pretty tense situations. I've never compromised my principles or backed down when I knew I was right."

Al looked over his shoulder. "Jill, get over here!"

She got up slowly, walked to the kitchen, and leaned on the wall. "This pissing contest had better be done pretty soon, or I'm going to give you both a piece of my mind, and then, I'm leaving." She looked at Mandy. "I'm truly sorry I dragged over two boys who don't know how to play nice."

Al appeared shocked.

"Don't look like you're surprised, Daddy. You raised me to stand up for myself. How else do you think I got through all those tomboy years. And you, Doug, shouldn't be surprised either."

Matt was ready to step between us, but something in Al's expression softened.

Al looked at Jill, then back at me. "I raised Jill like a son, and we're damned proud of what she's become. I imagine if Molly and I had raised a boy, he'd probably be as bullheaded and bristly as me."

He looked at Mom. "I gotta say, Ronnie. You raised a kid who knows how to stand up for himself, but he also knows right from wrong and good from bad." Al put out his hand. "I'd be proud if you'd call me Dad."

I shook his hand. "Dad it is."

I thought Matt was going to collapse in relief. "I'm going to put the shrimp on the grill."

Jill stared at Al and me, then pointed to the door. We walked outside, and she closed the door.

"I thought the two of you were housebroken! Geez. Don't either of you do that to me again."

287

Al smiled. "See what I mean, Doug. She's got spunk."

"I'll show you spunk!" Jill jammed her index finger into Al's solar plexus. "You start acting like a proud father and behave yourself." Then she turned to me. "Wipe that smile off your face. You're not off the hook either. You quit trying to hide the good things you do. You're a good detective, a good teacher, a good guy, and I pray to God that you'll be as good a husband as you are my friend. Are we done here?"

"Yes, dear," I said.

Jill poked me with her finger. "And quit saying that! It's starting to piss me off!"

Al started to laugh and slapped his leg, spilling his beer. Jill took a step back and couldn't help but smile. I tried to hug her, but she spun away.

"Okay. You've just about ruined Mandy's party. You two are going to apologize and act like perfect gentlemen the rest of the night."

I heard footsteps behind me and turned. Rachel was walking up the sidewalk with Ron Meland, who looked boyish out of his uniform. "I think we missed the fireworks."

"Dad, this is my partner, Rachel, and her friend, Ron. This is Jill's father, Al Rickowski."

They all shook hands, and Rachel looked at me and mouthed, "Dad?"

I nodded and mouthed, "Ron?"

Rachel glared at me. "You knew."

I smiled and nodded.

Chapter Twenty-Eight

Mandy and Matt were holding hands in the hallway, looking anxious, with Molly and Ronnie behind. Mandy saw our smiles and put her hand to her chest.

Molly pushed past everyone and grabbed Al's shirt. "You owe these nice people an apology."

"What did I do?"

"You acted like a bullheaded jerk, just like you do too often back home." She let go of Al, and her voice softened as she steered Jill aside. "Is everything okay?"

"The boys are going to play nice," Jill said loud enough for everyone to hear. "I had to interject a little reason into the posturing, but no one threw a punch, and the wedding's still on."

Ronnie's eyes got very wide. "You thought they were going to duke it out in the driveway?"

Jill shook her head. "It's just a figure of speech. Neither of them is really housebroken yet, and I had to set them straight."

Rachel started laughing. "Oh, that's so true. I knew Doug wasn't housebroken." That broke the ice, and Mandy showed up with a pitcher of margaritas in one hand and sweet tea in the other. Rachel introduced Ron to everyone.

Al brought two beers from the kitchen and handed me one, then steered me out the door. He made sure everyone could see his smile when he whispered to me, "We'll all play nice, and you can call me Dad, but if you hurt her, I'll kill you."

I managed to not flinch and maintain my own smile. "Both Jill and I have knocked around enough to know what life's all about. We're grownups, and we know we're going to hit some rocky spots, but we're both committed to making this marriage work. You've been married a long time, and you understand that."

Al ground his teeth. "You're one stubborn sonofabitch, aren't you?"

"What makes you say that?"

"I'm used to getting in the last word, and you always have to say something more."

"I've been a cop a long time, and I didn't accomplish that by backing down. People walk all over cops who look weak. But that's my public face. Jill's a strong woman, maybe stronger than me, and I'm strong when she needs it, but I can be as gentle as a lamb. That gentle part surprised her, but it's also the part she needs the most."

Jill pushed between us, standing eye to eye with her father. She stuck her finger into his solar plexus, which made him take a half-step back. "Aleksander Rickowski, I don't know what bullshit you're laying on Doug, but here's the deal."

I could see the fire in Al's eyes, and he looked over Jill's shoulder at me.

Jill poked him in the chest again. "Look at me!" When Al's gaze returned to her, Jill stared him in the eye. "I'm not sixteen anymore. You don't need to protect me from ranch hands with wandering eyes. Are we clear on that?"

When Al didn't answer, Jill poked him again. "Are. We. Clear?"

Al continued to smolder. "But…"

Jill put her hands on her hips. "There is no 'but.' If you can't accept that I'm an adult and I've chosen a decent, caring man for a husband, then you can climb back into your pickup and drive back to South Dakota."

Al glanced at me, and I could see that no one had ever spoken to him like that without getting punched. Jill grabbed his chin and turned his head, so he was looking at her. That, too, was something he'd never experienced.

"Dad, stand down," she said softly. "I've got this."

The fire dimmed in Al's eyes. "You're sure about this?"

Jill wrapped her arms around Al and kissed his cheek. "I've never been more sure about anything in my life."

Al put his arms around Jill and hugged her gently as Molly to us. She saw Jill and Al hugging and tears welled in her eyes. She looked at me, smiled, and went back to the table.

Jill released her hug and placed her hand son Al's shoulders. "Are you staying for the wedding?"

He glanced at me, then looked back at Jill. "I think I'm walking you down the aisle if you'll let me."

Jill turned him and pushed him toward the living room. "Go celebrate with the rest of them." When he stepped away, she hugged me. "Daddy told you he'd kill you if you hurt me, right?"

I smiled.

"There's lots of that going around. Ronnie told me I'd rot in hell if I hurt you like your ex-wife did. I gave her a softer version of what Dad just got."

I took a sip of beer. "We should've eloped and told everyone afterward."

Jill poked her finger into my chest. "You were the one who suggested having both sets of parents here at the same time. I believe you said it would create 'buzz.'"

"I didn't expect the theatrics."

When we walked out of the hallway, everyone was staring.

Jill smiled, and the frost started to melt. "The show's over. We can go back to partying."

Everyone restarted conversations, and Molly pulled Al into the kitchen to find out what had been said.

Jill grabbed her margarita and pulled me into the corner of the living room. "I'm glad I've had a margarita. It's not easy to stand up to Dad."

"You said exactly what he needed to hear."

Jill looked past me. "What's with Rachel and Ron? That seems like a quick rebound from Toby."

"It was Ron's baby that miscarried."

Jill spun me around and looked into my eyes. "Did she tell you that?"

"She didn't have to. Look at them."

"But Toby?"

"He was the one who wanted an open relationship. He probably thought that was a one-way street, and apparently, he was wrong. It's no different than your dealings with the young rangers. The rules have changed since we were young and dating."

Jill kissed me. "Thank you."

"For what?"

"For everything. I love you."

Mandy came off the patio, saw us holding hands, and smiled. "Everybody, find a spot at the table. The shrimp are done!"

* * *

Jill and I walked her parents to the mom and pop motel Mandy had located for them. Somehow Mandy had charmed the owners into letting Molly and Al stay in their one renovated room, and at a discount, she'd negotiated.

I kissed Molly on the cheek and shook Al's hand at their door. Molly was unaccustomed to the margaritas, so she'd been weaving while leaning on the doorframe when we walked away.

293

Jill intertwined her fingers with mine on the walk back to Matt and Mandy's. "You and Daddy are cool now, right?"

"We talked, and he understands I have no inappropriate designs on your virtue."

Jill pulled her hand free and dug a knuckle into my ribs. "Can you be serious for a minute?"

I stopped and rubbed my ribs. "Where'd you learn that move?"

"Dad used that to get cattle moving. I adapted it to boyfriends who got too 'handsy' at the drive-in movie." She paused. "Seriously. Have you and Daddy really settled down, and everything will be okay?"

"We're fine. He understands that I'm an okay guy, but it took a while for him to understand that I wasn't going to be treated like his hired help. I respect him and what he's accomplished, but I won't put up with his bluster and threats."

Jill grabbed my hand and pulled me along. "He's used to getting his way."

"I understand that, but he's a bit of a bully too."

"I know. He likes to throw his weight around."

Jill pecked my cheek. "So do you, dear." She pulled at my hand and glared at me. "And so help me, if you say, 'yes dear' to that you'll have a broken finger."

Mom was helping Matt and Mandy clean up and wash dishes. Ron Meland wiped down the grill while he and Rachel were having a serious discussion with the patio door closed. We didn't intend to intrude on their conversation, but we walked through the alley and overheard Ron making his pitch that she should move in with him. I stopped Jill, and we went around to the front door rather than interrupt them.

We didn't live far from Mandy and Matt, so the Margarita buzz was still going strong when I got Jill and Mom home. Mom slipped off her shoes and announced she was going to bed. I locked the front door and shut off the downstairs lights. By the time I got to the bedroom, Jill was already changed into her t-shirt top and boxer pajamas. She was flipping through the television channels when I closed the bedroom door.

"You're planning to watch television?"

"Just while you change." She stopped her selection at the local CBS affiliate. I was going to step into the bathroom when I recognized Scott Dixon's voice. I sat on the bed and listened to an announcer tease their upcoming exclusive interview with CCPD detective Scott Dixon about the arrest of the Padre Island strangler.

Jill looked at me and asked. "He's the guy you're working with?"

"Yeah." I stripped off my golf shirt and used the bathroom mirror to inspect the darkening bruise on my left rib, where Jill had inserted her knuckle. "You know, you could be arrested for domestic assault."

"The ads are over."

I pulled a fresh white t-shirt over my head and sat next to Jill, who was sitting with her legs crossed on the bed. I hadn't been able to do that since I'd reached puberty.

An attractive blonde with hair that looked like a helmet held the microphone in front of Scott. "Detective Dixon, I understand there was a breakthrough in the Padre Island strangler case this afternoon."

"The CCPD has been assisting the Park Service with the murder investigation for the past week. We'd been pursuing a number of leads, when Doug Fletcher, of the Park Service, put the pieces together this afternoon. He interviewed two men who were being held for several felony burglary investigations and an assault when one of them admitted witnessing the young woman's murder."

"Isn't it unusual for the Park Service to lead a criminal investigation?"

"In general, that's true, but the Park Service brought in their top criminal investigator, Doug Fletcher, and he was able to eliminate some red herrings that had the everyone stumped. He got a confession and then turned the case over to Jane Pruett of the U.S. Attorney's office. I watched a tape of his interview, and he should be teaching the witness interviewing class to the FBI students at Quantico."

"What happens from here, detective?"

"Ms. Pruett will bring the suspect in for an arraignment while the CCPD crime lab tests the last pieces of evidence."

"Why do you think the Park Service and your department were able to accomplish what has eluded the FBI?"

"We use local contacts and resources that aren't available to the FBI. Local informants get us inside information the FBI profilers don't have, and by using the CCPD crime lab instead of shipping the evidence to Washington D.C., we can get a much faster turnaround on the test results."

"This has been Holly Maxwell reporting from the steps of the Corpus Christi Police Department."

Jill looked at me. "You didn't tell me the FBI has been stymied on this case."

"The FBI hasn't done anything with this case, so I guess you could say they've been stymied."

Jill muted the television. "The FBI isn't going to like the way they were characterized as a second-tier resource, and Scott's comments about you teaching the interview class aren't going to make you any friends."

I did my best Clark Gable imitation. "Frankly, my dear, I don't give a damn."

"That's easy to say tonight. You might not be so cocky when the head FBI guy calls Matt tomorrow."

The weather report came on, and I unmuted the sound. The weather was going to be blustery with a chance of rain. I turned it off and set the remote on the nightstand. "I don't know how they can keep their jobs when they're wrong most of the time."

Jill drew back the sheet and crawled under the covers. She closed her eyes, but they popped open immediately.

I reached for the light. "What's wrong?"

"The room is moving."

"Ah, the margaritas are still working. I thought you learned your lesson last time."

She sat up and held her head. "They slide down so easy, and Mandy egged us on."

The guest bedroom door opened, and the bathroom door slammed. We heard the sounds of retching. Jill held her head.

"I guess you're not the only one suffering from too many margaritas." When Jill didn't answer, I added, "Mom's right, the walls really are paper-thin."

Jill continued to hold her head. "Do we have something to treat this?"

"Time."

I got a disgusted look. "I was hoping for something more immediate."

"Take it from a drunk. There's no remedy except sleep."

Jill slid out of bed and got a robe from the closet. "I'm going to brew some Chamomile tea. I'll ask Ronnie if she'd like some, too."

I listened to the groaning coming from the guest bathroom. "I suspect she'd rather stay close to the toilet for the time being."

Jill opened the door and looked back. "Are you coming along?"

"I'm going to sleep."

"No, you're not."

"Why not?"

"Because I'm miserable, and you want to make me feel better."

I pulled the sheet up to my chin and turned away from the door.

"Douglas, get your butt out of that bed and come downstairs and hold my hand."

"You sound like my mother. She's the only person who calls me, Douglas."

Jill's voice got sharper. "Fletcher, we're having tea. Come on."

"I don't think so."

"I'll come back to bed and throw up on you."

"That's underhanded." I threw back the sheet and slipped my feet into slippers.

Chapter Twenty-Nine

I made coffee. No one stirred upstairs, so I read the newspaper. When Jill came downstairs, I was working on the crossword. She looked at the yogurt I was eating and rushed past without comment. I heard her grab a coffee cup from the cupboard and pour from the carafe.

I carried my cup to the carafe. Jill had braced her hands on the counter and stared at the coffee cup.

"Are you okay?"

She shook her head. "It's too early to tell."

I refilled my cup. "Have you heard any stirring from the guest bedroom?"

"Nothing yet."

"The newspaper has a picture of Scott Dixon on the front page, and a short article that's continued on page four."

"I assume it's a repeat of the television broadcast."

"It's more complete. The television never has time to get into the details."

Jill dumped out her coffee and set the cup in the sink. "Are you the hero?"

"Hardly. The reporter did a very nice job of spreading the credit to the CCPD, the Park

Service, the Coast Guard, and even gave a nod to the Navy flight squadron."

"That's nice. I think I'll take a shower and let the water pound on me for a while."

"I told Al we'd meet them for breakfast."

Jill was climbing the stairs before she replied, "Go ahead."

I was walking to the Isuzu when I saw Charlie returning from his morning run.

He was dripping sweat and stopped at my fender, breathless. "I heard the Coast Guard relayed our message about the boat you were looking for."

"The message arrived, we shadowed the boat and caught them loading up at the county park. Thanks."

"But they weren't who you thought they were?"

"They were treasure-hunters, but not the murderers."

Charlie smiled. "I read the newspaper headlines before I ran. Interviewing them broke the case, and you personally nailed the murderer."

"There were a lot of people involved. I got more credit than I deserved."

Charlie put his hand on my arm and squeezed my bicep. "I think you're a better cop than you let on. I'm glad we met."

"Are you going somewhere?"

"I'm flying off the Ronald Reagan when it comes into Norfolk. Clarice will stay here with the boys and pack up the house, but she'll be

301

moving to Virginia as soon as I can find quarters for us."

I shook his hand. "Good luck."

Charlie was beaming. "I've always dreamt of being a fighter pilot. You can't imagine what it feels like when you light the afterburners and pull back the stick."

"Clarice sounds less enthusiastic about your career than you do."

"It's not easy being a Navy wife. She's tougher than she seems, and there's a whole contingent of officer's wives who support each other when the fleet is out."

"Good luck."

I was halfway down the street when I saw a Park Service pickup coming toward me. The pickup's headlights flashed, and I pulled over while Matt made a U-turn and pulled in behind me.

"What's up?"

"The shit hit the fan this morning. I've been on the phone since five o'clock."

"Who called?"

"First it was the FBI Special Agent in Charge, who chewed my butt for stepping on their investigation. Then, it was the chief of the CCPD thanking me for sharing credit with them and making the FBI look like glory hounds."

"That sounds like it's pretty balanced."

"Yeah, except we're Feds, and the FBI is supposed to have jurisdiction for crimes on Park Service property."

"Ah, that's true unless they decline to pursue the investigation. In that case, we can take the lead, or we can use local police resources, which is what happened in this case."

"The SAC thinks we skipped the step about asking for their assistance. They think we went right to the CCPD and used their forensic people for the murder investigation."

I leaned my head back. "I imagine they don't have a record of our call in their logs, and they're going to play politics to make someone squirm."

"It's too late for that. The FBI is jumping in and is taking over the investigation. The third call was from the federal prosecutor, who informed me your witness recanted his story when they brought in his lawyer. He says you promised to get him off if he turned in his partner, and said the prosecutor never agreed to a plea agreement."

"Someone in the Department of Justice is twisting Jane Pruett's arm."

"I have no way of knowing what's going on in the DOJ. All I know is that the FBI has announced their investigation into the Padre Island murder, and they're threatening to make us look like a bunch of idiots."

"Don't sweat it, Matt. The newspaper has all the information, and CCPD has a tape of the interview. They can squawk all they want, but CCPD has all the evidence, the interviews, and the newspaper and wire services have the story. There's going to be unbearable pressure on the FBI, and in the end, the federal prosecutor isn't going to let a murderer go free to make the FBI feel better."

Matt leaned against the pickup fender. "You're sure?"

"I'm sure. I'm going to pick up Al and have breakfast. Do you want to join us?"

"Mandy was a little green around the gills this morning after another night of margaritas, so all I've had is a cup of coffee. Sure, let's go to Art's Café and have some grits and red-eye gravy."

"If it's all the same to you, I think I'll stick with eggs and hash browns. I've never developed a taste for grits."

"You pick up Al. I'll get in line for a table. Art's gets a little busy Saturday mornings."

I knocked on the motel room door, and it opened almost immediately. Al was dressed in a western-cut shirt and jeans. He grabbed his Stetson and slipped out the door.

"Molly's not up?"

He shook his head. "I think she just fell asleep. I think she had an extra Margarita. She's not used to drinking, and she tried to keep up with Mandy, Jill, and Ronnie."

"It's Mandy they were trying to keep up with. Ronnie spent a lot of the night in the bathroom, and Jill made me sip tea with her until the room stopped spinning."

"You got a good breakfast spot?" Al asked as he got in the Isuzu.

"Matt's getting a table for us at Art's Café. It's a mom and pop place that reopened a couple weeks ago."

"What's with this hurricane stuff anyway? I remember hearing about Hurricane Harvey hitting Houston and all the damage there. I didn't realize there was much damage this far south."

"Harvey crossed over the coast just north of here, went inland a bit, and then came back across before turning north and hitting Houston. Mandy Mattson told me the reason no one heard about the devastation here is because the whole area got leveled. Rockport is where the eye crossed over, and it was virtually scrubbed bare. The town was gone: No newspaper. No radio. No apartment buildings. No Condos. No hotels. Everything was smashed and blown away. It's been two years, and they think it'll be mostly rebuilt in another three to five years."

Al looked at me. "That sounds like a Midwest tornado hit it."

"Think of a hundred-mile wide tornado hanging around for three days."

Al digested that as we drove past houses, businesses, and motels that were interspersed with empty lots. "I can't get my head around that much destruction. Where's FEMA?"

"They were here and assessed the damage. Then cut some checks and leaned on the insurance companies, but they're not equipped to hang around for four of five years to work through the recovery. I'm sure they've got a few people here in a trailer who are helping out, but

305

when whole towns are gone, they're overwhelmed too."

"I suppose once the news helicopters are gone, the Feds lose interest and move on."

I found an empty parking space a half-block from Art's and pulled in. Matt was at the counter, holding a couple stools for us. The rest of the café was filled, mostly with construction workers, who knew they could get a good meal at a reasonable price.

Al and I were sitting down when my phone chimed. Thinking it might be Jill, I told them to order for me and stepped outside.

"Fletcher," I said without checking the caller ID.

"We've stepped in it this time." I recognized Scott Dixon's voice.

"I heard the FBI didn't like your characterization of their role in the woman's murder."

"Yeah, we really poked the hornet's nest. The chief, the mayor, and a Congressman have all come through here, asking questions and shaking their heads."

"So, what's happening?"

"The FBI guy said they're through with us. He thought he was pretty smug, then the chief asked him if that was a promise, and if we could move into their offices when they left. Holy Hannah, did they start shouting then! The mayor heard the commotion and walked into the chief's office and got an earful, along with an order to fire the chief. Hoo-boy, did the mayor get hot then. He told the FBI guy to haul his ass out of the building and expect a call from the mayor's personal friend, Congressman Stanton. The FBI guy shut up, then said he ran his own shop, and he reported to the Department of Justice, not Congress. The mayor picked up the phone, dialed Stanton and asked him if he'd read the newspaper about the FBI stepping on their peckers while his department and the Park Service did their jobs for them. Then, he handed the phone to the FBI guy. I could hear Stanton yelling from my cubicle outside the chief's office. In the end, the FBI guy said, 'Yes, Congressman. I understand your concern, and we certainly won't stand in the way of the local police, who are doing a fine job.'"

"You listened in to all this, Scott?"

"Hell, yes! Half the floor heard it because the chief's door was open, and they were all yelling and swearing at each other. People started coming in from other areas and my cubicle was jammed with vice guys from one floor up by the time the FBI left."

"What's the final verdict?"

"Congressman Stanton is calling the director of the FBI and requesting they assign a competent Special Agent in Charge to the Corpus Christi office. I don't know if he's got enough clout to make that happen, but I suspect the FBI guy's career is going to take a hit."

"Wow. And what's happening to you?"

"The chief said he threw the FBI a bone, and I'm turning over all the evidence and files I've got about the silver coins that were stolen out of your boss's office. Our good buddy, Special Agent Mark Jones, just picked up all my files and the evidence, and I think he's on a personal mission to solve that burglary, so he can make you guys look stupid and maybe redeem himself and the FBI."

"Thanks for the warning. I'll check in after my honeymoon."

"Oh, shit. I forgot you're getting married soon. When's the big day?"

"Monday. As a matter of fact, my boss and future father-in-law are sitting inside, waiting for me to eat breakfast with them. I've got to run."

"Hey, good luck and the best of wishes. I'll text you or something if things start to heat up."

There were fried eggs, pancakes, hash browns, and grits sitting in front of my stool. I looked at Matt. "What's all this?"

Matt was grinning. "You said to order for you, and I wasn't sure what you wanted." Al just shook his head and sliced off some of his breakfast steak.

"I didn't get steak?" I asked as I sat on the stool and surveyed the banquet in front of me.

Al smiled. "We ordered it rare, and they didn't want to cook it until you came back."

I pushed the grits in front of Matt. "These are yours."

"I already ate a bowl of grits."

"Eat another," I said as a plate with a breakfast steak arrived.

The waitress looked at the plates already in front of me and realized there was no place to set the steak down. She was matronly and looked like she'd waited a lot of tables. She stuck out her hip and looked at me. "Honey, you better get eating, or I'm going to have to hold this here steak all morning."

I took the plate from her and slid the steak on top of the eggs. "Here you go. By the way, the guy wearing the Park Service uniform is paying the tab."

She looked at Matt, and he laughed. "Sure. It's on me."

Al leaned over and asked, "Was that call Jill and Molly looking for us?"

"I think they're still recovering. That was my friend, the detective from the Corpus Christi police."

"Matt said you were mentioned in a newspaper article today."

I glanced at Matt, who gave me a "so what" gesture.

"They interviewed the CCPD detective about a joint investigation we'd been on."

Al pushed his plate away, and the waitress topped off our coffee. "I hear you stepped out of the limelight again."

"I was part of a big team, and all I did was my job."

Al signaled to a guy on the other side of Matt, who was reading the sports page while drinking coffee. "Can I look at the front page?"

The paper came down, and Al folded it so Scott's picture was front and center. "This is your friend?"

"Yup." I left it at that while Al read the article, refolding the paper to get at the inside portion.

He finished and passed the newspaper back and tapped the article. "My future son-in-law solved that murder yesterday."

The man smiled and nodded at me.

Al sat down and pushed his dirty plates away. "You didn't say anything or celebrate?"

I piled the remnants of breakfast onto one plate and stacked the rest. "I guess getting closure on murder isn't something I can celebrate. Scott had to tell some poor woman's grieving parents that we knew who'd killed her and that we were going to take him to trial for the crime. That's terrible news to give to anyone. I'm proud we were able to close the case, but my heart is broken for her parents."

Al picked up his coffee and took a sip, then signaled for a refill. "I guess I've never thought of it that way." After our coffees were refilled, he held up his cup and tipped it toward me.

"What's that for?" I asked.

"That's for having character and knowing what's important."

"And what's important?" I asked.

"A grieving parent is a lot more important than dancing on a murderer's grave."

I nodded.

Matt paid the bill, and I left a $10 tip that made our waitress smile. Al and I were walking to the Isuzu when Matt pulled me aside. "What did Dixon want?"

"His chief and the mayor took on the FBI SAC. The mayor called a Congressman who threatened to have the SAC removed. Scott warned me that the FBI was now determined to solve the burglary from your file cabinet and make us look like idiots."

"When does it end?" Matt asked.

"When we roll over and let them walk all over us, or never. They are political. If we get in the way, they're going to push back."

"What should we do?"

Al realized that we had broken away, and he walked back to us. I took a step closer to him and said, "I'm marrying Al's daughter on Monday, and I'm not doing a damned thing until after the honeymoon."

Al smiled. "You've finally got your priorities straight. Let's go roust the women out of bed and do some more sightseeing. I've never been around here before."

Chapter Thirty

Molly was in the bathroom when Al unlocked the door. I waited outside the motel room while he found out if she was ready.

I called Jill's cellphone, and she sounded more chipper than I expected. "Your dad is checking on your mom, then he'd like to go sightseeing. How are you and Ronnie?"

"I'm tired, but I ate a piece of toast and had a cup of coffee. Ronnie is . . . hungover and in pain. She took a couple Tylenol, and now she's in the shower. We should be ready to do something in fifteen or twenty minutes as long as there's no food or alcohol involved."

I texted Scott Dixon, asking for an update. I didn't expect an immediate response but thought he might get back to me Monday morning before the wedding service. I'd hardly touched "send" when the icon told me he was typing, then my phone rang.

"Damned texting takes forever. The internet surveillance guys were told to stand down on the coin search. They did, to a degree, but continued to monitor online auctions, eBay, Craig's list, treasure-hunter sites, local pawnshops, and a few other places. The bottom line is that the market is flooded with Spanish silver coins. They're being bought up by collectors, and the bidding is slowing down a bit because there's a sudden glut, so that helps because the postings stay up longer."

"What's that mean for finding the coins from Matt's office?"

"You had some clumps of coins, and they're less common and more expensive, plus Matt had pictures taken from many sides. They thought they had it."

"*Thought* they had it?" I asked.

"Yeah, on Craig's list. There was a post with a phone number and address. The robbery guys cruised the address with an unmarked car, but it was an empty lot. The internet surveillance guys traced the phone number in the ad, and it's a throw-away phone the crooks bought from a local electronics superstore. These guys are not quite as dumb as the average crooks we arrest.

"A guy used that phone to call a pawnshop and tried to get someone from the store to meet him in the parking lot so he could show him the goods out of sight of the surveillance cameras, but the pawnshop owner refused, and told him it was because the caller's number was blocked. The store owner told him to call back after unblocking his number or using a phone with an unblocked number. Then the pawnshop called our burglary guys. They're sitting on the pawnshop, but the seller never called back."

"Thanks, Scott. Keep me posted if anything breaks."

Al opened the motel room door, and Molly stepped out, shielding her eyes. She ambled to their pickup, and Al walked over to the Isuzu as I hung up on Scott after asking for him to keep me posted.

"We'll follow you over to the townhouse. I think we might all fit in the crew cab and can go wherever Jill has planned."

I called Jill to warn her we were on the way.

Mom and Jill were standing on the steps when I pulled into the driveway. Neither looked chipper, but they were showered and dressed. Mom sipped from a thermal cup as she walked to the Isuzu. Al pulled up as I got out of the Rodeo and pulled the Sig from under the seat.

Jill pecked my cheek. "I'm never drinking another Margarita," she whispered.

"Al said we will all fit into the crew cab of his pickup."

Mom walked to the passenger door and talked to Molly. The short conversation moved Molly to the back seat and Mom up front. "I wonder what that's about?"

Ronnie is still queasy and needs to ride in the front seat, so she doesn't get car sick. She's sipping a tumbler of sweet tea to settle her stomach and get some calories into her."

"Hmm. Okay, where are we going?"

"The Indochino Mall has a couple stores that sell men's suits."

"I thought we were going sightseeing, "I protested.

"We've got lots of time to sightsee after we find suits for Daddy and you."

When I didn't respond quickly with excitement, Jill leaned close. "You promised to get a suit, and we're getting a little tight on time."

"Yeah, I get it."

I attached the Sig holster to my side waistband and untucked my shirt to conceal it.

Jill sat in the middle in the back. I put my arm around her shoulder, but she jerked away, "Your gun is sticking me in the ribs."

The mall was busy, but the men's suit store was quiet. A dapper young man came from behind the counter like a coyote ready to grab fresh meat. "How can I help you gentlemen, today?"

Jill followed us into the store and urged us ahead. "My father and fiancé need dark suits for a Monday wedding."

The salesman's smile faded. "Monday? We can't get alterations made that quickly."

"Then find them the best off-the-rack fit you can, and we'll call it good," she said.

"We pride ourselves in tailoring our suits for an excellent fit."

Jill gave him a withering glare. "What's the name of the other suit store in the mall? Maybe they're more interested in making a sale."

"Wait! We have some suits, and these gentlemen look like they might be able to wear something with our common inseam lengths and chest measurements."

Al was looking through the suitcoats on the closest rack. "None of these are Western cut."

The young man perked up. "Come with me to the rack over near the wall. Those are Western cut, and the pants are also boot cut."

We watched Al wander to the far side of the store with the salesman. "Honey, I don't see this going well."

Jill watched Al try on a suitcoat, the salesman adjusting his shoulders and checking the sleeve length. "Doug, make it work. I don't know quite what the holdup might be, but make it work."

"I'll try on some suitcoats on, but what if . . ."

"I'm buying a two-thousand-dollar wedding gown. The seamstress had to take in the bust and tighten up the butt to fit my figure. It's lovely, and it makes me feel girly and pretty. Please make an attempt to find something that'll make you look nice. You don't have to look like Prince Charming, but I'd really, really like to have a wedding picture I can hang on the wall that we can be proud of. Okay?"

"I'm not an off-the-rack size."

"You bought a Park Service dress uniform from a website that makes you look like a recruiting poster. I know you can find a suit that'll do the same thing."

"Maybe I could wear the Park Service uniform."

"Suck it up, Buttercup. You're buying a suit today. If not here, then the next store or the one after that."

"I hate shopping for clothes."

"Then pick something out here and put yourself out of your misery." She turned to leave.

"What are you girls doing?"

"We're buying dresses for mothers of the bride and groom."

"I thought we were going to do something fun today."

Jill smiled. "We are having fun."

"Shit," I said as a second salesman came out of the backroom.

"How can I help?" the thirty-something man asked.

"I need a dark suit."

"Western or English cut?"

"I don't even know what that means."

"Let's start over here . . ."

I was trying on coats when Al came out of a dressing room in a dark brown suit. He was smiling as he stood in front of the mirror. He noticed me watching. "What do you think?"

"You look nice. The pants are long."

The salesman appeared with what appeared to be a piece of soap, and he marked the cuffs.

"Excuse me. These are for a Monday afternoon wedding. Is there time to get them hemmed?"

"The seamstress is here at ten Monday morning. If I put these on top of the pile, he should have them hemmed and pressed by noon."

317

"Can you get him in today?"

"He doesn't work Saturdays."

I pulled out my wallet and unfolded the hundred-dollar bill I had shown to Captain Billy. "Do you have his phone number?" I flashed the corner of the hundred.

"I'm sorry, but Monday is the earliest."

"How much is the suit my father-in-law is wearing?"

The salesman reached for the tag on the cuff. "And how about the dark gray one over here? I kind of like it."

Al piped in. "I'd like to get a pair of nice boots. These shit-kickers are made for the barn."

Al's salesman was apparently the manager because he stepped over to me. "Sir, that's not how we do business."

"Is there another customer in the store?"

The manager glanced around.

"It's quiet right at the moment. If we left, you and your right-hand man could go back to your card game, or whatever you were doing when we came in. You'd miss out on the commission from the sale of two suits and a pair of boots. Personally, I don't give a shit where we buy our suits, but we're buying two suits and a pair of boots today and taking them home when we leave. You either figure out how to make that happen, or we'll find someone who will."

The manager stared at me, then glanced at the hundred-dollar bill. "I can make that happen, but you'd better have a VISA card with more than a hundred dollars on it."

I took out an American Express platinum card and laid it on the counter next to the cash register. "I'll be happy to pay for your suit and service, but if you waste my time or mess with me, I'll have the CCPD police here talking to you about fraud." I slid back my shirttail so he could see my badge."

Al stepped in at exactly the right moment. "I see you sell Tony Llama boots. Do you have any in ostrich skin?"

I saw a flicker in the manager's eyes as he tallied the commission he would make. He picked up the AmEx card and tapped it on the counter. He looked at me seriously for a second. "I'll call someone who can hem the pants this afternoon, but I'll run your AmEx for at least three thousand dollars by the time you've got suits, pants, shirts, ties, and Tony Llama boots."

I nodded. "Make it happen."

One corner of Al's mouth curled into a smile that left as fast as it arose.

The manager pulled out his cellphone and hit a speed dial number. "Jake, I need to make some alterations this afternoon."

He listened for a few moments. "There are five hundred dollars in it for you."

He listened again. "Monday is too late. That's why I'm telling you, if you come in now, there's five hundred in cash."

"Fine. I'll call Bitsy." He closed the connection and was entering a number when his phone rang. "Changed your mind?"

I could hear the vague heated comments of the man on the other end and saw him glance at the outline of the gun on my hip and my badge. "I know Bitsy isn't as good. But I've got a man here wearing a gun and badge who's handed me a platinum card and told me he wants his suits this afternoon."

He glanced at my badge again as he listened. He put his hand over the mic, "You're federal?"

I nodded.

"Jake, stop whining. One of the guys is a federal cop, and he's got a big gun on his hip. Get your butt in here and hem his pants and alter the jacket, so his gun fits under it. I'll give you five hundred cash plus pay you overtime."

The manager listened for a few seconds, then disconnected. "Jake's a drama queen at times, but I know he's got nothing going on until after dark. He's on his way. Let's try on some suits and see how we can accommodate your gun."

I was in a suit jacket, the pants already measured for hemming. Mick, the manager, was making a few marks on a coat when Al wandered over and stepped on a chair. I looked at his boots. The leather looked like it had large pimples spread around the tops.

"Genuine ostrich. I always wanted a pair but thought they were too expensive. My only daughter is getting married, and I thought, *'What the hell, this is the only wedding you'll ever attend where you can walk Jill down the aisle. Buy the damned boots.'*"

We finished with our fittings and had two hours to kill while Jake worked his magic, so I found a food court in the mall and bought some designer coffee.

"I know that guy's got your plastic card, but there's no need for you to pay for my stuff."

"It'd be my honor to buy your wedding suit, Dad."

Al nodded and ate his burger with a smile.

Chapter Thirty-One

We had the pickup topper filled with boxes, and the ladies were chattering again. Al drove while I navigated to the Corpus Christi Aquarium and the aircraft carrier. We turned and drove down the short road to the USS Lexington. At first, we only got a snippet of the ship, but as we got closer, it grew in size until we saw the immensity of the carrier.

The ladies went to the aquarium. Al and I walked down the block and went on a tour of the ship.

"I thought The Lexington sunk in the battle of the Coral Sea?"

"It did, but this was built and named for the original Lexington. This is a museum, but it's also a commissioned Naval vessel, and it can be deployed as required."

Al stood at one end of the flight deck and looked at the planes arranged on the deck.

"This looks big, but when you think about landing a plane on it, there's hardly a postage stamp of deck to land on in a big ocean."

My phone chimed, and I excused myself. Scott Dixon sounded excited.

"We've got a buy. The female cop on the burglary squad found an obscure website, and she contacted a guy who's going to sell her a clump of silver coins. The seller sent her a picture and it matches one your boss took. The guy's meeting her in front of the hobby store across the highway from the La Palmera Mall. We're meeting in our personal vehicles behind the IHOP across the highway to make plans for the bust."

"Are Rachel and I invited?"

"You're welcome to watch, but I've got a tactical team who are making the arrest after the sellers exit the parking lot. I've got another team ready to surround the seller's house until we can get a warrant once we identify them. Our buy is at eight tonight after the store closes. We're going to meet at seven."

"I'll call Rachel."

Al waited patiently behind an A-6 plane, talking with an older guy wearing a cap with a Marine Corps logo. I joined them, and Al introduced me to Roger Amundson, a WWII vet who lived in Corpus Christi and was showing Al around the deck.

"Roger had been a Marine guard on the original Lexington."

"Thanks for your service," I said, humbled by the experience the old man had lived through.

"You look like you might've been a vet," he said, looking at my haircut, and the way I carried myself.

"I was in Iraq with a Minnesota National Guard MP unit. Pretty quiet duty compared to what you went through."

Roger shook his head. "No one gets out of a battle without some scars."

I nodded my understanding. "Al, were you in the service?" Jill hadn't mentioned much about her parents other than life on the ranch while she was growing up.

"I was a teen between Korea and Viet Nam. There wasn't a draft, and I didn't volunteer because we needed everyone in a saddle to work the ranch. I was riding and knew how to repair barbed wire when I was eight." Al paused. "My father was a Marine in the South Pacific. He was on shore when the Navy pulled out of Guadalcanal, before they'd unloaded all their supplies and was wounded in a Banzai attack. He spent a year healing before they put him ashore on Iwo Jima, where he got his second purple heart."

"Wow," I said.

Al nodded. "Dad didn't abide anything Japanese on the ranch. If he couldn't find something made in the USA, we did without." I thought about my Isuzu Rodeo and wondered if it was part of the initial tension between us, even though the windshield sticker said it had been assembled in an Indiana GM plant.

Roger ended our discussion by announcing he needed to sit down. Al and I walked him to a row of folding chairs near the ramp to the pier.

"Was that Jill trying to track us down?"

"No, it was my friend asking if I could get away for a couple hours tonight."

"Scott wants you to go out for a toot?"

"It was Scott, but he's got a police issue tonight."

"You're helping?"

I shook my head. "My partner and I are invited to observe. We've been part of the investigation, and he's being polite and letting us be on the scene for the closure."

Al considered that while I called Jill. She'd found a little café around the corner from the aquarium, and we agreed to meet there.

It was the end of the lunch rush when we were seated. The ladies chose soup. I ordered a Rueben sandwich, and Al had a burger and fries. Al leaned close as the ladies ate soup and chattered at the other end of the table. "I'm amazed you've got room for a sandwich after that breakfast Matt ordered."

"It's an Army thing. Eat when you can. Sleep when you can. Use the latrine when you can."

"The ranch is like that when we're branding or shipping. The cattle are unpredictable. You've got to work them when you can, and you've got to keep an eye on them all the time."

"It's got to be a real logistics mess."

"It's a community get together. We all help each other out. The men work the cattle, and the women cook and serve. It's a bigger feed than Thanksgiving or Christmas. You'll have to come back in the spring when we're branding."

"Will I have to ride a horse?"

Al considered that for a bit. "Some of the young guys work the cattle with those ATVs. It takes something away from the experience, but I guess it's the future."

I excused myself and called Rachel. "Scott Dixon invited us to watch them arrest the guys who're trying to sell a clump of silver coins. We're meeting at seven tonight behind the IHOP by the Palmera Mall. I can pick you up at Matt's."

"Ron got the call half-an-hour ago. He's part of the regional SWAT team, and they're going to make the arrest. You can pick me up. Ron has to meet at the public safety building to get into his tactical gear, and he'll be riding down in the CCPD BearCat."

"I'll pick you up at six-thirty. And bring your vest."

"We're observers. The SWAT guys are making the arrest."

"Do you remember what I said about pistols and vests?"

"You don't need them until you need them badly and immediately." She paused. "I told Matt I was going. He wasn't excited about me being there, but I told him it was the payoff for the investigation."

"I'll pick you up tonight."

* * *

Jill navigated us around Corpus Christi, showing her parents much of the town for an hour in the afternoon. We went back to the townhouse and were discussing a light supper when I announced that I had to pick up Rachel for our police action. I put on my casual uniform, and when I came downstairs, Al followed me to the front closet.

"Any chance I could ride along?"

"Not when there's a chance there might be some violence. You're welcome to ride along with Rachel and me next week when we drive the beach."

"I thought it'd be interesting to see the fireworks tonight." He looked over his shoulder. "The estrogen levels get kind of high around here when it's just the women and me."

"I won't be late."

Al laughed. "You don't know how long an evening this could be for me."

Rachel was waiting in the driveway when I arrived at Matt's. She climbed into the Isuzu and frowned. "You're not driving the Park Service pickup?"

"Scott said they're going in their personal vehicles to minimize the chance of spooking the bad guys."

Matt stepped out and knocked on my window. "What's up, Matt?"

"You guys are just observing, right?"

"That's what Scott told me."

He leaned on the door. "I want you to be careful. This is a CCPD and sheriff's department

327

operation. You guys hang back. I had a call from the chief, and he said they're going in with heavy weapons and body armor. You're not equipped for what's going to happen. If you can't stay clear of the action, you're staying here and waiting for the blow-by-blow and after-action recap. Understood?"

We both nodded. Matt patted the top of the Isuzu. "Be safe."

* * *

There were six vehicles behind the IHOP, with seven cops standing around the hood of a pickup where Scott spread a crude drawing of the hobby store parking lot and the access roads.

"Linda and Kerry are going in for the buy. There's five thousand in the duffle bag with a tracking device. The BearCat is in an alley two blocks behind the store. When Linda says the deal is closed, the BearCat moves, and we tell them to go east or west, depending on which way the bad guys pull out. If the deal started to go south either Linda or Kerry will say, 'Whiskey,' and everyone moves in. Got it?"

"What're we going to do for the next half-hour?" One of the guys in the back asked.

"We're in front of an IHOP, Scott's buying coffee for everyone." That brought chuckles from everyone.

"Linda and Kerry are going in early. The rest of us will hang back."

I tapped Scott on the shoulder. "How about Rachel and I going inside the hobby store?"

"The store closed at six, and there won't be anyone inside except the manager and the night stocking crew."

"Do you have the manager's phone number? We could go in the back door and be inside just in case you need to backstop that escape route."

Scott looked at me. "The armored BearCat is taking them after they leave the parking lot. There's no need."

"It's a better vantage point," I argued. "We're not going to see anything from behind you guys."

Scott pulled out his cellphone and punched in a number. He talked briefly to the manager and shut the phone down. "The manager is actually relieved we'll have someone inside the store. They were feeling a little naked." He gave Rachel a handheld radio. "You can monitor the activity."

I looped down two exits past the hobby store and drove side streets to the store's back door. We carried the vests in a shopping bag, although our uniforms made us look more like cops than the cleaning crew if anyone had been paying attention. The manager, a thirty-something guy with thinning brown hair, opened the door nervously.

"I'm really glad you guys are in here. I agreed to let the cops use our parking lot before I thought about the crew that's here stocking shelves."

"Take us up to the front of the store and help us find a place where we will be concealed but can watch the lot."

The manager put me behind a display of woodworking supplies, and Rachel sat in a chair behind a cash register. We put on our light bullet-proof vests and were concealed except for our eyes and the tops of our heads. The manager moved his crew into the warehouse in the rear of the store.

We'd been deployed for five minutes when someone announced that it was eight, and there was no sign of the sellers. A minute later, a battered pickup pulled into the parking lot tentatively. Linda and Kerry were in a faded blue Camry parked in the center of the lot, so there was little question about which vehicle held the buyers. After a minute's hesitation, the pickup rolled slowly toward the Camry.

"These guys are really timid," Linda said. "I feel like they're going to rabbit at any time. You guys ready for a chase?"

I heard several radio mics click, indicating the team had received the transmission.

The pickup finally approached the Camry more quickly, and it came to a stop behind the Camry's trunk. Two men climbed out of the truck, looking around nervously.

"What nationality are the Park Service cleaning crew?" I whispered to Rachel.

"I think they're Haitian."

"Think these guys might be sons or brothers?"

"I don't know."

Linda and Kerry were out of the Camry talking with the two men. I couldn't hear the discussion but assumed they were deciding who showed first. One of the guys threw a tarp back from the pickup bed and lifted out a 5-gallon pail with some difficulty. Kerry got the small duffle bag out of the Camry when someone shouted over the radio, "What the hell?"

A dark car bristling with antennae came flying into the parking lot. It's red and blue flashers came on as it jumped the curb and raced forward. The guy with the bucket threw it into the pickup bed, and the other guy pulled a gun. He shot twice at Linda and Kerry, who ducked behind the Camry, then he fired several more shots at the oncoming car before he jumped into the pickup driver's seat.

"Whiskey! Whiskey! Whiskey!" Linda shouted into the radio. "Shots fired!"

"Who the hell is that?" Scott shouted over the radio.

Then there were voices talking over each other, a call for an ambulance, and I watched the dark car try to cut off the pickup. The driver in the pickup fired a couple shots at the dark car. The passenger started firing at Linda and Kerry.

The sedan rammed the rear of the pickup, and it lurched ahead as it was just starting to gain speed. The pickup driver cranked the steering wheel to the right, trying to place the Camry between him and the dark car.

Flashing lights came from every direction, and the BearCat raced in from the east. The pickup driver panicked and drove straight toward the front of the store, the only direction free of converging police vehicles.

"Get back!" I yelled at Rachel as I pulled my Sig and backed down an aisle away from the glass storefront. A second later, the glass exploded, and the pickup burst into the store, coming to a stop when it hit the row of cash registers.

I lost track of Rachel when I'd moved and realized the last place I'd seen her was now under the hood of the pickup.

The driver pushed his door open. He was obviously dazed but managed to step out and point some sort of short-barrelled machine pistol at the parking lot. It sounded like he was ripping cloth when the gun went off, and the muzzle flash didn't look like individual shots firing, but a tongue of fire spouted from the barrel for seconds.

I shouted, "Police!" But couldn't even hear myself over the gunfire. I pointed the Sig at the center of the shooter's chest and fired five shots before the shooter wavered. The muzzle went up, and the driver crumpled, and bullets ripped across the ceiling before the gun ran out of shells or the shooter's finger released from the trigger.

My ears were ringing, and I was still focused on the driver when I realized shots were coming from the other side of the vehicle, just before another ripping sound started. This time the muzzle flash wandered around the other side of the pickup into the store. I put my sights on the second shooter's head, the only part of him visible through the windshield, and I fired until the Sig was empty. I ejected the magazine, slapped another in and realized that the shooting had stopped. With the Sig pointed at the pickup, I slid out from behind the shelves and eased ahead until I kicked the machine pistol away from the driver's hand.

"Rachel!"

"What?"

"Where are you?"

I heard the police radio, now with discipline. "Dispatch, we need EMS at our location. Multiple gunshot victims. Officers down."

My heart sank. Somebody had screwed up big time.

"Doug, are you okay?"

"I'm good. You?"

Rachel walked around the front of the pickup with her Sig pointed at the passenger. The BearCat screeched to a stop, blocking the rear of the pickup, and black-clad cops in helmets and body armor poured out the doors.

"Clear! Clear!" I yelled. The SWAT team had great weapon control despite the tense situation. They trained their weapons back and forth, looking for bad guys, keeping their fingers outside the trigger guards of their weapons. No one came close to pointing their weapon at Rachel or me.

Dixon ran through the storefront, his shoes crunching broken glass. "Fletcher! Where the hell are you?"

"Rachel and I are here, in front of the pickup."

Scott raced to us as the SWAT guys checked the driver and passenger. I'd hit the driver five times in the chest, and I knew he wasn't alive. I edged around the pickup fender and saw six red splotches spreading on the passenger's white t-shirt. Rachel had done well. One of my shots hit the passenger in the back of the head, eradicating the top of his forehead.

Rachel held the Sig in her left hand. Scott approached her slowly.

"Randall, holster your weapon." She looked surprised to see the Sig in her left hand. She flicked the safety but struggled to shift it to her right hand, and finally twisted her left hand around and stuck the Sig in the holster on her right hip.

I'd holstered my Sig. "Who was in the dark car?"

"I don't know. It wasn't any of my people."

I saw the blood on Rachels right sleeve and dripping from her fingertips.

Oh, God, No! I stepped to her side and steadied her. "Scott, I need an EMT, now!"

Scott saw the blood and keyed his radio as Rachel's legs turned to rubber and I helped her gently to the floor. "Officer down inside the store!"

Chapter Thirty-Two

I sat in the Corpus Christi public safety building without a cellphone or weapon. Three different detectives had interviewed me, and I asked each of them to call Jill to let her know Rachel had been wounded and I was okay but would be late. None of them assured me that would happen.

Scott Dixon walked into the cubicle with a cup of coffee and a doughnut. "You probably need a fresh jolt of caffeine and sugar."

"Thanks. Has anyone told Jill I'm alive?"

"I called Matt. He knows you're okay, and he said someone named Mandy is at your house."

"She's Matt's wife." I paused. "Matt's not there?"

"Matt's at the hospital with Rachel," Scott said softly.

"How bad…"

"She was behind the cash registers when the pickup crashed through. She's got a broken arm and maybe a concussion."

"But she was shooting."

"She was shooting lefthanded. She got several rounds into the passenger before your bullet hit him in the head."

I thought back to Rachel's struggle to holster her gun with her left hand, and her bloodied right arm. I felt ill. "She's okay?"

"Like I said, she has a broken arm, lots of bruises, and a possible concussion."

"Back to my original question, who was the idiot in the dark car who didn't get the message about the stealth takedown?"

"FBI Special Agent Mark Jones and his partner, Special Agent Cal Dufresne."

"What? Where'd they come from?"

"It appears they were monitoring our frequencies and decided they weren't going to let us steal another arrest from them."

"They admitted that?"

Scott shook his head. I had a sudden memory of radio calls for EMS and reports of officers down. "They were hit?"

"Dufresne is banged up. Jones has multiple gunshot wounds and is still in surgery. They called in Mark's family and minister."

"Aw shit."

Scott nodded. "They're going to have a hell of a time spinning this one to make themselves look good. There were news vans there before we could cover the bodies."

"Are Linda and Kerry okay?"

"They're fine. They took cover behind the Camry. They're shaken up, but uninjured. I doubt either of them will volunteer to make an undercover buy anytime soon."

"Who were the sellers?"

"They were local gang members."

"They're the ones who took the coins?"

Dixon shook his head. "No, we think they were fences. Our forensic guys got the license plate number off the Nissan that raced past the entrance shack. It belongs to a college kid, who has a juvenile burglary record. He lawyered up, but he let it slip that he heard about the coins at a poker game. He'd camped at your park during spring break, so he knew how little night security you have and decided there wasn't much risk of getting caught."

"He heard about it at a poker game?"

"It's convoluted. We monitor the phone calls made from jail. Only one of your beachcombers called a lawyer. One of the others called a buddy, who went to a poker party, and slipped the information about the coins you seized to the guy who broke into Matt's office. He didn't know what to do with the coins with the 'experts' still in jail. He tried to pawn the coins, got cold feet when the pawnbroker started asking questions, and eventually fenced them to the gang members who showed up at our buy."

"You connected all those dots?"

"The guy who got the call from the jail cut a deal with the prosecutor. We can nail the original caller, and the guy who broke into Matt's office."

"You guys did good work. Thanks."

Dixon smiled. "Sometimes, the pieces come together. Sometimes, we just get lucky."

"Who else was interviewed by the shooting investigators?"

337

"Only you and Rachel discharged your weapons."

I shook my head. "I had writer's cramp after the last time I discharged my pistol at the canal."

"You never hit the guy in the boat. This time you took down two shooters. There'll be a ream of paper going to the county attorney. He'll have to review it and make a public statement. You guys will be okay."

I heard determined footsteps coming down the hallway. Scott peeked over the cubicle wall and stood up, looking toward the oncoming person. A slender, florid faced man stepped into the cubicle. His graying hair looked like he'd been pulled out of bed.

He looked at Scott. "Is this Fletcher?"

I stood. "Doug Fletcher. You are?"

"I'm the CCPD chief."

I had no idea what to expect from the chief, so I sat down and took a bite of the doughnut.

"I just spoke with my detectives, Fletcher. I hate to think what might've happened if you and your partner hadn't been inside the hobby store. We could still be sitting outside the store with hostage negotiators…or worse."

The chief stuck out his hand. I wiped the doughnut crumbs off my hand, stood, and we shook hands. "If y'all ever consider leaving the Park Service, you come talk to me."

I shook my head. "I prefer the quieter life in the parks."

The chief handed me his business card. "We could use someone like you. Give me a call Monday."

"Doug's getting married Monday," Scott said.

The chief hesitated to see if Scott was kidding. Seeing Scott was serious, he said, "I hope you're buying him a nice present because he saved your bacon tonight."

I heard my phone ringtone as we sat down, and Scott pulled it out of his shirt pocket. "Sorry. I was supposed to give this back to you."

I fumbled to answer it before it rolled over to voicemail. "Fletcher."

"Where are you?" Jill sounded distressed.

"I'm in the CCPD having coffee and doughnuts with Scott Dixon."

"What? I'm worried sick, and you're drinking coffee and eating doughnuts with a cop? There's this invention called a cellphone. It works anywhere. All you have to do is take it out of your pocket, hit my speed dial number, and I answer it."

I handed the phone to Scott. "It's for you."

He took the phone, giving me a strange look. "This is Scott Dixon."

I could see he was getting the same lecture, but couldn't get a word in. Jill must've taken a breath because Scott stopped nodding and spoke. "He's been interviewed by our shooting investigation team, and he had to surrender his phone as part of our standard operating procedure. I'd just returned the phone to him when you called." He paused. "Yes, he was in a gunfight." He paused again. "Yes, really."

"Sure, I'll give it back to him in a second. But first, go to your computer and pull up the Corpus Christi newspaper website."

Scott handed me the phone and walked away. "Hi."

There was a delay before Jill responded. "I'm sorry I teed off on you, but I was worried."

"I should've called, but they didn't let me use a phone." That was true, but with all the adrenaline and questioning, calling home hadn't been on my mind. I needed to become a husband instead of the Lone Ranger.

"When are you coming home?"

"I think I'm free to go. I'm not sure where the Isuzu is right now." I struggled to get past the stress and missed sleep. "I suppose it might still be behind the hobby store. I'll see if I can get a ride, then I'll drive home."

Jill gasped. "Oh, God, I forgot to ask. Are you okay? Rachel's in the hospital."

"What's the situation?"

"Mandy's on her way. I don't have any details beyond that. Are you okay?"

"I'm just tired. I'll be there soon."

"Doug."

I rubbed my eyes and yawned. "Yeah."

"I love you."

The haze lifted, and I was glad I was alive. I was about to share the rest of my life with someone who cared. "I love you too."

"Hang on. Daddy found the newspaper website on my laptop. He's all smiles. I don't know what he's reading, but he just gave me a thumbs up. I take it you did something good."

I thought about the scene in the hobby shop, the dead guys, and the realization that my partner was in the hospital. "I hope I never fire my weapon again."

Chapter Thirty-Three

Mandy demanded that Jill and I go to church, followed by a meeting with the minister, which turned out to be a pre-marital counseling session. Ron Meland, Matt, and Mandy spent Sunday morning in the hospital waiting room while Rachel was in surgery and the recovery room. We joined the vigil mid-afternoon after she'd been taken from recovery to a surgical floor. We went in, two at a time, for short visits. Rachel was sleepy and mostly unaware of our presence.

The FBI special agent in charge had shown in the waiting room up late in the evening. He'd never met any of us but shook hands politely with everyone until he introduced himself to me. He quickly corralled Matt, and they had a heated conversation in the hallway.

Rachel fell asleep and the nurse told us all to go home and get some rest.

* * *

The phone rang early Monday morning while I was drinking coffee and working on the crossword puzzle that I hadn't had time for

Sunday. Mom and Jill were still in bed, and I scooped up the phone before it woke them.

"Fletcher."

"Hey, Doug. Jane Pruett."

"What can I do for the Assistant U.S. Attorney?"

"Can you meet me at the hospital in half-an-hour?"

I struggled to find a reason she'd want me at the hospital and came up blank. "Why the hospital?"

"Meet me in Rachel Randall's room. I don't want to discuss this topic on the phone."

"I'm getting married in a few hours."

"This won't take much time."

I left Jill a note and grabbed my keys.

* * *

Rachel was still on the surgical floor. Like I had on Sunday, I noticed the scent of flowers before I walked in the door, but Sunday's two floral arrangements had turned into a garden. Rachel looked up from her breakfast tray of grits and Jell-O. I was struck by how pale she still looked, but she smiled and raised her left hand to wave. Her right arm, recovering from surgery to repair the broken bones, was swaddled in gauze and supported by a sling. There were flowers on every flat surface. Ron Meland was in uniform, sitting next to the bed. He got up when I entered.

"Doug, I was hoping you'd come by again today." He put out his hand. "Thank you."

343

"For what?"

He glanced at Rachel. "For putting the bad guy down. If you hadn't hit him, I don't think Rachel would be here."

I nodded to my partner. "Rachel was defending herself admirably."

Rachel smiled and lifted her right arm. "Some training officer you are. You never told me I'd have to shoot left-handed to save my life. I was shooting, but I'm amazed I hit anything."

"You hit the bad guy."

"The leader of the shooting team was here earlier and had me sign the statement they'd taken in the emergency room. I hit the bad guy in his left hand, left leg, grazed his torso four times, ripped open his right pants pocket, and nicked his left ear. That's out of a full magazine. All the other shots missed."

I reflected on the man's body. He'd had bloodstains on his shirt, but none would've been fatal, or would've stopped him from reloading and killing Rachel, me, or others. My mouth went dry.

Meland hugged me, then stepped back. "That's from Rachel. She's not really ready to hug anyone right now." He pecked Rachel's cheek and shook my hand. "I'm on duty, so I've got to dash off."

I got misty, so I looked around the room to avoid Rachel's gaze. "Who sent all the flowers?"

"I haven't read all the cards, but I know the one on the windowsill is from Matt and Mandy. There are some from the CCPD, the county sheriff's department, my mom, and the FBI. The big one on the counter is from you and Jill."

I looked at the huge arrangement and took out the card. It said simply, "Jill and Doug." I knew nothing about it, but Jill knew how important it would be for me...us to show our support. I held back my tears and was saved from facing Rachel's gratitude by Jane Pruett.

Jane walked into the room with purpose. She stopped when she saw me putting the card back in the flowers, and then she looked at Rachel. "I'm Jane Pruett, the Assistant U.S. Attorney. You've had quite a week, young lady."

Jane was in dark slacks and an ivory blouse that I guessed was silk. She walked to the bedside and squeezed Rachel's left hand. "I'd like to talk to you for a bit if Doug would give us a moment alone."

I was happy to escape and walked into the hallway, closing the door behind me. Jane was with Rachel for almost ten minutes. I thought I heard crying through the door but couldn't decide if I was hallucinating or hearing sounds from down the hallway. Jane came out looking for me.

"I just talked to your partner, and I want to run something past you before I meet with the magistrate."

I froze. "What are we talking about?"

"Toby Sanderson. I've been negotiating with his public defender, and we've got a plea agreement. He's willing to plead guilty to Class D felony assault and accept the maximum sentence with no financial penalty if I drop the charges claiming great bodily harm. That would've made it a Class C felony and could've added another dozen years to the sentence if he'd been convicted. I wanted Rachel's okay before we meet with the magistrate."

"Rachel's okay with that?"

"She doesn't want to testify against Toby. I could show the jury the pictures and medical reports, but it's not as compelling without Rachel's testimony."

"I hate this kind of deal. He was using her for years, and then he beat her. He should be in jail until he's old and gray."

"He won't see the outside of prison until he's in his forties. His life is over. He'll never fill out a job application without telling them he's a federal felon. He won't ever own a gun. He won't ever vote. By the time he gets out technology will be different, and he won't be able to make a phone call without help."

I mulled her comments while staring at the ceiling. "If Rachel's okay with that, I won't stop you."

"There's one other matter."

"The FBI, I suppose."

"They're playing nice, for now, but you've got to quit stepping on their feet. They have long memories. They keep files on people and tap into them at inconvenient times."

"You think they'll try to torpedo my career?"

"They won't try to get you through the Park Service—you've got too much support at very high levels, but I don't think you should run for office."

"I've got no interest in being a politician."

"I understand, but you get my drift."

I looked Jane in the eye. "They've got some dirty laundry too, and I've got a couple people who know pieces of it. If something happens, they'll put the pieces together, and their dirty laundry will be flying."

Jane looked me in the eye. "Can I call you Doug?"

"Sure, that's my name."

"My name's Jane, and there aren't a lot of people I allow to call me that. Jane is reserved for my friends, and I'd like to consider you a friend."

"I don't trust a lot of lawyers."

She hesitated for a moment, then put out her hand. "Give me your cellphone." I unlocked it and handed it to her. She opened my contacts and entered her phone number. "That's my DOJ cell number. Please reserve it for emergencies."

I couldn't help but smile. "Good luck, Jane."

She shook my hand. "You're a good cop, Doug. You're too modest, but you get the job done, and you've got people who have your back. Good luck."

When I walked back into Rachel's room, her eyes were red from crying. I sat on the edge of her bed and swept some stray hair behind her ear. "Jane Pruett told me about the plea agreement."

Rachel's eyes filled with tears again, and I handed her the box of tissues from the nightstand.

"Toby treated you like shit, then he beat the hell out of you. He deserves more than he's getting."

Rachel nodded. "It's hard," she sniffled.

"I think Ron will help you through it."

Rachel nodded. "Toby and I were through. I just couldn't cut the cord. I never thought it would end this way."

I decided to change the subject. "We'll have to take you out to the firing range when you're back on duty. You'll have to qualify lefthanded."

She sniffled and smiled. "You should've thought of that *before* I had to shoot someone."

"So, it's my fault?"

She cracked a smile. "Damned right!"

A doctor walked in, carrying an iPad. He was oblivious to our conversation. "Looks like you get to go home tomorrow."

"Let me out of here, now. I'm fine."

"We'd like to keep you here another day for observation."

"I'm going to my partner's wedding this afternoon whether you release me or not."

The young resident studied the iPad and looked at the breakfast tray. "You've eaten and used the bathroom?"

"Yes, and I don't need to do either of them again in the hospital."

"I'll finish the paperwork in a minute, but you can get dressed and," he looked up, "maybe your dad can pick up your painkillers at the pharmacy."

Rachel shook her head. "Yeah, Dad, will you pick up my pain pills while I get dressed?"

The doctor handed me a prescription and walked out.

I looked at Rachel's bandaged arm. "Do you need help?"

Rachel pushed herself up and swung her legs over the side of the bed, trying to keep her legs covered by the hospital gown. "You are not helping me get dressed. Go pick up my pills."

"I'll get your clothes out of the closet." I found a plastic bag marked "patient belongings," and I was about to hand it to her. I saw her tan shirt on top of the clothing pile spattered with blood and other pink tissue. I realized how close Rachel had been to the shooter when I'd taken the killing shot, and it rattled me. I closed the bag. "I'll call Mandy and have her bring you some fresh clothes."

"Mandy can't get here before I'm discharged. I can wear my uniform."

I pulled out the shirt and threw it in the wastebasket. "The EMTs had to cut you out of it." I unbuttoned my shirt, pulled it off, exposing my t-shirt, badge, and the gun on my hip. I handed it to her.

She looked at the shirt. "You're literally giving me the shirt off your back."

"I'll be back when I've got your pills. Then I'll give you a ride to Mandy's."

I turned to leave as she said, "Thanks, Dad."

I stopped and looked over my shoulder. "I'm not old enough to be your father."

349

"The doctor thought so."

Jill's voice came from the door. "What did the doctor think?"

"That Rachel can go home. You can help her get dressed."

Jill looked at my gun and white t-shirt. "You forgot to wear a shirt."

I pulled her into the hallway. "Rachel's uniform shirt is splattered with the dead guy's blood. I threw it away and gave her my shirt. Don't let her go digging in the trash."

Jill's eyes went wide. "She was that close to the gunman when he was shot?"

I nodded. "And that close to being killed."

"Where were you?"

"I shot the guy." I saw the shock on Jill's face as she processed my words.

"There was blood on your uniform shirt too. You were close enough to . . ."

"I've got to get her pills. We're going to drive her to Mandy's after she's dressed."

Chapter Thirty-Four

The armpits of my new shirt and suit were soaked. Matt, in a black suit, was at my side. Reverend Lind, who looked young enough to be my son, stood behind me. The small Port Aransas Episcopal Church was empty except for the front row with Mom, Rachel, and Ron Meland sitting on the groom's side. Molly, Clarice, Charlie and the boys on the bride's side of the aisle. The organist had been playing for what seemed like a half-hour when Mandy appeared in the aisle wearing a long lavender dress, smiling from ear-to-ear. She stopped at the bottom step, then stepped up and took a half-step aside.

The wedding march started, and there was motion in the narthex doors as our few guests stood. Jill's veil was backlit by the afternoon sun, making her look like an angel with an aura. Al stepped into view and took her arm. They walked slowly, Jill's eyes never leaving mine until her father stopped her at the steps. He kissed her cheek and guided her up the steps, giving her hand to me.

She was beaming. I was close to tears. Mandy took the bouquet. Jill took my hands.

Reverend Lind cleared his throat to get our attention. "I've married dozens of couples. Many in their teens and twenties. Some in their thirties. A few who were more…mature, like Doug and Jill." I heard chuckles behind us. "I usually counsel them several times to explain what love and marriage are about. Because of the short notice, I was reluctant to perform this ceremony, this sacrament, without having those counseling sessions. But Mandy Mattson came to me and assured me that Jill and Doug weren't naïve or unsure of the meaning of love or the gravity of this wedding sacrament. Well, those of you who know Mandy, know she can be persuasive." There were more chuckles.

"So, I met Jill and Doug briefly yesterday after church for one counseling session. I knew in two minutes that they were like no other couple I'd ever married, and that Mandy was right. They weren't naïve or moonstruck. What she didn't tell me was that they are past the teen infatuation and other stages of relationships people go through on the way to a lasting marriage. I asked Jill what she saw in Doug. She took his hand and looked me in the eye and said, 'He's my best friend.'

"No one has ever said that before, and I was taken aback because young people always talk about their deep love. Then I realized the reason people stay married for decades is because they're in love, but much more than that, they've become best friends. I could see in Jill and

Doug's eyes there was nothing I could teach these two about love or marriage."

Reverend Lind turned to Jill. "Please read your wedding vows."

I expected Jill to open a sweaty piece of paper, but she looked at me and said, "I've waited a lifetime for someone to love. You gently taught me what true friendship and trust were, and I surrendered my heart and love to you. I want to be your best friend, your partner, and your wife for eternity."

The reverend turned to me. "Doug, please read your wedding vows."

I was reaching for the notecard in my pocket, then I decided just to speak from my heart. "Jill, I've loved you since our first dinner. I had to earn your trust and love. We're still individuals, Doug and Jill, but we've become one. I promise to love you, respect you, and be your best friend. I know you're the missing piece that's made me whole, and I want to be at your side for eternity."

The reverend placed his hand on top of ours. "By the power vested in me, I pronounce you husband and wife. Doug, you may kiss Jill."

I lifted Jill's veil and saw the tears in her eyes. I kissed her gently, our eyes staring at each other, knowing we were now one in the eyes of the church, an affirmation of what we'd both known in our hearts.

"Can we have cake yet?" I glanced up and saw Danny pulling on Clarice's sleeve. "Can we?"

Clarice swept Danny up in her arms. "Soon. Wait just a little bit longer."

Jill and I walked down the pews, kissing our parents and shaking hands.

Rachel hugged me and buried her face in my shoulder. "We could've been killed."

I leaned down and whispered to her. "Cherish every day like it's your last."

Then I shook hands with Ron Meland and whispered to him, "Treat her special."

He nodded and took Rachel's hand. "Rachel needs to catch the bouquet." Then he winked at me.

After hugging Molly and Al, Clarice pulled Jill and I together, and we did a group hug. She whispered, "I wasn't sure I was going to move to Norfolk until I heard your vows and saw the looks on your faces this afternoon. Thank you for reminding me what love is."

We both looked at her with concern, but she smiled. "Come visit us in Norfolk."

Charlie was in his Navy whites with brand new gold wings on his chest. I shook his hand. He pulled me close and asked, "What was that about?"

"Clarice invited us to Norfolk after you get settled."

"Absolutely!"

Allen looked sober when I knelt and shook his hand. "My dad said you're a good cop."

"That's kind of him."

"He showed me your picture in the newspaper and said you could've been hurt, but you caught some very bad people. I'm glad you live by us."

I had to drag Danny from behind Charlie to shake his hand. "Are you married?" he asked.

"Yes."

"Can we have cake now?"

Jill and I led the small procession outside, and Mandy announced the reception was going to be at the newly refurbished VFW.

Mandy shooed everyone to their cars and then intercepted us before we got to the Isuzu. "The realtor called, and the sellers declined your counteroffer. They're convinced they can sell the shell of the house even though they're now obligated to disclose the mold. Glenda has another listing further down the canal. She'd like to show it to you tomorrow."

I helped Jill gather her dress and get into the Isuzu. We drove to the VFW and walked into a roomful of local friends, rangers, county deputies, CCPD, and PAPD police officers. One thing you can depend on; cops show up for free food and beer.

Mandy steered Jill toward a group of young rangers and made introductions. The CCPD chief cornered me. "Are you ready to get back to real police work? I'll up the ante. I spoke with Scott Dixon, and we'd like you to be his partner."

I thanked him but declined.

Jill found me talking with Matt by the beer tap. "Mom asked if we had plans for Thanksgiving. I think she wants to show you off to the neighbors."

"It's snowy and cold there in November, and I gave all my winter gear to the Salvation Army before I left St. Paul. I said I'd never move north of the Mason Dixon line."

"I know. But Mom never asks anything of me. Please."

"Sure."

Jill's eyes lit up.

"I'll tell Mom and Daddy. You and Daddy can go riding and see the ranch." Jill gathered her gown and waded through the crowd.

I watched the smiles on Al and Molly's faces as Jill told them we'd be in Spearfish for Thanksgiving. I smiled back, nodded, and thought, *"Way to jump in over your head, Fletcher. Horses. Really?"*

I felt someone at my elbow and saw Rachel smiling. "I didn't know you could ride."

"I'm afraid of horses."

She shook her head. "Try not to break anything."

The End

Dean Hovey is the award-winning author of **Family Trees**, *A Pine County Mystery* and twelve other mysteries. His three previous Doug Fletcher mysteries are set in Arizona and Texas.

Dean and his wife split their year between northern Minnesota and Arizona.

BWL Publishing

bwlpublishing.ca

Made in the USA
Monee, IL
07 April 2020